THE WIDOW'S HUSBAND

NATASHA BOYDELL

B
Boldwood

First published in Great Britain in 2025 by Boldwood Books Ltd.

Copyright © Natasha Boydell, 2025

Cover Design by Head Design Ltd.

Cover Images: Shutterstock

The moral right of Natasha Boydell to be identified as the author of this work has been asserted in accordance with the Copyright, Designs and Patents Act 1988.

All rights reserved. No part of this book may be reproduced in any form or by any electronic or mechanical means, including information storage and retrieval systems, without written permission from the author, except for the use of brief quotations in a book review. This book is a work of fiction and, except in the case of historical fact, any resemblance to actual persons, living or dead, is purely coincidental.

Every effort has been made to obtain the necessary permissions with reference to copyright material, both illustrative and quoted. We apologise for any omissions in this respect and will be pleased to make the appropriate acknowledgements in any future edition.

A CIP catalogue record for this book is available from the British Library.

Paperback ISBN 978-1-83533-330-3

Large Print ISBN 978-1-83533-331-0

Hardback ISBN 978-1-83533-329-7

Ebook ISBN 978-1-83533-332-7

Kindle ISBN 978-1-83533-333-4

Audio CD ISBN 978-1-83533-324-2

MP3 CD ISBN 978-1-83533-325-9

Digital audio download ISBN 978-1-83533-327-3

This book is printed on certified sustainable paper. Boldwood Books is dedicated to putting sustainability at the heart of our business. For more information please visit https://www.boldwoodbooks.com/about-us/sustainability/

Boldwood Books Ltd, 23 Bowerdean Street, London, SW6 3TN

www.boldwoodbooks.com

PROLOGUE

He has finally come for me. I can't breathe, can't move. His presence in this house again overcomes me, paralysing me in terror. The warning signs have been building up to this crescendo, but I ignored them. I told myself it wasn't possible, that I was imagining things.

I was wrong.

I can sense him behind me. I can *smell* him. The air between us is electric, making my skin tingle and my hairs stand on end. The panicked barks of my dog, trapped in the kitchen, amplifies my fear to an unbearable level. It has gripped me by the throat and is squeezing mercilessly. I should never have come back here and now it's too late to turn back. Fate has led me down this path, on a terrifying journey that I can't comprehend or control.

I buried this man a year ago. My husband. I grieved for him as a widow should do and then I began to rebuild myself. I tried to let him go. Yet somehow he is still here. He has defied all that we are taught about life and death, lingering in this world, haunting me day and night. He is not ready to leave because he has unfinished business. And that business is me.

My mind is frantic, but reason begins to force its way through the wall of chaos. I have to think straight. This can't be real, it's my brain playing cruel tricks on me. My spiralling anxiety has plunged me into paranoid delusions and made me see and feel things that aren't really there. If I can just force him out of my mind, then I can make this stop. I cling to this hope like a life raft, summoning my inner strength to banish this demon once and for all. I will myself to open my eyes and look in the mirror on the wall in front of me. I tell myself that I will see nothing but my own reflection and then I will be able to breathe again.

A floorboard creaks and I choke, terror suffocating me once again. Reason disappears because I can no longer deny the truth. Somehow, he is in this room and he's getting closer. I can feel death in the air. It engulfs me, consumes me. And it's coming for me.

Defeat trickles through my veins, like a hunted animal who knows they've been caught. There is no escape now. Keeping my eyes closed will not protect me from what is about to happen because my moment of reckoning has finally come. *You will never live without me.*

Another creak. As I slowly open my eyes to look in the mirror, I brace myself for what I will see. There is a shadowy figure standing right behind me and as I adjust to the darkness our eyes meet in the reflection. I stagger forwards, clutching my chest. My legs buckle underneath me and I begin to fall. The last thing I see before I crash to the floor is a pale face, two large, dark eyes glistening with malice and a haunting smile. It is the face of evil.

1

EIGHT MONTHS EARLIER

I stare at the two steaming mugs of coffee sitting on the kitchen counter and frown. I don't remember making them, but I must have done. There is no one else in the house but me. How did it happen? How could I have gone through the motions of making two cups of coffee without even realising what I was doing? What is happening to me?

I tighten the belt of my flannel dressing gown and pick up one of the mugs, the one with the cartoon dogs on, because the other one is his. *Was* his. With my free hand I pick up the newspaper and walk to the living room, sitting down on the faded patchwork armchair. I put my coffee down and try to read the front-page news, but I give up after a few paragraphs. I toss the newspaper to the side and stare out of the window instead.

A woman walks past the cottage with a dog. She is probably around my age, but she looks younger. Her bare arms are toned and there is no middle-aged spread protruding from the belt of her khaki shorts. Her long, highlighted hair is tied back into a stylish ponytail and her cheeks are glowing. I imagine she does yoga and eats kale. I wish I was her.

I sigh and reach for my coffee, taking a small sip. It is like a hit of liquid gold and I take another, larger gulp, wincing as the hot water scalds the back of my throat. The dog walker has gone and the window is a blank canvas as I wait for the next passer-by. This is my life now, watching other people live in the world that I have retreated from.

My stomach rumbles and I contemplate making four slices of toast and slathering them in butter and jam. And then I remember the dog walker's muscular arms and I remain on the sofa, battling with indecision. I want to look after myself better, but I have no reason to get back into shape. There is no one to impress, no one to care what I look like. No one to hide from as I stealthily snaffle an entire pack of chocolate digestives.

It should be liberating, but instead I descend further into misery.

My husband has been dead for four months. The tasks of contacting relatives and organising the funeral are behind me. The sympathy calls and letters have dried up. His belongings have been neatly packed into bags and stored in the spare room until I take them to the charity shop. The financial matters, as bleak as they are, are all in hand. The busyness that comes with death has passed and there is nothing left for me to do. In a strange way, I miss the admin because it kept me distracted and prevented me from facing reality. Now I am alone with my thoughts, and they follow me around all day and haunt me at night. It's like I'm living in an echo chamber, and I can't find my way out.

I have not left the house in weeks. I'm the one who is still alive and yet I've become a ghost, wandering aimlessly around the empty rooms, opening the door only to the postie and the grocery delivery driver. It is no way to live, I know that. And yet every time I try to step out of the door, fear grips me and I quickly close it again and retreat into the safe sanctuary of my house, where I don't have to face the world. I'm trapped in a pattern of lethargy and agoraphobia. If I'm not careful, I'll become a recluse. Perhaps I already have.

I haven't been on my own for over thirty years. I've forgotten how to do it, how to be my own person. When you live in the shadow of someone for your entire life, it seems inconceivable to step out into the light again, no matter how much you yearn to do it.

I am fifty-one years old and yet I feel like a centenarian. Maybe it's my punishment, for being alive, when he died. He was always the stronger one, the one people gravitated to. I was nothing compared to him, no one would have missed me if I'd been the one to pass. I doubt anyone would have come to my funeral, except for the friends and colleagues of my husband, out of a sense of duty. Perhaps it should have been the other way around.

Because it's not just fear that's imprisoned me, it's guilt. I broke the wedding vows I made to my husband when I didn't look after him properly. I was a failure of a wife and I know this because he told me all the time. I didn't take care of myself. I didn't fit in with the wives of his colleagues. I couldn't give him children. I didn't cook or clean properly. I ignored his stress and turned a blind eye when he refused to take life-saving medication.

I was not a good wife. But he was not a good husband either.

I finish my coffee and as the caffeine courses through my veins, it gives me a surge of optimism. Today will be the day that I leave the house. I will go for a walk around the village, stretch my legs and breathe in the scent of summer. Cut grass and flowers. My body needs it. *I* need it. With a renewed sense of purpose, I stand up and climb the stairs to take a shower. I turn the radio on and the silence is filled with the energetic voice of the breakfast DJ, reminding me that while I've been self-imprisoned, life has continued without me. And I want to reach a hand out and grasp it again. I want to *live*.

After my shower, I dry myself and slip into a shirt and skirt. I blow-dry my hair and put on some make-up and then I gaze at my reflection in the mirror. If the dog walker passed me on the street, would she smile at me? Would I have the confidence to say something to her? Just a simple 'good morning'? Perhaps we might even engage in some small talk about the weather. But as my gaze drifts down to my frumpy shirt, hope seeps out of me. The dog walker probably wouldn't even notice me, because I am invisible.

I sit down on the side of the bed, my earlier enthusiasm depleted. I will not go out today after all. I will go downstairs, read the newspaper, watch a bit of television, and eventually succumb to the multiple slices of toast I have been craving since I woke up. The radio is playing a ballad now, someone singing about a lost love, and it pierces through my heart, painful and overwhelming, a reminder of what my life could have been.

I can't listen to it any more. I turn the music off and then I look out of the bedroom window at the sunlight streaming in, and the tops of the trees. I think about the extra mug of coffee I accidentally made this morning, which is still sitting on the kitchen counter, cold and curdling. I close my eyes and imagine a thousand days, each one the same, a void of loneliness, until eventually I die, and no one notices. I picture the police turning up months later, when a neighbour complains about the smell, and finding my decaying body.

No, this will not do.

My eyes snap open and before I have time to change my

mind, I march down the stairs, put my shoes on, take my handbag from the peg and throw open the front door.

The bright light engulfs me and I shield my eyes from the sun, rummaging around in my bag for my sunglasses. I head tentatively up the garden path and onto the pavement. My legs feel wobbly from weeks of inactivity, but I force myself to keep going. I have no plan for where I will go, or what I will do, I just need to be out. I glance at the neighbour's house as I pass, at the children's bikes abandoned on the front lawn and the garden gnome who watches me intently. We have lived here, in this quaint Hertfordshire village, for three years and yet I don't even know my neighbours' names. I don't know anyone's names.

It wasn't always like this. There was a time, long ago, when I had friends. When I socialised, gossiped, laughed and lived. It feels like a million years ago now. But I still have it in me, I know I do. As I walk, the sun warms my face and memories come flooding back of a forgotten time. Working in the Mexican restaurant and giggling with the other wait staff. Scoffing fajitas after my shift. Drinking white wine spritzers in pub beer gardens on a Saturday afternoon. Jogging and weekend walks. Fun and laughter and companionship. I want it again so much it hurts. Each step I take reminds me of what I crave. There is room in this world for a widowed middle-aged woman to enjoy life, not as I did in my twenties but in new and different ways. There is nothing stopping me but myself. And yet the fresh air and the exercise is giving me hope and I raise my head to the sun, push away my crippling insecurities, and let the warm rays drench me with small ambitions.

A young couple are walking towards me on the pavement and I smile. They give me a nod as they pass and I glow with satisfaction. They'll have forgotten about me in a minute, but that tiny interaction will stay with me for the rest of the day. It emboldens me, as I walk towards the centre of the village, which is little more than a church hall, pub and scattering of small shops. Perhaps I'll go into the cafe and have another coffee. I'm feeling braver now and I walk with determination towards the high street, my gaze fixed on the cafe door. At the last minute I swerve, narrowly avoiding a woman pushing a buggy, mutter my apologies and keep walking. I will go tomorrow. Today, just being outside is enough.

As I pass the pub, which is still locked at this early hour, I see a poster stapled to a noticeboard outside. Looking around self-consciously, I stop to read it. It's advertising a psychic supper, taking place the following Saturday evening. *Everyone welcome to attend this community event*, it says. *Pre-booking advised*. A thrill runs through me. I don't believe in the paranormal, but it still feels like a sign. Is this my opportunity to attend a local event and meet some new people in the village? Perhaps even make friends. I can't be the only person thinking of attending on my own, surely? The idea of walking into a busy pub terrifies me, but fear is now competing with anticipation. This is my chance to re-engage with society. If I can just find a way to make myself walk through that door, it could change my entire life.

I'm going to do it, I decide triumphantly. I take a photograph of the poster on my phone so I can buy a ticket online when I get home. This is the start of a new chapter and I imagine joining the community that I've been watching from my window for so long. Book clubs and dinners and walks with like-minded friends! I wonder if the dog walker will be going to the event and I feel nervous and excited, but at least I'm feeling something.

As I begin to walk home, I think about browsing the M&S website for a new outfit to wear. One that makes me feel more confident about myself. I pass some more people on the pavement and I smile shyly at them, each small interaction a personal victory. I can already feel the psychological shackles that have chained me loosening. I am allowed to move on, there is nothing stopping me any more, no one standing in my way but myself.

But it's enough for one day. I'm exhausted, my stiff legs are complaining and my stomach is rumbling. I'll go out again tomorrow, and the next day. Maybe even start clearing out the spare room and taking boxes to the charity shop. The world, dull for so long, gleams with possibility and it's intoxicating and addictive. I want more of it.

When I get back to the cottage, I'm suddenly aware that I am being watched. I look up, half expecting to see my husband's face in a window, home early from work, his gaze fixed on mine. But of course there's no one there. Yet the sensation persists and an uncomfortable feeling settles over me. I glance anxiously behind me and spot a black cat, sitting on the pavement, staring at me with sleepy eyes. We gaze at each other for a few seconds and then I crouch down and reach a hand out towards the cat. It looks at me, unblinking, for a few moments before getting up and slinking away.

I stand up with a wince, open the door and step into the cool hallway. Take off my shoes and return my bag to the peg, grateful that my mind is busy with jobs to do. I need to buy a ticket to the psychic supper, look for an outfit, choose the first lot of things to take to the charity shop. But then I feel it. Despair. It's been waiting for me and now it creeps over me, rising from the tips of my toes to the top of my head, until it has covered me like a blanket.

You will never live without me.

And, once again, the joy evaporates until I can't imagine it ever having been there.

2

The pub is full when I push the door open and glance inside. It's noisy and suffocating. Nerves churn my stomach as I look left and right, trying to decide where to go and what to do with myself. My hands are trembling. This was a mistake, a monumental error in judgement.

To calm myself, I try to concentrate on the surroundings. The pub decor is somewhere between a traditional village boozer and a modern, gastro-style eatery. Original exposed beams painted white. Floorboards varnished until they shine. It's probably designed to be warm and inviting, but I still feel like an unwelcome guest. My body is drenched with sweat and my new navy M&S dress is clinging to my clammy skin. It's even more oppressively hot in the pub than it is outside, and I begin to feel light-headed. I sway in the doorway, my eyes wide and my mind frantic. I think I might faint.

I'm just about to turn around and flee when someone calls out.

'Hi there!'

I look up in alarm to see a man striding towards me.

'Are you here for the psychic supper?' he asks.

'That's right.' My voice sounds shrill and unfamiliar. I haven't spoken to another human being in weeks. I reach into my bag and produce the ticket I printed at home, proffering it to him shakily. He takes it and gives me an encouraging smile.

'Welcome, I'm Mark, the pub landlord. I hope you have a wonderful evening. Take a seat wherever you like. Dinner will be served in half an hour.'

I glance anxiously around and see that the pub tables have been set, bottles of red and white wine placed in the middle of each one. Many tables are already full but on others there are some spaces. The sound of chatter fills my ears, echoing around my head. I wanted company, but this is too much. It's too loud and intense. I should have started off with something smaller, like the cafe or the library. What on earth was I thinking?

I could still leave. No one would care or even notice. But then I catch a woman's eye and she beckons to me. I take a deep breath and slowly make my way over.

'Hi.' She smiles warmly at me when I reach her. 'Are you on your own too?'

'Yes.' My voice is husky and out of practice.

'Thank goodness! Come and join me. I'm Beth.'

The woman extends a hand and I shake it, ashamed of my sweaty palms. 'Maggie.'

'Hi, Maggie.' Beth gestures at a chair. 'Red or white?'

I glance at her full glass of white wine. 'White please.'

Beth pours me a glass and I take it gratefully. The wine is cool and crisp, and it goes straight to my head, reminding me that it's been a long time since I've had a drink.

'This is Gary.' Beth points to a man around my age sitting opposite her. 'And this is Alyssa.' Alyssa smiles at me and I recognise her as the pretty young woman with the buggy who I nearly crashed into outside the cafe. If she remembers me, she doesn't show it.

'We're all here on our own too,' Beth continues. 'So I guess this is the singles table!'

I laugh nervously at the joke. I suppose I am single, but I've never really thought about it. It hasn't once occurred to me that I might meet someone else, only that I might find a way to live on my own. That would be more than enough for me. Despite not previously knowing each other, my companions seem to be at ease already, but this is the first time I've socialised with anyone since my husband's funeral, if you can call that socialising, and I wonder if I can still remember how to do it. I take another bracing sip of wine.

'What brings you here?' Beth asks. She has an open, inquisitive face. I do a quick appraisal and decide that she's probably in her early forties. She has thick, long red hair and freckles across her nose. She's lovely, in an outdoorsy and wholesome way.

I shuffle in my seat self-consciously. 'An opportunity to meet new people, really,' I reply. 'Get to know some others in the village. How about you?'

'Curiosity. I've always wanted to go to a psychic supper.' She leans in and says quietly, 'And I recently lost my partner so I'm hoping that he might have a message for me.'

'I'm so sorry to hear that,' I say automatically, but Beth's words have triggered an internal panic alarm. I have been so consumed with the idea of getting out that I haven't considered the true purpose of this evening, beyond some sort of fun show. What if the psychic has a message for me? I can't even bear to think about it.

I talk some sense into myself. There's no way that the psychic can really communicate with dead people. This event is just for entertainment purposes, a chance for people grieving their loved ones to have some comfort, and while I do not judge anyone who hopes otherwise, I am not a believer. There is nothing to fear beyond my own social incompetence.

I tune back into Beth's words. 'It's been hard,' she is saying, her eyes filling with tears. 'I still miss him every day.'

I try to empathise. 'My husband passed recently too.'

She puts a hand on my arm. 'I'm so terribly sorry. I know how it feels.'

This woman has no idea how it feels. I've only known her for five minutes, but I can tell she's a good person. She was probably a wonderful, loving partner in a happy relationship. I imagine a content couple, going on long hikes, holding hands, putting the world to rights. I, on the other hand, failed my husband and he never forgave me for it. I'm the reason why our marriage fell apart because I was so useless at everything. Why there were no children to carry on his family name. No little boy to play football with or little girl to worship. Why he ate, drank and worked himself to death because there was nothing else to do. Does this make her more entitled to her grief than me? I think it does.

She looks at me intently. 'Do you feel guilty sometimes? When you laugh at something or forget what happened for just a few, short seconds?'

'Yes,' I whisper.

'I'm so glad you said that. Because I do too.'

We don't know each other, yet the conversation is so intimate, it's like we've been friends forever. The wine and the connection with this stranger make me giddy. But I need to be on my guard because I don't want to put my foot in it and say anything stupid. If she realises that I'm a sad old woman with no friends, she'll probably keep her distance.

Beth refills my rapidly depleting wine glass. 'Do you live in the village, Maggie?'

'Yes. Bridge Street. How about you?'

'Just a few miles up the road. Harpenden.'

Beth turns to Gary and Alyssa, bringing them into our conversation. I learn that Alyssa is married with two sons aged eighteen months and three, and this is her first night out in months. She recently moved to the village from London and is adjusting to the change in pace. She's young and energetic and her enthusiasm is infectious. Her dark black curls are shiny and her skin is flawless. I'm almost captivated by her beauty, but her mannerisms suggest that she doesn't know just how pretty she is. Gary is divorced and lives with his son whose wife is expecting a baby. I'm not surprised when he tells us he's a landscape gardener because he has sun-bleached fair hair and the tanned, firm arms of a man who spends time working outdoors. But his beer belly suggests that he likes a drink and he goes to great lengths to tell us he is here tonight because he's good friends with the pub landlord and not because he believes in 'all this hocus pocus nonsense'.

I wonder what they make of me, but they all seem friendly and eager to engage in conversation. Although, they're so chatty that it's hard to get a word in edgeways and that suits me just fine. I listen to their stories without feeling under too much pressure to join in and slowly, I begin to relax. What a delight it is to be out. To hear other people's stories and laugh at their jokes. I can't believe I've been depriving myself of this for so long. The loudness of the pub is no longer intimidating, it's comforting. It's just like riding a bike, I tell myself, remembering what it was like to have friends and to have fun. And if they're just talking to me because they feel sorry for me then so be it. I'll take that over another evening in the cottage on my own, staring into the abyss.

As the wait staff bring over our starters, little parcels of ravioli that melt in my mouth, and the wine numbs my nerves,

I ease into the evening. I talk as little as possible about myself, explaining that I've lived here for a while but haven't really got to know anyone yet. There are murmurs of agreement or sympathy, but no judgement. Alyssa gives me a smile that suggests she knows how I feel. Beth advises me to check out the noticeboard in the cafe, where she's seen flyers for various local clubs that might interest me. I thank her and deflect attention away from myself again by asking Alyssa about her boys.

She tells us all about her busy family. Her husband works in London most days and she's a full-time mum. Her elder son is at preschool, but the younger is still at home. I feel a pang of sadness as I always do when people talk about their children. I imagine the different life I could have had if I'd had my own, the love and happy chaos that would have filled my home, drowning out the silent disapproval, banishing the loneliness. But tonight is about living in the moment, not dwelling on the past, and I try to focus on Alyssa.

'So then Thomas asked me if I was meeting Robin, and I couldn't work out what on earth he was talking about until I realised he thought I was going to a sidekick supper, not a psychic supper! He was disappointed that superheroes wouldn't be there.'

Gary and Beth hoot with laughter and I join in, enjoying the sensation of it.

'Do you have children, Maggie?' Beth asks me.

Shame consumes me on cue. 'No, I don't.'

'Me neither,' Beth says cheerfully. 'I've never felt maternal. I've got nothing but admiration and respect for women who have babies, but they're not for me.'

I envy Beth intensely in that moment. Her satisfaction with her life and her control over her own decision-making. And then

I remember that she has lost her partner and I feel guilty for thinking, even for a split second, that she has it easy.

'I thought I was done with babies,' Gary confesses. 'But there'll be a newborn in the house in a matter of weeks.'

The conversation moves on to extortionate house prices, which is why Gary's son and his wife had to move back in with him, to save money for a deposit. By the time we've been served our main courses, I've almost forgotten the reason why we're here.

But then a silence descends as a woman walks into the middle of the room and naturally commands our attention. We all turn to gaze at her. She's not like how I imagined her to be. She's wearing normal clothes. She looks just like one of us. She's probably been in the room all evening without me even noticing her. But from the authoritative way she stands and casts her eyes around, I know she is the psychic.

She begins to talk, introducing herself as Zara and explaining how the evening will work. We listen, rapt, as she says that this will be a fun and informal event and warns us that she will not have messages for everyone. *Thank God*, I think. I don't want to attract any attention to myself. I want to blend into the background and be a passive observer. To enjoy other people's reactions to Zara's messages and witness their healing.

As Zara walks slowly around the room, I begin to feel nervous again. I keep my eyes lowered, avoiding eye contact and hoping she'll get the message that I don't want to interact. I'm a spectator tonight, not a participant. She takes her time, wandering from table to table, and when she reaches ours, I hold my breath. But she moves on and I exhale again.

She goes over to another table and stands in front of an apprehensive-looking woman.

'Your sister is here with us tonight,' Zara says. The entire room inhales and even I'm getting a little caught up in the moment. I glance at Gary and he rolls his eyes.

'Mary,' the woman gasps.

Zara nods. 'Yes. She wants you to know that you need to stop feeling guilty over what happened to her. It wasn't your fault.'

The woman begins to cry, and her husband comforts her.

'You kept telling her to go to the doctor, but she wouldn't listen,' Zara continues and the woman nods vehemently. 'She says that she was too stubborn and nothing you could have said would have made any difference. But she wants to you know that she's okay. She says it's time for you to move on and be happy again.'

We all watch, enthralled, as the woman sobs; grief and relief spilling out of her. Even Gary is looking a little moved by the tender moment.

'And she also says she's sorry for stealing your clothes when you were younger. Especially the red dress, which she never told you about.'

'I *knew* that was her!' Now the woman is laughing through her tears and the whole pub joins in. Some people are wiping their eyes. But the interaction has unnerved me. How does Zara know all of this? It's so specific, so convincing, I can almost sense this woman's dead sister in the room. Could Zara really be talking to her?

Zara is on a roll now. She walks around the room, giving out messages, some funny, some sad. The audience cries and laughs and cheers. I should be enjoying myself but with each message my fear accelerates. Why did I come here, of all places? This woman is eerily accurate, and I dread what message she might have for me. I fear it will not be a message of love, like the others, but one of reproval or, even worse, threat, which will expose my marriage for what it was. What I tried to ignore. I will be humiliated in front of all these people. The food, wine and nerves make me nauseous and I'm becoming increasingly claustrophobic. I must leave, before it's too late. I stand up and clutch my bag, aware that I'm drawing attention to myself, but I don't care. I need to get out of this pub.

Zara appears in front of me, blocking my exit. Her commanding presence makes me sit back down obediently, as meek as a schoolgirl. I'm shaking, despite the heat.

'Your husband is here,' she tells me, and I hear a collective intake of breath from Beth and Alyssa. The food and wine are curdling in my stomach and I think I might vomit.

'He says the back door key is in the plant pot on the dresser.'

Everyone in the pub laughs except me. I stare at Zara, wide-eyed. Of all the messages she could have given me, I was not expecting this. Is it some kind of a joke? Anyway, she's wrong. The key is in a kitchen drawer, where it always is. I've kept it in the same place ever since we moved to the cottage although I rarely use it because I don't go out into the garden. Come to think of it, I haven't seen the key in weeks. Suddenly I need to know where it is. It is of critical importance because if the key is in the drawer, where it is supposed to be, then I'll know for sure that Zara is a fake. But she's not done yet. She's still hovering over me and I wonder if this is just the start. If Frank has something else he wants to tell me.

You will never live without me.

Zara pauses. Frowns. And then she shrugs. 'I can't reach him any more, I'm very sorry. It happens sometimes. I'm sure there was much more he wanted to say to you.'

She moves away to the next person and I remain stock-still, stunned by what has just happened. I picture the dresser, the old plant pot sitting on the middle shelf. I need to get home and see if the key is there. I won't be able to rest easy until I do.

'I have to go,' I say, standing up again. The others look at me with concern.

'Wait.' Beth reaches for her bag. 'You're upset. Let me walk you home.'

'No, it's okay, I don't want to you miss the rest of the evening. I'm fine.'

'Give me your number then, and perhaps we could meet for coffee?'

This is exactly what I wanted, the opportunity to make friends. Beth and I got along well, so the invitation to meet again should please me. But as I hastily give her my number, I just want to escape. An uneasy sensation has crept over me. Is Frank really here? Is he watching me? I rush towards the exit and few people glance at me, but no one says anything.

It's a relief to be outside but the fresh air does nothing to soothe my anxiety. I half walk, half run back to the cottage, fixated only on looking for the back door key. It cannot be in the plant pot. It will not be in the plant pot because I have never once put the key there.

I'm sweating again and gasping for breath when I let myself into the house. I dash into the living room, wiping my clammy forehead with my hand. There it is, the blue glazed pot. It must have had a plant in it once, but not for a long time. I take a deep breath, lift it carefully off the shelf and peer inside. I see a matchbox in there, some used batteries. A couple of business cards. I close my eyes and exhale with relief. No key.

My pulse begins to return to normal. Already I'm thinking about putting the kettle on, perhaps having a bit of chocolate to take the edge off as I missed dessert in my haste to leave the pub. It was the wine that did it, it set me on edge. I've never been a big drinker, even when I was young, and I'm well out of practice. I'm embarrassed now about how I reacted. I ran out of the pub like a madwoman. What must Beth, Gary and Alyssa think of me? And the rest of the people who attended? What if I become known as the village crazy woman? Then I remember that lots of people became emotional this evening, not just me. And anyway, Beth asked for my phone number, so I can't have scared her off.

I can't believe I thought, even for a second, that my husband might be there. He's dead and buried. I'm delirious with relief and I laugh out loud, the sound of my voice cutting through the silence of the room. I begin to put the plant pot back but change my mind. I'll get rid of those batteries, goodness knows how long they've been in there. And I'll put the old business cards into the recycling. Maybe I'll buy a new plant to brighten up the room. As I reach in to lift the detritus out, I see a glint of something silver at the bottom and I gasp. The batteries I'm holding fall to the ground with a clatter and roll across the floorboards.

I turn the plant pot upside down and tip out the contents, which scatter messily across the floor. I scan the ground frantically, my eyes searching for what I fear the most. And then I see it, the dull silver metal reflecting the evening light, and the world closes in on me.

It's the back door key.

3

Frank and I were teenagers when we met. I was sixteen and had a summer job working in a shoe shop. He was buying a new pair of trainers. I fell in love with him the moment that I saw him.

I attended a Catholic girls' school at the time, and I had limited experience with boys, particularly ones as good looking as Frank. So when he walked in and asked for some assistance, I couldn't hide my blush. He was tall, with piercing brown eyes and hair so dark it was almost black. His stubbly chin made him look masculine, so different to the boys who hung around outside the school gates on Friday afternoons, waiting for departing girls to chat up. He was only three years older than me but back then the age difference seemed vast.

I was a pretty girl. My long, fair hair gleamed, thanks to my diligent 100-brushstrokes-a-day routine and I'd started experimenting with small amounts of make-up. Even though I went to a girls' school, I was of the age where I was acutely self-aware and wanted to look my best. I was curvy in a way that I knew boys admired, from their appreciative gazes when I walked past them on the pavement. Some of my friends had older brothers or invited boys to parties, and I'd had crushes and a few awkward kisses, but I'd never had a boyfriend.

As Frank talked to me, I couldn't tear my eyes away from him. It was as though he was imparting some great wisdom of the world, rather than informing me of his shoe size. When I realised that he was holding out a trainer, waiting patiently for me to take it while I stared at him, I turned a shade of beetroot and from the way he smiled, a little smugly, I knew he knew what I was thinking. I felt exposed, and it was terrifyingly thrilling.

In the back room, I fanned myself with an old discarded slip of paper and tried to calm myself down. But when I emerged a few minutes later with a pile of shoeboxes, the sight of him sent me into a nervous frenzy again. He was so relaxed, so handsome and so, so cool. I tried to keep my wits about me, as I took the tissue paper out of the shoes and loosened the laces for him. When he reached down to take the trainer from me, our hands briefly touched and a jolt of electricity ran right through me.

To my disappointment, Frank bought the first pair of trainers he tried on and a few minutes later, he was gone. I was deflated, certain that I would never see him again. Resigned to going back to my boring life, which now seemed empty and meaningless without him in it, I battled through the rest of my shift, smiling benignly at mothers bringing their wriggly children in to buy new school shoes. Elderly people looking for a comfortable pair of flats. Women buying heels for upcoming weddings. And I wished I lived a different life.

I left work a few hours later to find Frank hanging around outside, smoking a cigarette. I still remember the flutter I felt in my stomach at the sight of him. The realisation that he was waiting for me and that dreams really could come true. He stubbed his cigarette out and drifted over to me, his gaze on mine, and when he invited me for a walk, he might as well have been asking for my hand in marriage. I was his, for as long as he wanted me.

But he didn't want me, or at least not then. Frank would soon be going back to university for his second year and he had no desire to leave town with a girl back home. He told me about his new digs, the housemates he would be living with, and I learned then that it was possible to be bitterly jealous of strangers that I would never meet. I was a brief summer flirt to him, a walk in the park, a kiss on the swings and nothing more. We talked, or more accurately, I talked and he listened and smoked. He kissed me as often as he could and I didn't protest when his hand wandered up my T-shirt. He told me I was beautiful and he teased me about my innocence, but he made no promises, no declaration of faithfulness. I convinced myself that a fortnight with Frank was better than nothing. That my heart could take the strain.

It couldn't. When he left, I tormented myself with thoughts of what he was doing, the girls he was taking home to his bed. I knew that students wouldn't be as prudish as I was and there was no denying that Frank was infinitely more experienced than me. I only hoped that he wouldn't fall in love with anyone. But I also knew that, although it crushed me, I had no claim to him and he could date whoever he wanted with a clear conscience. My hope that he would call me from university faded with each week that passed. I tried to concentrate on my schoolwork so that I might get good grades and impress Frank. But my mind constantly wandered as I dreamed about being with him again, seeing him standing on my doorstep and declaring his love for me. I got detentions for not paying attention in class and the local boys labelled me stuck-up when I spurned their advances. But I only wanted Frank.

He didn't return the following summer. I went back to my job at the shoe shop and waited for him to walk through the door and take me in his arms. At home, I gazed out of the window and imagined him suddenly appearing, one hand tucked in his pocket and the other holding a cigarette. I imagined the look on my parents' face when this older boy knocked on the door asking to see me and planned how I would sneak out if they banned me from going with him. In the end, I didn't need to worry because there was no sign of Frank.

And so life went on. I tried to push him out of my mind. I concentrated on my A levels, made it through the exams and celebrated leaving school with my friends. It was nearly two years since my summer romance with Frank, and I should have forgotten all about him. I should have been excited about the carefree summer I had been looking forward to and a future full of possibilities, but Frank was still there, consuming my thoughts. Would he return again this summer and would he come and find me?

One scorching July day, I was hanging out with some friends on the high street when I saw him. His hair was shorter and his clothes smarter, but he was just as devastatingly handsome. When he spotted me, he smiled his lazy, confident smile and headed in my direction. My friends parted like curtains, watching this captivating stranger walk up to me with wide, curious and greedy eyes. I vowed then that I was never going to let him go again.

My vow was decimated less than half an hour later, when Frank told me that he was moving to London in a few weeks. He'd come back to visit his parents for the summer before starting his new graduate job. I could no longer deny my feelings and I immediately burst into tears. I think it was then that Frank realised just how much I adored him, how he had held the key to my heart for this entire time. He asked me, so very casually, if I wanted to go with him and I didn't hesitate to say yes. I didn't care that my parents would go ballistic, or that I barely knew this beautiful man. There was no doubt in my mind that I was going to London with Frank. In the years that followed I came to realise that Frank's invitation was spur of the moment. The reality, as harsh as it was to accept, was that if we hadn't seen each other that day, he would have gone off to London without a second thought for me.

And I've wished to God that I'd never bumped into him.

But at the time, I didn't consider any of this. As far as I was concerned, it was the most romantic thing that had ever happened to me, and it proved that Frank loved me too. I had a conditional place at a local university, pending my A level results, but I knew I'd turn it down. Moving to London with Frank was a far more enticing option than spending the next three years living with my parents and sleeping in my childhood bed. It was the most dangerous and rebellious thing I'd ever done in my life. It was the Frank effect.

Saying yes to Frank that day sealed my fate in ways I could never have imagined. I was too young, too naive, and too willing to give Frank every part of me before I even knew who *I* was. The truth is that I was lost before I'd even found myself and by the time I realised what I'd done, and who I had become, there was no way back.

But I don't tell Beth any of this as we sit in the village cafe, sipping lattes. She messaged me a few days after the psychic supper, asking if I was okay and suggesting a coffee. The truth is that I am not okay, not after what happened. I've been going round in circles trying to make sense of it, my theories becoming more outlandish as my paranoia grows. Was it a coincidence? Did Zara somehow plant the key to boost her credibility?

And the worst one. Is Frank watching me?

Today, I try to forget about it and concentrate on enjoying my coffee with Beth. I hadn't been out much since the psychic supper and it's good to have something to do. But I'm nervous too, my keenness to impress Beth competing with my social anxiety. I don't want to ruin the chance to make a friend and yet I can't think why she wants to see me again.

'You didn't miss much after you left,' Beth tells me, as she rips apart a croissant and dips it into her drink. 'Zara didn't have a message for Alyssa, Gary or me.'

'I'm sorry,' I say, wishing that I had been spared too.

'Was the key where Zara said it would be?'

I give a small nod.

'Oh my goodness, that's *so* freaky!'

'Yes.'

Beth's brow furrows with concern. 'Are you okay? It must have been unsettling.'

'Yes,' I repeat, fiddling with my coffee cup.

Beth leans forward and puts a hand over mine. 'You're missing your husband.'

I don't miss Frank, but I feel his absence. He was my life for more than thirty years and even when our love, and then our marriage, eroded, I still couldn't imagine a world without him. He was a constant, and now he's gone, I'm struggling to recalibrate.

'Do you mind if I ask what happened to him?' Beth asks.

'He had a heart attack.'

'Oh Maggie, I'm so sorry.'

'Frank wasn't in great health,' I explain. 'And he had a family history of heart problems. His doctor had been trying to get him to take statins for years, but he wouldn't have it. Said he didn't want the side effects, but I think he just believed he was invincible.'

'That's awful. When did it happen?'

'A few months ago.'

'So recently. It must be terribly raw. I think you're doing wonderfully.'

'I don't feel like it,' I admit.

'Of course you don't, that's natural. But you shouldn't be afraid to live your life. I'm sure Frank would want you to move on and be happy.'

I grimace inwardly. 'Perhaps.'

'Not perhaps.' Beth is looking intently at me. 'It's harder for the people left behind. We have to battle with so many conflicting emotions and find a way to live without the ones we've lost. It will always be hard, but it does get easier, I promise.'

'What about your partner?' I ask her. 'When did he pass away?'

'It's been over a year now.'

'What happened to him?'

'It was a freak accident. He was driving home from work one evening and there were some loose horses on the motorway. He swerved to avoid them and collided with the barrier. He died on the scene. It was his birthday too.'

I'm horrified. 'Oh gosh, I'm so very sorry.'

Beth's eyes fill with tears. 'He was called David. I was waiting for him at home that night. I'd cooked a special birthday dinner. The table was set, the wine poured, everything. But he never came home. Instead, I got a knock on the door from the police.'

I'm so stunned by this tragic story that I don't know what to say. I search my mind for some words of comfort, or any words at all, but I'm speechless.

Eventually, all I can muster is, 'That's absolutely terrible. I really am sorry.'

Beth smiles sadly as she wipes her eyes. 'Life can be cruel, but we have to find a way to survive and eventually thrive again. I know it's what David would have wanted for me.'

We sit in silence for a minute or two, both lost in our own thoughts, before Beth finally breaks it. 'Anyway, let's talk about something a bit cheerier, shall we? I exchanged numbers with Alyssa and Gary and I'd love to arrange a dinner. Are you free next Friday?'

'Oh yes, that would be lovely.'

'Great. I'll set up a WhatsApp group. Do you have WhatsApp?'

She thinks I'm a dinosaur. And I'm not that much older than her. 'Yes, I do.'

'Fabulous!' Beth starts fiddling with her phone and a few seconds later, a WhatsApp notification pops up on my own screen. 'All set up,' she says triumphantly.

'Thank you. I must say, it's exciting to have something to look forward to.'

'I think we all need it,' Beth admits. 'After you left the other night, Alyssa told us that she's been feeling really isolated. She's struggling to adjust to village life and she hasn't met many other mums yet, so she's mainly on her own with the boys. Her husband still commutes into the office most days and gets home late, and her parents live in Birmingham.'

'What about Gary?'

'He's desperate to get out of the house and give his son and daughter-in-law some space. I think he's very self-conscious of being in their way.'

I wonder what the rest of Beth's story is. She seems like a sociable type and probably has plenty of friends. Is this a pity gesture? Does she want to take some lame ducks under her wing and help us fly again? Or is she just as lonely as the rest of us, still mourning the tragic loss of her partner and seeking comfort and company? I have a strong, almost motherly, urge to protect her. And then I wonder where all her friends are, the ones who should be rallying around her.

As though she can read my mind, Beth leans forward. 'All my friends have settled down and had children. We still see each other but their lives are so different to mine. And although they'd never say it to my face, they think I'm strange because I never got married or had kids. And now I'm on my own again, I swear they think I'm going to seduce their husbands or something.'

'I get it,' I tell her. 'I never had children either and often felt excluded.'

Beth nods in understanding. 'Although to be honest, I don't know how I would have coped over the past year or so if I had children. Losing a loved one is so hard but at least I only had myself to look after.' She smiles suddenly, as though eager to break the sombre moment. 'And besides, at least we can take great holidays at the drop of a hat!'

'Do you do that often?'

'Oh yes. I love travelling. Life is short and I want to enjoy it.'

That's what I want too. To enjoy my life, or what I have left of it. An idea forms of Beth and I becoming close friends. Going on holiday together. Maybe a yoga retreat where we eat kale. Then I steady myself. This is just a quick coffee, not a lifelong friendship. And I don't want to scare her off with my eagerness. But still, I feel a surge of hope. Getting out of the house has lifted my spirits again and I'm cautiously optimistic.

Then I remember the back door key and a shiver runs up my spine. I've been on edge ever since I found it in the plant pot, jumping at the slightest noise and I don't like it. Living alone for the first time is hard enough without this, and it almost feels like I've taken one step forward and two steps back. But I tell myself it was a one-off. The key is now in the kitchen drawer where it belongs, and nothing else out of the ordinary has happened.

Still, when Beth suggests a post-coffee walk, I'm pleased to have a reason to delay my return home. We stroll through the village until we reach a public footpath which takes us through some farmland. Beth is fitter than I am, but she walks at my pace and we chat easily. Butterflies dance around us and cows graze in the field next to the path. It is so beautiful here. So peaceful and serene. Why have I not done this before? Why did Frank and I not go out together at weekends, for a country walk and a drink in the pub? Why could we not have been a normal, married couple? What went so wrong for us? People talk about the strain that having a family puts on a relationship, but not about the impact of *not* having children. The intensity between two people, the pressure without anyone else to dilute it. Deep down I know our marriage was not destroyed by my inability to conceive, but it's easier to blame it on that. Because, as Frank told me often enough, it was entirely my fault.

As we walk, Beth tells me more about her life. She's an architect and mainly works from home. She is heading off on a charity cycling trip to France in a few weeks and she's decided to add on a couple of days in Paris to soak up the atmosphere. I listen to her, absorbing her adventurous life and hoping it's contagious.

'I love France,' she tells me. 'Have you been away recently?'

'Oh.' I try to think back. It's been years since I went abroad. 'We went to Greece once. Maybe seven or eight years ago.'

Beth raises her eyebrows. 'Really?'

'We didn't go away much, Frank and me. I mean, Frank travelled a lot, so he was often away, but we didn't go away very often together.'

Beth is quiet and the silence is uncomfortable. *She thinks I'm a freak.* Desperate to fill the void with words, I say, 'Greece was wonderful though. What a beautiful country.'

'Oh yes,' Beth gushes. 'Stunning.'

I'm worried that I've made things awkward, but Beth is off again, talking about the things she's hoping to see and do in Paris and by the time we return to the village, I'm tired but relaxed again. We walk to her car and she offers me a lift.

'Thanks, but I need to do some chores first, so I'll walk home.'

'No problem, I'll see you next week for dinner,' she says.

'I'm looking forward to it.' As I say it, I realise how much it's true.

Beth beeps her horn as she drives away, and I head towards the village shop. I've decided to go more often rather than relying solely on online deliveries. I'm sure most people aren't gripped by fear at the prospect of visiting their local shop but I am, and yet I know the more I do it, the easier it will get. Before I go in, I check to make sure I have everything I need. Reusable bag. Check. Debit card. Check. Shopping list. Check. I'm ready.

Ten minutes later I'm back out on the street with milk, bread and tomatoes. *See, that wasn't so hard, was it?* I put the bag on one shoulder and walk home with aching legs. I haven't walked so far in years, but my discomfort is satisfying. It feels well earned. I pass the pub and Mark, who is cleaning tables outside, waves at me. I wave back. Gosh, just look at me. A couple of weeks ago I refused to leave the house. Today I've been for coffee and a walk with a friend and then to the shops. And if I can achieve that in such a short space time then the possibilities are endless. Buying tomatoes has never been so liberating.

The familiar sense of dread trickles in as soon as I turn into Bridge Street and grows stronger with each step I take towards the cottage. I have been struggling to adapt to living alone but now what consumes me is the fear that I am *not* alone. That Frank is somehow still here. Having conversations with psychics. Telling me where the back door key is.

I shake my head and walk resolutely towards the front door. I'm being ridiculous. Getting worked up over a silly key. But then I hear a noise and I feel like I'm the one who's having a heart attack. I spin around in fright and see the black cat meandering up the footpath, miaowing at me. It's been hanging around for the past few days, getting gradually bolder as it becomes accustomed to my presence. I don't know who it belongs to but it looks well fed so I doubt it's a stray. Suddenly I have an idea. I leave the front door open as I go inside and head to the kitchen to rummage around in the cupboards for some tuna. As I open the tin, I glance sideways at the door. The cat is on the threshold, watching me. I scoop the tuna into a saucer and pop it on the floor, and then I step back.

The cat hesitates and then scurries inside, devouring the food in eager gulps. I know I shouldn't be feeding someone else's cat, it's irresponsible. But I like the idea of having some company in this quiet, lonely house. I don't want to be on my own.

The cat finishes the tuna, licks its lips and sits down, eyeing me expectantly. I crouch down, groaning as my legs complain, and reach out a hand. It sniffs it and then lets me stroke it, lying down on the tiles and purring. But after a couple of minutes, it grows bored of me and, with a flick of its tail, it turns and scurries back out of the house.

I'm sad that it's gone because I'd hoped it would stay awhile. But I remind myself that it's not my cat and it doesn't live here. I stand up slowly and stretch my legs and then something on the kitchen table catches my eye. I stagger backwards as a jolt of fear ripples through me. No, that's not possible. This can't be happening, not again.

Because right in the middle of the table, sitting between my empty breakfast plate and some unopened bills, is the back door key. The key that should be in the kitchen drawer.

4

When Frank and I first moved to London I thought I was living the dream. But it didn't take long for the first cracks to begin to show. We were basically strangers and the gulf between us became even more pronounced in the huge, chaotic city. Frank adjusted easily to our new life. He had a burgeoning career and colleagues to meet after work, while I had nothing to do with my days but wait for him to get home. And when he did, all he wanted to do was take me to bed. We had, it seemed, little to talk about. Or maybe Frank just wasn't a big talker.

But I still worshipped him, perhaps even more so. Because the less he needed me, the more I needed him. I was desperate to impress him, to make sure he didn't regret inviting me to come with him. I kept our poky flat clean, learned to cook, asked him about his day each evening. His answers were always brief, but I was determined to make him open up to me. I wanted to be the one to change Frank, just like he had changed me. He had made me a woman. *His* woman. I was absurdly grateful, indebted to him, and he knew it.

After a few weeks, I started looking for a job. But while Frank had a finance degree, I had scraped my A levels, turned down my university offer, and my only work experience was in a shoe shop. My parents, who had begged me not to go to London, had reluctantly given me some money when I'd refused to back down, but it wouldn't last long.

It was Frank who got me some work, at a Mexican restaurant, close to the flat we had rented in Clapham. He had seen a notice in the window and gone in to enquire on my behalf. I was so thrilled that I'd be able to financially contribute that I didn't stop to think about the fact that I was perfectly capable of getting my own job. I started the following night, and I was so proud when I walked in for my first shift. With me working, Frank and I could finally start our exciting new life together for real.

Only it wasn't exactly how I had expected it to be.

It was evident from the start where the balance of power lay, in all areas of our lives. Frank was in charge of everything. I didn't mind back then, in fact I welcomed it. I had lived a sheltered life and I was overwhelmed by the big city and all its inhabitants. I was terrified of navigating the Tube network or being out late at night, and I was more than happy to have someone looking out for me. When Frank got back from work, he would walk me to the restaurant for my evening shift. Sometimes he'd stay, nursing a beer at the bar. Other times he'd leave but he'd always be there to walk me home again. The other waitresses fluttered their eyelashes at him and told me I was lucky to have such a chivalrous boyfriend, and I beamed with pride. They asked me if he had any handsome friends, which made me realise I'd never met a single one.

When I asked Frank about it on the way home, he told me his friends were from work and that girlfriends weren't invited to his office nights out. I suggested a weekend event, so I could meet them, but his only response was to light a cigarette. Worried that I'd annoyed him, I moved in closer to him, enjoying the flutter I felt at simply touching him. Frank may not have been a talker, but the physical attraction I felt towards him was more than enough.

In the bedroom, Frank had quickly and expertly taken my virginity and before long he was introducing me to things I'd never imagined. He liked to play games and I was too inexperienced to understand that this was not something all couples did. I was the naughty girl who had to be punished. It scared me and sometimes it hurt me. But I never said no. It was like a dark secret between us and it made me feel worldly and sophisticated. I imagined my old friends from school stuck at home, bored, waiting for life to happen to them. Life was happening to me, right here. And as soon as I got Frank to open up to me a little more, I knew that we were going to be so happy.

Over time, Frank moved between jobs, slowly working his way up the ladder, his salary increasing incrementally. I suggested I get a Monday to Friday job so we could spend more time together, but he said our routine worked just fine. So I stayed at the Mexican restaurant. I made friends with the other wait staff and I saw them during the week when Frank was working. At the weekends, if I didn't have a shift, Frank and I went out for dinner or drinks. At home we watched television or had sex. There wasn't anything else Frank wanted to do.

I was happy though, I really was. I was infatuated with Frank and the life that he had given me. I felt proud to be on his arm. He was my world and I was his, and I didn't want anything else. I lost touch with my schoolfriends and rarely went back to visit my parents. We spoke on the phone but with each call I felt

The Widow's Husband 37

increasingly distant from them. I knew my mum and dad loved me, but we'd never been close or affectionate with each other. We'd been a typical, reserved British family and it delighted me that my relationship with Frank was the opposite. We were passionate, intimate. We were untouchable.

And so it was easy to banish any doubts I had about him. The fact that he never invited me out with his colleagues. That he seemed to control every area of my life. That sometimes I felt more like his plaything than his beloved. I rationalised everything. Frank didn't use words, he expressed his love for me physically. My friends at the restaurant said we made a beautiful couple. I never, ever wanted to go back to the boring life of my childhood.

When Frank asked me to marry him, I cried with happiness as I accepted. The wedding was planned quickly, a simple affair because Frank didn't want to waste money. My parents came, along with Frank's mum and two brothers, and we had a ceremony at the registry office followed by a party at the restaurant I worked at, with my friends and some of Frank's work colleagues, who I finally had the opportunity to meet. They were all friendly and told me they'd heard a lot about me, and this extinguished any tiny doubt I'd had. I was on a high that night, clinging to Frank as we smiled for photographs. I still couldn't believe how lucky I was to call this handsome, successful and powerful man mine. To be Mrs Frank Rossi.

Later that evening, a waiter called Juan invited me to dance with him. I'd known Juan for years and I also knew that he had a boyfriend, so I had no qualms in throwing myself into his embrace and letting him swing me around the dance floor. I wrapped my arms around him and laughed in delight as he clasped me tightly. But when I looked up, Frank was watching me and the expression on his face wiped the smile from my own. When the dance finished, I went over and tried to take his hand, but he snatched it away. I giggled, tipsy on champagne.

'Are you jealous?' I teased.

He wouldn't answer me. His face was stony and I became self-conscious of the other guests who were watching us. I tried to take his hand again and this time he stormed out of the restaurant. I followed him, smiling at everyone I passed, trying to make out that all was well. Outside, Frank was pacing up and down the pavement.

'What's wrong, Frank?'

'Are you sleeping with him?'

I stared at him in shock. 'What? What are you talking about?'

He grabbed me then, his hands digging into the tops of my arms. I winced at the pain but I didn't try to move away. I was afraid, scared that I had done something wrong. That I had upset my new husband on our wedding day.

'Frank,' I insisted. 'There's nothing going on between Juan and me.'

'You're mine,' he hissed. 'Mine.'

'Yes,' I insisted. 'Of course I'm yours.'

'I'm going to beat him up.'

'Stop it, Frank. Juan's a friend, he's not interested in me. He has a boyfriend.'

'That's what he told you,' Frank scoffed. 'To make you trust him.'

'No! No, honestly.' I was crying now, all my emotion from the day coming to the fore, mortified that what was supposed to be the best day of my life was turning out like this.

'You can't keep secrets from me, Mags. I'll find out. I'll always find out.'

'There are no secrets!' I was almost shouting now. 'There's nothing going on.'

His grip on my arms loosened. I covered his hand with mine and this time he didn't move away. But when he looked at me, his eyes were hard. 'If you ever cheat on me, I'll kill you.'

And in that moment, I didn't doubt it. Not for one second.

It is this memory I wake up to, gasping for breath. It takes me a minute to work out where I am, to realise that it was a bad dream. I look at the clock and see that it is 5 a.m. As my breathing gradually returns to normal, I wonder why such an old memory has resurfaced now, after all this time. Is it this business with the key? The message from the psychic? Or is it simply age, which is yanking me back into the past, reminding me of long-forgotten times.

I lie there for a few minutes, as the sun begins to rise and flood the room with light. Eventually, I decide to get up and start the day. Tonight, I am going out with Beth, Alyssa and Gary and I'm looking forward to it. It's the distraction I need because I've been dwelling on the strange incidents with the key all week. The only explanation I can think of is that I left it on the table after all. I'm growing senile because I spend so much time alone. I don't want to entertain any other theories because I simply can't deal with the implication.

What I need is to get out and about. Starting with this evening. I am going to wear the M&S dress again, I decide, as I put the kettle on and reach for a mug. This time I only get one out and I heap some coffee granules into it and open the fridge to get some milk. I think about the key again and I go to the kitchen drawer to check it's in there. Thankfully it is.

As I make my coffee, I think about what I will do today. I've been trying to get out every day and I'm feeling the difference. I'm more energetic and less anxious about seeing people. Just the other day I passed the dog walker, the one with the toned arms who probably eats kale, and she said good morning to me. I stopped to pat her dog and she told me she got him from a local rescue centre. It was a brief exchange, but it meant everything because it proves I'm not invisible after all. She will never know what an effort it was for me just to make polite conversation with her. But it's getting easier. With each day that passes, it gets easier.

The weather is unsettled and, in the end, I go for a quick walk around the village and return home. I watch some television, do some tidying and will the time to pass. By four o'clock I'm so desperate for my evening to start that I get ready and then I feel silly, sitting on the sofa in my frock, my hair blow-dried and my make-up caking on my face. Having too much time is a curse because I begin to feel anxious again. I worry that I will say something daft and start to wonder if I should cancel, feign a headache or a brewing virus. But I don't want to do that, I want to see Beth, Alyssa and Gary. I want to have a dinner that wasn't prepared in the microwave. And so before I can talk myself out of it, I get up and leave.

As a result, I'm forty-five minutes early but Gary is already there, sitting on a bar stool, chatting to Mark, the landlord. He waves me over and offers to buy me a drink. I ask for a gin and tonic, reminding myself to nurse it so I don't get too tipsy. As I perch on a stool next to him, my nerves are at an all-time high, but Gary doesn't seem to notice.

'How are your son and daughter-in-law?' I ask him, racking my brain to think of some other questions I can use to fill any awkward silences.

'Great,' Gary says. 'Sophie is due in a couple of weeks, and they've been busy getting the nursery ready. There's baby stuff everywhere. I tripped over a toy rabbit this morning.'

'It'll be strange for you,' I say. 'Having a baby in the house again.'

'Yeah.' Gary takes a drink from his pint. 'To be honest, I've been thinking about moving out and letting them have the place to themselves. They're a young family, they don't want me hanging around and getting in the way.'

'They might be grateful for your support though.'

'I'm not very good with babies,' Gary admits with a self-deprecating smile. 'Back in my day, we went to work and let our wives do all the heavy lifting at home.'

'It's very different now.'

'Don't I know it. Chris, my son, is taking shared parental leave, whatever that is. Fair play to him. These are the moments that matter in life. The ones we should cherish.'

I ignore my habitual feeling of regret. 'Do you have any other children?'

'Yes, but my daughter lives in Australia.'

'Lucky her.'

Gary is easy to talk to. But after a while I've run out of things to ask him and I'm relieved when Beth and Alyssa arrive together. Beth looks beautiful in denim shorts and a vest top and Alyssa is resplendent in a multicoloured sundress. I feel frumpy and old, but I remind myself that they invited me to dinner. They want me here.

We go over to the table we've reserved and order a bottle of wine.

'Cheers,' Beth says, holding up her glass. 'To new friends.'

New friends. I like the sound of it. We're an odd group. Alyssa must be nearly half my age and I can't help but think she should be hanging around with people she has more in common with. And Beth's busy life and successful career feels alien to me. Perhaps Gary and I are most alike, even though he seems to come from a completely different walk of life. But somehow it just works. The conversation flows easily and I realise that I have nothing to be afraid of. It feels natural, being here with these three lovely people.

'I'm thinking of getting a dog,' I say, voicing an idea that has only been a tiny seed in my mind until now. It must be the wine.

'How exciting!' Alyssa enthuses. 'I love dogs. What type?'

'I'm not sure. I was going to go to the rescue centre and see what they have.'

The truth is that I'm craving company in the cottage more than ever. And I like the idea of having a pet. It will give me a reason to leave the house and a purpose for my aimless walks. I've always wanted a dog, but Frank didn't like animals. Now Frank is not here though, and I can do what I like. It will take some time for this to really sink in, but the more I talk about it with Beth, Alyssa and Gary, the more I realise that I want to do it.

'The manager of the local rescue centre is an old mate,' Gary tells me. 'It would be good to see him again. Want me to take you?'

Is there anyone Gary doesn't know? 'That would be great,' I say, already looking forward to it. To having another engagement to fill the empty pages of my diary.

By the time we've finished dinner and paid the bill, I'm more than tipsy. But I refuse Beth's offer of a lift home because I want to walk. To digest the rich food I've eaten and enjoy the warm night. We leave Gary having one for the road at the bar and say goodbye to Alyssa who lives in the opposite direction. Beth gives me another hug and climbs into her car. I walk home, feeling pleasantly intoxicated by the alcohol and the fun I've had.

I'm woozy when I reach the house, and I let myself in and collapse into the armchair. It's the first time I've got home and not felt dread building up inside me. *I can do this*, I think. *I can find a way to move on, to be on my own, to forge a new path. It's not too late.* I pass out within minutes with a smile on my face, sleeping the sleep of the inebriated.

But with sleep comes dreams. Nightmares. Demons. And the words which have haunted me for three decades. Which still haunt me now, even after he's gone.

I'll kill you.

5

Gary picks me up in a battered old Jeep. As I clamber in, he hastily brushes some empty crisp packets and scraps of paper off the passenger seat.

'Thanks for the lift,' I say. I've never learned to drive, something which didn't bother me when we lived in London, but which has become a hindrance in the village.

'No problem. Get home okay the other night?'

I think back to Friday evening, when I woke up in the middle of the night, my mouth dry and my limbs stiff from my uncomfortable position in the armchair.

'Absolutely fine,' I tell Gary. 'You?'

'I stayed until closing,' he admits. 'And then for a little longer after that. It's safe to say that I was feeling sorry for myself on Saturday.'

'At least the baby hasn't arrived yet. I can't imagine the sound of crying is good for a hangover.'

Gary chuckles and then puts the radio on. As pop music fills the car, I relax. I don't know Gary well, but I feel comfortable around him and I'm grateful that he offered to come with me to the rescue centre. I still can't believe that I've made new friends in such a short space of time, I almost want to pinch myself. Tomorrow I'm going for another walk with Beth and afterwards we're going to meet Alyssa for lunch. Our motley crew is fast becoming the thing that I'm living for each day.

I haven't forgotten how it all started at the psychic supper. But as the weeks go by, it's becoming easier to push it to the back of my mind. To find rational explanations for the irrational. To ignore the attacks of trepidation that still ambush me at unexpected moments. *You will never live without me.* Well, he was wrong. Here I am, not just existing but living. Making friends. Getting a dog. Looking to the future. And something is beginning to change inside me. I've spent so long believing I was the one to blame. That I gave up on life and in turn I ruined Frank's too. But now the narrative is shifting in my mind. The bad dreams frighten me but I'm also wondering if they are serving an important purpose. Reminding me what he did to me. What he made me.

And I'm starting to think, perhaps, that none of it is my fault.

We park up at the rescue centre and as soon as I get out of the car, I hear barking in the distance. The manager comes out to greet us, his footsteps crunching on the gravel. I called ahead and he is expecting me. He pats Gary on the back affectionately and they exchange some light-hearted banter before he turns his attention to me.

'I've been through your application form,' he says. 'And I think I may have the perfect dog for you.'

I'm almost bursting with excitement. 'I can't wait to meet them.'

'He's called Benji and he's a crossbreed,' the man explains as he leads us towards the kennels. 'He's seven years old and he came here two months ago when his owner died. You said you didn't mind rehoming an older dog?'

'That's right,' I say. 'I can hardly discriminate when I'm no spring chicken myself. And anyway, I want to give an older dog a chance. I imagine the puppies get snapped up.'

'They do,' the man agrees. 'And poor Benji is desperate to find his forever home.'

He opens the door to the kennels and I'm overwhelmed by all the dogs who are standing at the doors, barking or gazing longingly at us. My heart breaks and then breaks again. I had been looking forward to this but now it's making me sad. All these unwanted animals. I want to take them all home with me, to turn the cottage into a sanctuary. I imagine the look of horror on Frank's face and a surge of defiance runs through me. It's my home now and I can do what I like, including adopting every single dog here.

But sense tells me that one is enough for now. And there, at the end of the row, is a medium-sized dog with wiry brown fur and the sweetest look on his face.

'Is this Benji?' I ask, squatting down with a rush of satisfaction when my legs don't complain as much as usual. My daily walks are doing me the world of good.

'Yes, this is Benji.' The manager opens the door and I step in. Benji immediately rushes towards me and I give him a stroke. He's trying to climb onto my lap and I breathe in the musty smell of him and know immediately that he's the one for me.

'I love him,' I say. 'Can I take him home today?'

The manager laughs. 'I'm so pleased you like him. But we encourage you to visit a couple of times first. Get to know each other. We want to make sure it's a good match.'

My disappointment is palpable, but I know that it's the responsible thing to do. The manager suggests that we take Benji for a walk and I'm beaming as he clips on a lead and hands it to me. We go outside and Benji is clearly overjoyed because he darts about, but he's also considerate of me, hardly pulling on the lead at all. By the time we've returned to the kennels, I'm so in love with him that the idea of leaving him here is excruciating.

'Can I come back at the weekend?' I ask.

The manager smiles. 'Sure. And if you're both happy, I reckon you can take him home then.'

I want to hug him. 'Thank you. Thank you so much!'

In the car on the way home I'm buzzing with excitement and when Gary suggests a quick half at the pub, I'm pleased. We sit at the bar again and he orders me a shandy.

'I can take you again at the weekend if you like,' he says.

'Thank you so much. I do appreciate it.'

'Is this your first dog?'

'Yes. Frank, my husband, didn't like animals.'

'My ex-wife wasn't keen either. Maybe I should get a dog too.'

'Oh you should,' I enthuse. 'Then we can go for walks together.'

Gary looks rather pleased by this suggestion. 'Although I'll have to hold off for now. A new dog and a new baby isn't the best combination.'

'Are you still thinking of moving out?' I ask.

He shrugs. 'I've been looking around but I can't afford the rent on an entire property and I'm a bit too ancient for a house share.'

As the shandy goes to my head, I have an impulsive idea. 'You could always rent my spare room.'

Gary looks at me in surprise. 'Really?'

'To be honest, you'd be doing me a favour,' I admit. 'I haven't paid the mortgage off on the cottage yet and things are, well, they're a bit tight.'

'But didn't your husband have life insurance?'

'I thought he did,' I admit. 'But I found out after he died that he hadn't renewed it.'

Gary is aghast. 'That's awful.'

'It's my fault,' I say quickly. 'I should have known. Sorted it out.'

'Do you have savings?'

'Yes.' I don't know Gary well enough to tell him the truth, so I give him as much as I am prepared to. 'But they won't last forever and I'm well below pension age. Plus, I haven't worked in so long, I don't think anyone would hire me now.'

'What was your previous job?'

'I was a waitress.'

Gary's looking thoughtful. 'Why don't you get a job here?'

I look around. 'At the pub?'

'Why not? They're always looking for staff.'

'Aren't I a bit old?'

Gary laughs. 'You're not old at all.'

'I'm not sure,' I say hesitantly.

Gary shrugs, unconcerned. 'Think about it,' he says. 'And I'll think about the room.'

I can't believe I've just invited a man to move in with me. Is this a midlife crisis? Early onset senility? I have no idea and already I'm beginning to regret it. But Gary hasn't accepted my offer and it's possible that he won't bring it up again. Perhaps we can forget it happened.

Frank would be turning in his grave. That's what I think after I've said goodbye to Gary and I'm walking home. I remember the back door key again. Is Frank really watching me? Is he witnessing how I'm behaving now he's gone? What must he be making of all this? What will my punishment be? And for a moment I'm petrified, a deer caught in the headlights.

But then I see the dog walker again, the kale-eating one, and I tell her that I've just been to the rescue centre and I'm hoping to adopt a dog. She says there's a dog-walking group that meets twice a week in the village and invites me to join them. Then she adds that she can't wait to meet Benji and offers me some advice on settling in a new dog.

By the time I've said goodbye and continued my journey home, my mind has reset itself and I'm just me again; a widow, slowly getting on with my life, finding a way to readjust to my new normal. I see the black cat outside the cottage, and I give it a quick stroke, but I don't feel the urge to entice it inside, because hopefully in a few days Benji will be coming home with me. Anyway, the cat doesn't belong to me.

Like I don't belong to Frank. Not any more.

I make a cup of tea and take it out into the garden, sitting on one of the rotting wooden chairs and looking at the overgrown grass and the flowers that need pruning. That's my next project, I decide. I'm going to tidy up the garden and that will keep me busy for a while. It will be great exercise too. I glance at the shed, wondering if I should strike while the iron is hot and get started this afternoon, when I see something at the back of the garden, moving behind the shed. A shadow, too big to be an animal. Fear jolts through me like electricity.

'Who's there?' I shout, my voice shrill.

There is no response and I clamber up from the chair, torn between running inside and locking the door and confronting whoever is at the back of my garden. Adrenaline starts pumping through my veins, giving me a strength I didn't know I had and so, instead of retreating, I make my way across the garden, calling out again.

'Who's there?'

I reach the end of the garden, trying to hold my nerve, and

peer gingerly behind the shed. But there's no one there. Was it my imagination? A trick of the light, perhaps? I glance uneasily at the shed, steeling myself to open the door and look inside, just in case there's an intruder hiding. I wonder if I should call Gary, or Beth. And even then, at the height of my fear, I feel relief that I have people I can call. People who are looking out for me.

But I don't want to overreact. The garden is quiet and I can't hear any movement inside the shed. It's possible that I've got myself into a tizz for no reason. I slide the bolt and open the shed door, peering inside. It's crammed full of stuff and there's barely room for a cat, let alone a human being. Satisfied that no one is in there, I close the door again and walk back down the garden.

I decide to take my tea inside anyway because I'm still on edge. I close the back door and lock it, putting the key in the drawer. Soon, with any luck, Benji will be here with me and I'm looking forward to his reassuring presence more than ever.

Later, when I've pottered around the house and calmed my nerves, I go out into the garden again to see if the rusty old lawnmower still has any life in it. And when I open the shed, I know immediately that something is different. I look around, trying to work out what it is. And then I realise that it's not what I can see, it's what I can smell. It's aftershave, a scent so familiar to me, one that evokes a tsunami of old emotions: arousal, power, fear.

It's the smell of Frank.

6

Frank bought a two-bedroom flat in South London a few months after we married. After years of renting, it was the first home we'd ever owned and although Frank was paying the mortgage, I was still proud and hopeful that this was a new start. I tried to put our wedding night behind me and look forward to our future together.

I didn't go back to work at the restaurant after we got married. Frank thought it would be better if I gave Juan a wide berth and I was too eager to please him to argue. I quit my job and ignored all the phone calls from my friends until eventually they stopped. With no job and no one to talk to, I was isolated and this made me even more reliant on Frank.

I focused on being a good wife. I devoted myself to furnishing our new home and looking after Frank. I made sure that dinner was always on the table when he got home. I gave him everything he wanted in the bedroom. And I prayed for a baby.

While I retreated from the world, Frank embraced it. He'd charmed his way in with the senior management of the company he worked for and had his eye on a promotion. It seemed that he needed a woman on his arm now that he was mingling with the bosses, and we started being invited to dinner parties and client functions. Frank held court at these events, displaying a charisma that he didn't bring home, making the men guffaw and the women flutter their eyelashes. It was the Frank effect again, but in a different way. I hung off him, smiling at everyone, uncomfortable in the smart dresses that Frank picked out for me to wear. The ones he said would make me fit in with the other wives.

I did not fit in. The women were older than me and they treated me with, at best, suspicion, and at worst, contempt. Some of them were high-flying career women, others were busy raising their children. And what was I? I was nothing. I had no job, no children, no higher education and little to talk about. The only thing I had going for me was my looks.

Frank didn't notice any of this or if he did, he ignored it. But what he couldn't ignore was the looks of admiration the other men gave me at these events. How their expressions glazed over as they looked down my body towards my ample cleavage. I didn't encourage it in the slightest, but I couldn't help it. It wasn't my fault.

Still, Frank didn't like it. In fact, he loathed it. I saw the way his eyes flashed with rage, even though he deftly hid it from the men he was trying so hard to impress. He punished me when we got home though. Stripped me down, tied me up. Told me I was a naughty girl. I gave up trying to argue with him. I let him do what he needed to do to feel powerful and in control. To prove just how much I loved him, that I would do anything for him.

Because I still loved him, with all my heart. And when he said he couldn't live without me it was music to my ears because I couldn't live without him either. I was addicted to him.

'You are mine,' he said, over and over again, in those intimate moments.

'Yes,' I whispered back, giving my whole self to him. 'Yes I am.'

* * *

Gary takes me back to the rescue centre at the weekend, and after spending some time with Benji, I'm allowed to take him home. I ordered some pet supplies online in preparation and have everything I need waiting for us back at the cottage. Still, I can't resist buying a few extras from the rescue centre shop. Then I sign some paperwork and take Benji's lead, feeling pride, excitement and nervous trepidation.

In the Jeep, Benji looks out of the window, his tongue lolling. I keep glancing back at him in disbelief. I can't believe that I have a dog. It feels so surreal, like I might wake up from this dream at any moment. It also feels a little impulsive but instead of worrying me, it excites me. Gary drops us off at the cottage and gives us a wave before speeding off, no doubt to the pub where he seems to spend most of his spare time, and I'm left standing in the front garden, on my own, wondering what the hell I've just done.

Benji spends the first half an hour darting around the house, hurrying from room to room, sniffing everything. As I watch him, my panic begins to subside. He's a gorgeous dog and I know we're going to get along just fine once we get used to each other.

Still, I wonder if he's hungry, if he needs the toilet, if he should go for a walk. In the end I decide to take him out for a wander around the village and as soon as I reach for the lead, he scurries up to me, paws skittering on the kitchen tiles, his eyes bright.

I quickly learn that having a dog is the easiest way to make friends. Everyone we pass stops to admire him. Benji laps up the attention, letting people stroke him, and I feel a rush of pride. When we pass the pub, I see Gary sitting on a table outside, and I go over to say hello. Benji, who has already decided that Gary is a friend, throws himself at him.

'He really is a super dog,' Gary says, rubbing Benji's ears.

'I know. I'm already in love with him.'

Benji may be a rescue dog, but I think I need him more than he needs me. I've been getting terribly worked up, convincing myself that I can smell Frank's aftershave. For the past few nights, I've been unable to sleep. I lie awake listening to the creaks and groans of the house, terrified there's someone there. My heart pounds against my chest and I drip with sweat. I put the radio on to drown out the silence and only then do I eventually drop off.

I'm too embarrassed to tell any of my new friends. They'll think I'm some batty old loner. And deep down I know that it's not real because it can't possibly be. There's no such thing as ghosts, especially not ones who smell and move keys. Frank is gone.

Sometimes I wish I'd never gone to that damn psychic supper. But then I would never have met Beth, Gary and Alyssa. I might not have adopted Benji. That evening set off a chain of events in my life and led me to where I am right now: sitting outside the pub in the glorious sunshine, chatting to my friend and clutching on to my new dog's lead.

Gary's phone rings and I can tell from his expression that something has happened. When he hangs up, he looks at me with wide eyes.

'Sophie's gone into labour,' he says. 'They're on the way to the hospital.'

'You should go,' I tell him.

'Do you think they want me there?'

'I'm sure they would.' I look down at Benji. 'I'd come with you, but I don't want to leave Benji on his own when he's only just arrived.'

'Of course, I understand.'

Gary stands up, looking uncertain. 'Right then. I'll be off.'

I smile encouragingly. 'Good luck!'

Once Gary's gone, I get up and continue my walk. I know I should take Benji home and let him settle in but I'm enjoying the fresh air and I'm reluctant to be in the cottage. Hopefully Benji's presence will banish my paranoia once and for all. I've considered selling up more than once, but I can't afford it, not until I've paid off some more equity. No one is going to give me a mortgage because I haven't worked in thirty years, so I'd need to be able to pay for any new home in cash. Anyway, I have nowhere else to go. My parents died years ago, I don't have any siblings and despite being middle-aged, I have no old friends either. It's a sobering thought. But it also reminds me that I need to start standing on my own two feet, I've put it off for too long already and my dwindling savings won't last for much longer.

On impulse, I change direction and go into the pub, striding up to Mark before I can chicken out.

'Is it okay that I've brought Benji inside?' I ask.

Mark beams. 'Of course. We're a very dog-friendly pub. He's a lovely chap.'

'I only got him today,' I tell him as he comes around the bar and crouches down to make a fuss of Benji. And then I add hurriedly, 'I don't suppose you're looking for staff?'

Mark looks up at me in surprise. 'As a matter of fact, I am. Are you asking for yourself or someone else?'

'Myself,' I say, my stomach churning with nerves. I haven't

had a job interview in decades. Not that you could call this a job interview but it's the closest I've had to one.

Mark stands up and smooths his trousers. 'Do you have any bar experience?'

'I used to work as a waitress at a restaurant in London,' I explain and then add, for the sake of transparency, 'It was a long time ago though, so I don't have a reference.'

Mark appraises me but his gaze is friendly. 'How about a trial run? Do you want to come in and do a shift on Monday? See how you get on?'

I try, and fail, to hide my enthusiasm. 'Oh yes, that would be wonderful, thank you!' And then I have a thought. 'Can I bring Benji with me, or is that too much? It's just that he's only just arrived and I don't want to leave him alone all day.'

The landlord strokes Benji again. 'He seems like a gentle sort. Bring him with you. It'll be nice to have a pub pet.'

As we make the arrangements and I leave the pub again, I can't stop grinning. A job behind the bar might not be every middle-aged woman's dream career, but for me, it's everything I could have hoped for. A chance to meet some more people, a reason to leave the house – and stay out of the house – every day. Something that will tire me out and make me sleep better at night. And of course some much-needed income.

I never got involved in the finances. That, like everything else, was Frank's job. I had a credit card to pay for things like groceries, household goods and so on. And I never bought anything else. I didn't go out for dinner or have expensive gym memberships. I cut my own hair. I lived extremely frugally, despite Frank's successful career. It wasn't until after he died that I realised he had not done the same.

When I sat down with the solicitor, who Frank had named as executor of his will, I had expected to be told that I would never

The Widow's Husband

need to worry about money. I didn't need a lot to get by and I was sure that we had ample savings to cover my costs. When he showed me the bank statements, I thought there must be some mistake. It couldn't be possible. But it was.

Frank had lost almost all our savings and had liquidated his business without my knowledge. Some people were claiming he owed them money and the solicitor was trying to make sure that I wasn't liable for any of it. I also learned that Frank had cancelled our life insurance so the mortgage would not be paid off upon his death.

He had, quite frankly, dropped me right in it.

Guilt had mingled with my anger. I hadn't worked. I hadn't contributed financially so why did I feel my husband, who had worked hard all his life, owed me? But it was more complicated than that. I hadn't worked because Frank didn't let me. I had been imprisoned in my own home because that was where Frank insisted I stay. That was where he wanted me.

And even when he didn't want me any more, he didn't want anyone else to have me either.

I had considered the obvious explanations for our dire financial situation. Affairs. Gambling addiction. Extravagant spending on his work trips. A simple case of a business venture gone wrong. They were all plausible, but I'd never know the truth. And the more time that passed, the less I wanted to know. Perhaps Frank had lived a better life than I thought. And while it upset me, it also, somehow, made the guilt of our failed marriage easier to bear.

I'm ready to move on now. I'm getting braver and bolder with each day that passes. Now here I am, on the cusp of starting a new job, and I'm so excited. I can't believe how far I've come in such a short space of time. How easy it's been to re-engage with life. And I ignore the voices in my head chastising me for not doing it sooner. I've done it now and that's what matters. The shadow that has shrouded my life is lifting.

But as Benji and I make our way home, and the cottage comes into view, I smell it again. His aftershave, wafting in the air. How is it possible? Could someone else in the village wear the same aftershave as him? Yes, that must be it. It doesn't explain why I smelled it in the shed but it's an explanation that causes me the least stress. Perhaps the neighbour likes to slap on a bit too much in the mornings. I know Frank did.

I continue walking until I reach the garden path, stopping to open the little gate, and persuading myself that I have nothing to fear from my own home. Then I look up and see the smashed window on the ground floor, and all my self-reassurance evaporates into thin air.

7

'Ghosts don't smash windows.'

I try to absorb Gary's comforting words, willing them to soak into my mind. I'm standing behind the bar, polishing glasses, on the third day of my new job. Benji is lying by Gary's feet, snoozing. The lunch rush is over and the pub is quiet so I don't have much to do. I sailed through my trial shift and I'm now on the staff rota, working three days and two evenings a week. I should be proud, but instead I'm living in a constant state of panic.

It's all become too much and today I've told Gary about what's been going on. He's a pub regular, popping in most days for a pint, and I find him incredibly easy to talk to. The words tumble out of me before I can stop myself and although I know it sounds irrational, especially to someone as pragmatic as Gary, at least he hasn't laughed at me.

'It was probably an attempted break-in,' he says. 'Was anything taken?'

'No, nothing.'

'Maybe it was kids then. Perhaps they kicked a ball through

the window and legged it before they got caught. I often see them playing out on the street.'

'Perhaps.' I hope it's true. I want it to be true.

'Did you call the police?'

'No. When I realised nothing had been taken, I decided not to.'

Gary rubs his head. He looks exhausted. His new granddaughter, Emilia, is home from the hospital and is already ruling the roost. Apparently she doesn't sleep. At all.

'At least you have Benji now,' he tells me. 'He'll alert you to any intruders.'

I look down at my beautiful, placid dog, fast asleep and snoring. 'Maybe.'

'Do you really believe the house is haunted?' Gary's eyebrows are raised.

'I don't know. I'm tired. I'm not sleeping well.'

'But your husband died in the house, right?'

'Yes.'

Gary is thoughtful. 'You know what you said the other week? About me renting your spare room? Maybe it's not such a bad idea.'

I look at him with interest. I'd been hoping that Gary would forget all about my offer, but suddenly the idea of someone else being in the house holds a strong appeal. Especially a man, who could protect me. I'm painfully aware that I'm regressing. Just as I finally emerge from relying on one person, I'm attaching myself to the next. But this is different. Gary is not Frank, he is not my husband. He's just a friend, whose company I enjoy. And whose rent money I could really do with. I'm in control of this situation.

'The offer still stands,' I tell him.

'How much rent were you thinking?'

I pluck a random figure from my mind and from the look on

Gary's face, I know it's probably too low. But it will still be a huge help to me, in more ways than one.

'When can I move in?' he asks.

'Whenever you like.'

'How about this weekend? I really want to give my son and his new family some space. We're all climbing over each other and it's not fair on them. And, if I'm being selfish, I desperately need a good night's sleep.'

That makes two of us, I think. I imagine sharing my space with someone again. Bumping into Gary in the kitchen. Will I be self-conscious in my dressing gown? Will we have the same taste in television shows? It'll take some getting used to, that's for sure, but I'm becoming increasingly convinced that it's the perfect plan. And it's only temporary. There won't be any contracts or twelve-month agreements, so if it all goes horribly wrong, then he can move out again. I can't believe that someone I've only known for a few weeks is about to share my house but there's another feeling inside me which is fighting for attention. An impulsive recklessness that I'm doing something so un-'me' again. And I like it.

As Gary starts talking about packing up his things and bringing them over on Saturday, my mind wanders. To the back door key, the smashed window. The smell of Frank. Even having Benji in the house hasn't given me the feeling of safety I crave. He's a wonderful dog and I love having him around, but he's so sweet and friendly that I doubt he'd scare off a mouse, let alone an intruder. Or a ghost.

But I don't believe in ghosts. Do I?

With Gary keeping me company, my shift flies by and by the time I've finished, Alyssa and Beth have arrived. We're having an early dinner together and I take Benji for a quick walk before returning to the pub and sitting down beside Alyssa.

'How's the new job going?' she asks me.

My eyes light up. 'Oh, it's wonderful. I'm really enjoying it.'

'I must say, I'm a little jealous. I miss working.'

'Will you go back, when the children are older?'

'I don't know. Dylan says I don't need to. He thinks I should enjoy the time to myself when the kids are at school.'

I think about Frank. When he'd told me that I didn't need to work I'd thought he was being loving and generous. Now I realise that it wasn't a gesture, it was an order.

'I think it's good for women to keep some independence,' I tell Alyssa. 'If you want to go back to work, you should. It doesn't matter what your husband thinks.'

She looks at me with interest. 'Hmm, perhaps you're right.'

'What did you used to do? Before the children?'

'I worked in finance. That's how I met Dylan.'

Frank also worked in finance. I gaze at Alyssa and wonder if she ever crossed paths with my late husband. But the chances are slim and, anyway, I don't want to bring up Frank. I don't want to taint this moment, or my friendships with these people.

'Shall we tell them the news?' Gary is looking at me like an excited child.

'Oh yes,' I say. 'Do.'

'Maggie and I are going to be housemates. I'm moving into her cottage.'

Beth claps her hands with delight, but a look of concern flashes over Alyssa's face before she covers it up with a smile. 'Oh wow. When did that happen?' she asks.

As Gary talks, I study Beth and Alyssa. Beth seems thrilled for us, but Alyssa is quiet and I make a mental note to ask her about it later. Why would she disapprove of this arrangement? Is she worried for us because we barely know each other? It is quite a spontaneous thing to do but I'm determined to only look at the positives. I have a new job, a new dog and soon I'll have a new housemate. I'm fitter and healthier than I've been for years and my confidence is growing. I don't want anything, or anyone, to rain on my parade.

After dinner, Beth dashes off in the car and Gary goes home to start packing, so I offer to walk Alyssa home. She doesn't need an escort but I'm keen to ask her why she's got reservations about Gary moving in with me. As we stroll through the village, basking in the evening sunshine, I tentatively bring it up with her.

Alyssa scrunches up her nose. 'I'm just looking out for you, Maggie. You're a single woman, living alone, and I don't like the idea of a stranger being in your house.'

'But Gary's not a stranger, he's our friend.'

'We haven't known him for very long. And he's...' Alyssa pauses. 'Never mind.'

'What is it? What were you going to say?'

I can tell that Alyssa is battling with something. 'I'm just not sure about him.'

'Why?'

She shrugs. 'I can't put my finger on it. It might be nothing.'

But alarm bells are ringing now. 'Alyssa, tell me, please.'

She turns to me, conflicted. 'I met Sophie, his daughter-in-law, the other day. She was taking the baby out for a walk in the pram and I was by the pond with the kids, feeding the ducks. We got chatting and she told me that her father-in-law is a nightmare.'

I frown. 'In what way?'

'She said he's lazy and always getting in the way. He hasn't lifted a finger to help with the new baby. And he drinks. A lot.'

I process Alyssa's words. Are these red flags or simply the complaints of an exhausted and overwhelmed new mother in conflict with her father-in-law? Gary's been honest that he's from a different generation and not good with babies. It's one of the reasons he wants to move out because he feels like he's constantly getting in the way. It doesn't paint him in the best light but I'm not sure it makes him a monster. And I know that he drinks because I see him at the pub every day I work there, but I've never seen him drunk, not once.

I haven't met Sophie, but I've spent time with Gary, and I decide to give him the benefit of the doubt. 'It's only temporary. If it doesn't work out, I'll ask him to leave.'

'What if he refuses to go?'

I hadn't thought about that. Have I just made a huge mistake in inviting Gary to live with me? But then I think about Mark, my new boss at the pub. He's got nothing but positive things to say about Gary and he seems a good judge of character. And Benji adores Gary. Don't people say that dogs are excellent at reading humans?

'Look,' I tell Alyssa. 'I really appreciate you looking out for me. But I think it will be fine. I'm looking forward to having some company, to be honest.'

She touches my arm. 'I know. I'm sorry. And I don't want to worry you.'

I fix a smile on my face. 'You haven't.'

'It must be hard for you, living alone after being with your husband for so long.'

'It was at first,' I admit. 'But I'm getting used to it.'

'I think you're doing brilliantly. Can I ask, what's your secret to a happy marriage?'

I almost laugh out loud. If anyone knows the secret to that, it's certainly not me. I could give Alyssa a generic answer, gloss over the truth, but I decide to be honest for once. After all, Frank isn't here any more to contradict or punish me.

'Our marriage wasn't a happy one, Alyssa. We got together when I was very young and I was absolutely infatuated with Frank. So much so that I was blind to who he really was.'

She looks at me curiously. 'What do you mean?'

'Frank was jealous and controlling. For a long time, I thought it was because he loved me and wanted to protect me. I realised too late that his intentions were selfish.'

Alyssa's eyes are wide. 'Were you afraid of him?'

I consider the question, marvelling at how time is a healer. How I can talk about this with Alyssa when previously it would have been incomprehensible to say the words aloud.

'Yes, I was. But it's complicated.'

'You don't have to talk about it.'

'It's not that I don't want to talk about it. I just don't know how to explain it. Frank was a powerful man in his youth. And I liked that about him. Being his girl made me feel safe.'

Alyssa nods but I know she doesn't understand. These modern women are strong and independent. They're not the naive, delicate flower that I was when I met Frank.

'It wasn't until after we married that I realised I wasn't his wife, I was his possession. Things got worse after that, but by then I was isolated. Frank was all I knew and all I had.'

'You never thought about leaving him?'

'Yes, I did. But I knew that I wouldn't. I had nowhere to go. No friends, no family. No money or job. I'd lost my confidence. That's why I told you to keep working, if you want to. It's good to know that you can stand on your own two feet, if you ever need to.'

'You're right.' Alyssa stands up straighter. 'You're so right.'

'Not that you'll ever need it,' I add quickly. 'I'm sure your husband is lovely.'

'He is. He's so supportive and he's great with the kids. You never had children?'

'We tried for years. But it didn't happen for us.'

'I'm so sorry. Did you ever consider IVF or adoption?'

I shake my head. 'No. IVF wasn't as widely available as it is now and anyway Frank flatly refused to have someone examining his tackle, as he put it. I suggested adoption once and it didn't go down well. He said he wasn't raising someone else's child.'

'But what about you?'

'I wanted children.' I'm welling up just talking about it. 'I wanted them so much.'

'Surely Frank could have considered it, knowing how much it meant to you?'

'That's not how Frank worked. Anyway, when it became clear that I wasn't going to be a mother, I kind of gave up on myself. I was lonely and depressed and that led to a chronic inertia. I didn't look after myself, I stopped taking care of the home.'

'And how did Frank react to that?'

'With disgust. He told me I was useless, pathetic. He locked me in the flat as punishment, but it's not like I had anywhere to go anyway.'

Alyssa's eyes fill with tears. 'Oh Maggie.'

'You shouldn't feel sorry for me,' I say. 'It's my own damn fault.'

'No, it's not.'

'I felt so guilty that I'd failed him as a wife. I thought I deserved my punishment. I convinced myself that if we'd had children, our marriage would have been perfect.'

'But Frank would still have been Frank. He wouldn't have changed.'

'You're right. I know that now.'

'And yet he's still controlling you, even though he's dead. Because you still blame yourself. You think you're a failure.'

It's like she can see into my soul. 'Yes,' I say quietly.

Alyssa grips my arm. 'You are not a failure, Maggie. He failed *you*.'

'We failed each other, that's the truth of it. We should never have married. I was not the wife that Frank wanted me to be.'

'And he wasn't the husband he should have been.'

'Perhaps.'

'Quite frankly, Maggie, he sounds like an absolutely good for nothing arsewipe.'

The sound of my laughter cuts through the tension that has been building up around me. And once I start, I can't stop. Soon I'm doubled over.

'Oh Alyssa,' I say, when I can finally speak.

'Well, someone needed to say it. Look, Frank is gone. He can't control you unless you let him. So don't let him. Be the strong woman you wished you were when you were younger. And stop feeling guilty for things that simply aren't your fault. You can't change the past, but you can change your future so don't make the same mistakes again.'

Her words are music to my ears. Already I can feel the burden of guilt lifting from my shoulders. I don't want to look back, I want to look forward. I just hope Frank will let me.

'I can feel him,' I confess. 'In the house. I can smell him too.'

'He's gone, Maggie. You have to let him go.'

Is that the problem? Is it me clinging on to Frank, rather than the other way around? Refusing to let him go? Is that why I feel like he's haunting me? He was such a dominant presence in my life that perhaps it's just been hard to accept that he's really gone.

We reach Alyssa's door and she leans in to hug me. 'I'm always happy to talk.'

I give her a squeeze. 'Thank you.'

As I walk home, with Benji at my heel, I think of ghosts. Frank's. The children we never had. The young, pretty version of me who had her whole life ahead of her. The world is filled with dreams never realised. Are these what really haunt us? It's sad but it's comforting too because it's something I can control, something I can banish. Talking to Alyssa was like having a therapy session and I'm so grateful that we had the chance to discuss it. She's right, Frank is gone and it's time to stop letting him control me.

But as I walk up the path to the front door, Benji suddenly starts barking furiously, and I wonder if he can see them too. The ghosts that refuse to leave me.

8

It was Frank who started encouraging me to eat. I'd always had a good figure and took pride in my appearance but with no job, no social life and no babies to distract me, I craved *something* and it didn't take much persuasion. Frank would come home laden with junk food and sweet treats and I would dive in, enjoying the sugar rush. I did no exercise and when I started to gain weight, Frank told me not to worry about it. I had always assumed he would want to keep me young, beautiful and desirable, so I'd look good on his arm. I realised too late that he wanted the opposite, because it would stop men gawping at me.

Frank didn't like me going out alone. I acquiesced to his demands, because by then the idea of leaving the house on my own frightened me anyway. I never went clothes shopping and Frank had long stopped buying me new dresses, so my wardrobe became increasingly limited as my size changed. As the years went by, I became no threat to the other wives. At the dinner parties their husbands' gazes no longer skimmed over my body and rested on my breasts. I was invisible to them now, just another ball and chain, as they referred to their wives, guffawing loudly, their masculinity dominating the room. The wives never truly accepted me, but their hostility mellowed. If anything, I think they pitied me.

But I was no longer a naughty girl either. Frank and I had been together for nearly ten years and I could feel his sexual interest in me waning. The electricity that had sparked between us in the early years was fizzling out. I told myself that this was part and parcel of married life and that it happened to all couples. I'd gained a bit of weight and Frank was tired a lot. He worked long hours and often travelled. We had even less to say to each other. How could I talk about my day when I hadn't left the house? How could I make him look at me in the way that he used to when I felt about as desirable as a rubbish bin?

I was convinced that children would solve everything. We were a family without a family, that was the problem. We were ageing in a natural way but were struggling to adapt. The problem was that Frank and I were intimate less and less, which made me anxious. But I was too afraid to bring it up, too worried about making Frank angry.

I could feel the dynamic shifting between us again. Frank still had the power, but he used it in different ways. To diminish me. To tell me I was useless. He'd come home from work and scowl that there was no dinner on the table. He'd ask me what the hell I'd done all day. He'd wrinkle his nose at the un-hoovered carpet. And I'd apologise and promise to make more of an effort. But the next day, after he'd left for work, I'd sit around in my pyjamas, watching daytime television and working my way through the stash of food in the cupboards. I dreaded the moment when I would hear his key in the lock at the end of the day.

Frank started telling me I was disgusting. He seemed to conveniently ignore the fact that he had enabled me and said the reason why we couldn't conceive was because I was overweight. Because I didn't exercise and ate so much junk food. I was hurt and confused because I thought it was what he wanted. What he had encouraged. I was also ashamed because I knew he was right. But by then I was in a cycle of destruction and I didn't know how to escape. The more depressed I became, the more I craved salt and sugar.

I couldn't please Frank, no matter what I did. I couldn't say the right thing, do the right thing. He started going to the dinner parties without me, telling me I was an embarrassment. Saying I'd have nothing to talk to the other wives about because I was so boring. I suggested that I get a job and he laughed.

'Who would hire *you*?' he said.

And I believed him. No one would hire me because I was useless.

And yet, for some obscure reason, we couldn't live without each other. Frank could have left me at any time. He had money and I'm sure he had attention from women. He was still attractive, he hadn't given up on himself yet. But he always came home to me. Was it because somewhere, deep down, he truly loved me? Or was it because he needed to control me to thrive? Clearly it fed his ego, his pride, his power. It made him who he was and so without me, perhaps he was also nothing. He was still possessive, even though he rarely wanted me sexually any more.

'If I ever see you with another man, I'll kill you both,' he told me once, when we were watching a movie about a woman having an extramarital affair. In the film, the husband finds out about the affair and kills the man his wife is sleeping with.

'I would never do that,' I replied immediately.

And he looked me up and down. 'No one would have you anyway.'

* * *

Gary turns up in his battered old Jeep, heaving with belongings. I look on in horror. Where is it all going to go? The spare room is a double, but it's not huge. Is Gary going to take over the entire house with his stuff? What have I done?

Benji is more excited than me. He dashes out and starts running around the Jeep, sniffing furiously, his tail wagging. Gary climbs out and pats the dog before turning to me.

'I've just brought a few essentials,' he says. 'I can go back for the rest.'

I gulp. 'Lovely. Cup of tea?'

'I'd kill for a beer.'

It is eleven o'clock in the morning. I think of what Alyssa said to me and then push it to the back of my mind. Moving house is stressful and if Gary wants a beer then who am I to judge? I head into the kitchen and open the fridge. Yesterday I bought a six-pack of lager, knowing it was Gary's favourite, and I wonder now how long it will last. I take one out of the fridge, open it and go back outside.

'Thanks, Maggie.' Gary takes it from me and drinks deeply.

I look away. 'Need any help?'

'Nah, I'm fine. You carry on with what you were doing.'

'I was just about to take Benji for a walk, actually.'

'Good idea. By the time you come back, hopefully I'll be a bit more settled.'

I hand over the set of keys I've had cut for him. 'These are for you.'

'Nice one.'

With a last look at the Jeep, I call Benji, clip on his lead and begin to walk. It is late September and the weather is changing. Benji is skittish, and he jumps around, chasing fallen leaves. As soon as we reach the fields, I let him off the lead and he dashes off, seeking out squirrels. I walk with my arms crossed defensively, although I'm not sure why. I have been looking forward to Gary moving in so why am I in a funk about it now? Are Alyssa's words playing on my mind? No, that's not it. With a start I realise that it is Frank who is monopolising my thoughts, not Alyssa. *If I ever see you with another man, I'll kill you both.* But Frank is no longer around to carry out his threat. And in any case, nothing is going on between Gary and I, we're just friends. So why am I feeling uneasy about him moving in?

A noise startles me and I turn, half expecting to see Frank striding towards me, his face contorted with anger. But it's Beth who approaches me, waving furiously.

'I thought it was you!' she calls. 'I'm just out for a morning hike. I've walked all the way from Harpenden along the public footpath. Oh, it's such a lovely route.'

Beth looks the picture of health, her long legs wrapped in jeans, her hair loose around her shoulders. She reaches me, slightly breathless.

'Has Gary moved in?' she asks.

'He's there now, unpacking. I thought I'd give him some space.'

Benji comes rushing over and Beth crouches down to stroke him. 'How are you?'

'I'm fine,' I say.

Beth looks up at me. 'Are you sure? You seem a little off.'

'It's just the change, I think. You know, having someone new in the house.'

'Of course, I understand. But actually I think it will be good for you both. And, well, you never know. Perhaps love will bloom?'

My face contorts. 'No, Beth, we're just friends,' I snap.

She looks at me curiously. 'I was joking, Maggie.'

'Sorry.' I am ashamed by my reaction. 'I'm just feeling a bit strange today.'

'Do you want to get a coffee?'

I smile gratefully at her. 'I'd love that.'

In the cafe, Beth fetches the drinks and a bowl of water for Benji, while I find us a table. By the time she's come over with our coffees, I've composed myself.

'I'm sorry I was touchy earlier,' I say. 'I'm just wondering if asking Gary to move in was a good idea.'

'Is it Frank?'

The mention of his name on her lips startles me. It's like two lives colliding and although I've talked about him briefly to Beth, I've compartmentalised them in my mind.

I nod. 'Yes.'

'But as you said, you and Gary are just friends. You're not replacing him. And to be honest, even if you were, I wouldn't judge. People have to move on.'

'Have you moved on?'

She smiles. 'No. It's a bit of a pot calling the kettle black situation.'

'I really think you should, Beth. You're young. You deserve to be happy.'

'So do you, Maggie.'

'I still get two mugs out in the morning sometimes,' I admit. 'I've even made two coffees on occasion. Old habits are hard to break.'

'Oh, I know, I got two bikes out of the shed the other day,' Beth confides.

'Do you ever feel like your partner is still here?'

Beth frowns. 'How do you mean?'

'Like he's in the room with you.'

'I talk to him sometimes. Well, more than sometimes to be honest. And often I'll walk into a room and half expect to see him. But I know he's gone, if that's what you mean.'

'What if he's not?'

Beth is looking at me curiously. 'Where has all this come from?'

'I don't know.' I look away. 'Forget I said anything.'

'Is it this business with the back door key? Because honestly, I wouldn't worry about it. People leave keys in pots all the time. It was probably a lucky guess.'

'You're right.' I don't want to talk about it any more. 'Tell me what you've been up to.'

Beth starts chatting away about a work project and by the time we've finished our coffee, my equilibrium has been restored and I'm ready to go home and see how Gary's getting on. The thought of not returning to an empty house cheers me and I tell myself that this was a good idea after all. I'm not working tonight so perhaps I can cook a nice meal and we can have a chat and get to know each other better. And I'm sure I'll sleep well tonight, knowing I'm not alone. My mind and body crave a good night's slumber.

When I return to the house, Gary's sitting on the sofa, his feet up on the coffee table, drinking a beer. I suspect it's not the same one I gave him a couple of hours ago.

'All unpacked?' I ask, even though I know what the answer is.

'Well, everything's inside, so I thought I deserved a quick break.'

'Were your son and daughter-in-law sad to see you go?'

Gary laughs. 'They're probably drinking a bottle of champagne to celebrate.'

I don't want to pry but I can't stop myself. 'Do you get on with Sophie?'

'She's a lovely woman and her heart's in the right place but she's a little bit, shall we say, *uptight*? And she thinks I'm a lazy good-for-nothing, always getting in her way.'

I sag with relief. There we are then. Gary's openly admitting his own faults and it corroborates what his daughter-in-law complained to Alyssa about. There are no skeletons in Gary's closet, he's an open book and that's why I've warmed to him.

'I thought I could make us some dinner tonight,' I say.

Gary springs up from the sofa. 'I'll do it,' he replies. 'It's the least I can do after you've invited me to stay with you. I'll go to the shops now.'

He's clearly making an effort and I smile warmly. 'Lovely.'

Gary returns a couple of hours later and I suspect he stopped at the pub on the way back. But he arrives laden with bags and sets about chopping vegetables. I offer to help but he won't hear of it and so I sit at the kitchen table, watching him.

'Do you cook a lot?'

'I learned after the divorce. Couldn't survive on oven chips and pub grub forever. But I'm not exactly a Michelin-starred chef. It'll be chicken, potatoes and veg.'

'Sounds delicious.'

'What about you? Do you cook much?'

'I used to when I was younger. But then, I don't know, I lost the enthusiasm for it. After that, it was ready meals most of the time.'

I think of Frank. The doctor's warnings that he should eat better. The endless ready meals. And then I shiver, as though someone has walked over my grave.

'I'm making more of an effort to cook from scratch now,' I add. 'I'm eating better than I have done in years and I've lost a bit of weight.'

'You can tell, Maggie, you're looking great.'

His comment makes me blush and I look away. 'Thank you.'

We eat at the kitchen table, sharing a bottle of wine. The food is delicious and I tuck into the potatoes with gusto while Gary tells me about his work, sharing anecdotes that are so ridiculous they make me snort with laughter.

'This one wealthy client had some stone statues in her garden, including a naked man,' he says. 'I was moving one and accidentally dropped it, and its tackle broke clean off!'

I lean forward, enthralled. 'Did you manage to stick it back on?'

'I had some superglue in the van, but I was so stressed about fixing it before the lady got home, I slathered it on and then grabbed the wrong side, sticking my hand to it.'

I clap my hands with delight. 'What happened then?'

'My colleague had to prise it off me and together we managed to get it stuck back on. The lady never said a word. But to this day, I wonder if it stayed in place.'

'That sounds a lot more exciting than my job at the Mexican restaurant.'

'Was that the only previous job you've had?'

My smile evaporates and I look away. 'Yes. Frank didn't want me to work.'

Gary is nonplussed. 'My ex-wife didn't work either.'

The difference is that Gary's ex-wife was raising their children. I was sitting at home doing nothing. But I'm not that person any more, I remind myself.

'Tell me more stories about your work,' I urge Gary, craving laughter again.

When we've finished eating, I wash up and Gary dries, and then he suggests we put on a film. We sit down together on the sofa and choose a comedy. It's odd, being in such close proximity to a man, and I feel uncomfortable and self-conscious at first.

But I soon relax, especially when Benji jumps up and settles himself between us on the sofa. Gary starts laughing uproariously at an amusing punchline and his easiness is infectious.

I go to bed just after ten. Gary is still watching television and I say goodnight and then head upstairs to use the bathroom. By the time I'm in bed I'm so shattered that I fall asleep immediately, Benji dozing at the end of the bed by my feet.

I awake with a start a few hours later, immediately on edge without knowing why. Did I have a bad dream? But then a feeling creeps over me and chills me all the way to the bone. There's someone in the room. I can feel their presence, an instinct that I'm not alone.

I sit up, my eyes adjusting to the gloom, and then I see it. There is a dark shadow on the other side of the room, in the corner. It is still and silent. And it is watching me.

9

I scream, gasping for breath, and as I scramble around frantically to turn on my bedside table lamp, I knock it to the floor and Benji starts barking furiously. There is a flurry of activity on the landing and then the room is flooded with light.

Gary is standing there in his boxer shorts, his hand on the light switch.

'What's going on?' he demands.

'There was someone here, in my room.'

Gary looks around. 'Are you sure?'

'Yes!' I cry. I point to the corner of the room. 'They were right there.'

'Stay here.'

Gary calls for Benji and I hear them racing down the stairs. I remain in bed, clutching on to the duvet and shaking with fear. Why is this happening?

If I ever see you with another man, I'll kill you both.

Asking Gary to move in was supposed to make me feel safer but the opposite has happened, and I can't help but feel I'm being punished. Frank is angry that I'm moving on. He is furious that I've invited another man into our home.

No, this can't be happening. It makes no sense. It must have been a bad dream. And yet I'm sure I was awake when I saw the shadow. And I was definitely awake when I smelled Frank's aftershave and when I found the back door key in the pot.

Oh God.

I can hardly breathe. I think I'm going to have a panic attack. All the old feelings that I've worked so hard to bury are rising to the surface again and I'm terrified. I will never be free of Frank because he will never let me be. I will be trapped forever.

Gary reappears in the doorway. 'There's no one here, Maggie, I've searched the whole house. And there's no sign of any forced entry either.'

Perhaps I should be relieved but I'm even more afraid. At least a burglar would explain what has just happened. I can just about cope with a human being trying to break into my house. What I can't cope with is the prospect of it being someone else. *Something* else.

Gary is watching me carefully. 'Are you okay?'

I'm trying to catch my breath. My body is slick with sweat and my hair is stuck to my face. All I can do is nod.

'I think you had a nightmare,' Gary says, still looking at me intently.

'Perhaps,' I say weakly, because I don't know what else to say.

'Shall I stay with you for a while?'

I imagine Gary climbing into my bed in his boxer shorts. And then I think of Frank. 'No, I'm fine, thank you,' I manage to say.

'Can I get you a cup of tea?'

'No.'

Gary looks uncertain but he begins to turn away. 'Well, I'll leave you to it then. Goodnight, Maggie. Shout if you need anything.'

He goes, although I notice that he leaves the landing light on, and I don't hear the sound of his bedroom door closing. I lie back down, resting my head on the pillow. But I can't go back to sleep. Even with the light on, I still feel like I'm being watched. Eventually I reach for the book on my bedside table and start reading, craving the distraction of other people's fictitious lives. But I'm jumpy and every creak or groan of the house sets my pulse racing again. I'm sticky with sweat. Benji must sense my unease because he remains on alert for the rest of the night, like a canine sentry. I've never been more grateful for his company.

When my alarm goes off, I haven't slept a wink and it takes a great deal of effort to heave myself out of bed and go downstairs to make a cup of coffee. I'm working at the pub today and I'm worried about how I'll get through my shift as I'm so exhausted. It's quiet upstairs so I suspect Gary is still asleep. I let Benji out into the back garden and stand in the doorway, watching him as I sip my coffee. In the morning light, I'm feeling a bit better. I'm more rational despite my tiredness. It was a bad dream, a trick of the light, that's all. It's almost funny, I tell myself out loud. Fancy getting all worked up about ghosts at my age! But it's bluster, because I'm using reassuring words to cover over the cracks of my spiralling fear.

By the time I'm dressed and ready to leave for work, Gary is still in his room. I call to Benji and open the front door quietly so as not to wake our new lodger. I can't believe he can sleep so late but then he had a disturbed night, thanks to me. I'm a little early so I detour past the playing fields so that Benji can have a good run before he spends the afternoon at the pub and I see Alyssa in the playground with her boys.

'Alyssa, hi!' I call out to her and she waves back and comes over.

'I'm exhausted,' she says, rubbing her eyes. Even without make-up on, she is still beautiful and I want to tell her to make the most of it. To enjoy her youth while she still has it. But she's a mum and she's shattered and I know that what she sees in the mirror is very different to what I see.

'Long night?' I ask sympathetically, thinking of my own lack of sleep.

'Yes, the boys took it in turns to get up throughout the night and Dylan's gone to visit his mum so I'm on my own. And to think I used to find weekends relaxing.'

'Oh no, you poor thing.'

'I'm feeling rather sorry for myself,' Alyssa admits. 'It's all got a bit much.'

I have an idea. 'Why don't you and your husband go out this evening? I can babysit.'

Alyssa looks at me with excitement. 'Really?'

'Of course. I love children and I'd be more than happy to help.'

'Dylan and I haven't been out together for months.' Alyssa is already reaching for her phone. 'I'll message him and see what time he'll be home. Are you sure?'

'Quite sure.'

'We'll just go to the pub, we'll only be a couple of hours.'

I look at Alyssa's two boys who now seem to be wrestling, and wonder what I've let myself in for. It's true that I love children, but I have no experience with them. This is the new me though, the brave me, and I want to help my friend.

'Take your time,' I assure her. 'We'll be just fine.'

'You're a star, Maggie, thank you.'

I smile, enjoying the feeling of being useful. And busy. I say goodbye to Alyssa and make my way to the pub, with Benji at my heel, and for a while it's easy to banish my dark thoughts. To forget about what happened the previous evening and to remember that I am free now. Free to live my own life. To help out my friends whenever I want.

The friendly banter with the regulars distracts me from my tiredness and my shift flies by, but by the time I get home I'm exhausted again and I only have an hour before I'm due at Alyssa's. I'm looking forward to a cup of tea and a quiet sit down but when I open the door, the television is on full blast and my heart sinks. Having Gary in the house will take some getting used to, but I remind myself of the benefits of his company, the fun we had together last night, and the extra income I'll now have.

I poke my head around the living room door and Gary is sprawled on the sofa, a bottle of beer in his hand. The coffee table is a mess, littered with empty crisp packets and dirty mugs and plates, and I wonder if he's been there all day. Gary is self-employed but he seems to have more days off than he does on and this is clearly one of them.

'Hi, Gary,' I say.

He starts at the sound of my voice and hurriedly starts clearing up. 'Sorry, Maggie, I'll get this shipshape in no time.'

'That's okay,' I lie, looking at the mess. 'Don't worry about it.'

I frown as I realised that the fruit bowl, a wedding present that survived the test of time, is missing. It's usually in the middle of the coffee table. Perhaps Gary relocated it to make more room? But I glance around the room and can't see it anywhere.

'What happened to the fruit bowl?' I ask.

Gary looks around, running his hand through his unkempt hair. 'What fruit bowl?'

'The one that was on the coffee table.'

'I haven't seen it.'

'It was there this morning.'

'Sorry, Maggie, I've got no idea.'

I go into the kitchen and look around for the bowl but it's not there. So where the hell is it then? And a thought creeps in.

Frank.

He's messing with me. Showing me that he's there, that he's watching me. I stand, stock-still in the middle of the kitchen, too afraid to move. I'm unravelling and I don't know how to fix it. I don't know how to make this go away.

Gary wanders in with an armful of dirty crockery and starts washing up, stealing a glance at me over his shoulder. 'You alright, Maggie? You look like you've seen a ghost.'

He has no idea. And I'm too shaken to tell him. Suddenly I can't wait to go to Alyssa's. To get out of this cottage and immerse myself in the chaos of two young children.

'I'm babysitting for Alyssa tonight,' I tell him, reaching for my bag. I'm early but I just want to get out of here as soon as possible. 'I'm not sure what time I'll be back.'

'I'll be at the pub,' Gary replies. 'Stop in for a drink on the way home if you fancy.'

I smile weakly. 'I'll see what time it is.'

I feed Benji, give him a cuddle and then leave. Being outside is like coming up for air after being underwater for too long, and I can breathe again. But I'm still shaken and when I arrive at Alyssa's she looks at me with concern.

'Are you okay, Maggie? You're very pale.'

'I'm fine,' I assure her, suspecting that Alyssa is worried I'm going to back out. She looks stunning and I can tell she's made an effort for her date night. Her long black curls are glossy and she's wearing skinny jeans with a fitted white top. 'You look lovely, Alyssa,' I say earnestly.

She beams. 'Thank you. Come in, Dylan's not home yet but he'll be here any moment. The boys have had their baths and will be going to bed shortly.'

I follow Alyssa into the living room and see her two boys lying on the floor, watching a cartoon. The toys have all been cleared up and there's a box of chocolates on the table.

'Those are for you,' Alyssa says, pointing at them. 'To say thanks.'

'That's very kind.' I stare at the television absent-mindedly.

'Are you sure you're okay, Maggie?'

How do I explain it? How do I tell Alyssa that I'm getting worked up over a missing fruit bowl? But the words come spilling out of me before I can stop them.

'A fruit bowl has gone missing. It was a wedding present and I don't know what's happened to it.'

'I'm sure it'll turn up. Have you checked all the cupboards?'

'It was on the coffee table. It's been there since we moved in three years ago.'

'Did you ask Gary about it?'

'Yes, he said he hasn't seen it.'

Alyssa is looking at me with a worried expression, probably wondering why I'm getting so stressed about this. But that's because she doesn't know the full story and I can't bring myself to tell her. Or maybe it's just that I can't say the words aloud.

'Check the bin,' she says.

'Excuse me?'

'Check the bin.'

'Why?'

'Perhaps Gary broke it, and he doesn't want to tell you.'

I hadn't thought of that. 'But I wouldn't be angry with him. These things happen.'

Alyssa shrugs. 'Still. Check the bin.'

Dylan arrives home at that moment and both the boys jump up to greet him. He comes over to shake my hand, a child hanging off each leg. It's the first time I've met him and he's a handsome man so I can see why Alyssa fell for him. I just hope he's good to her.

Alyssa and Dylan take the children upstairs to bed and leave shortly afterwards, telling me to call them if I need anything. They must have bribed the boys with sweets or something because they don't come back downstairs and although I listen keenly for any noises, the house is silent. I'm almost disappointed. Although I was nervous about babysitting for the first time, I was looking forward to spending some time with the children too.

After half an hour, I creep upstairs to check on them and they are both fast asleep, probably exhausted from their adventures the previous night. I watch them sleep for a while, absorbing their innocence and I can feel myself being pulled down into the past as I imagine what my own children might have looked like. They would be adults now. I might even be a grandmother. I imagine us all sitting around a table, laughing. Frank at the head, holding court and carving a chicken. I had always believed that Frank would idolise our children. That he would treat them like princes or princesses and in turn, his behaviour towards me would change too. As the mother of his children, I would no longer be a failure in Frank's eyes. We would be a happy family and it was all I ever wanted.

But the longer Frank is gone, the more I doubt the alternative story I once wove in my mind. As Alyssa said, if we'd had children, Frank would still have been Frank. Would our children have witnessed the way he treated me, the way I *let* him treat me? Or would I have found the strength to stand up to him or even to leave him? And I'm beginning to wonder if I cultivated a fantasy life which was never going to become a reality. If I was looking for strength in the wrong places. If I shouldn't have risked it and run from him long ago.

Perhaps if I had, he wouldn't still be haunting me now. Or maybe he would have done what he threatened to do when he was alive – find me and kill me.

I don't know how long I stand there for but when one of the children stirs, I plummet back to reality again. I back away and tiptoe back down the stairs. In the living room I turn the television on and half watch the first thing I find. But I'm lost in my thoughts, hurtling back in time again to when Frank and I first met. Why did I not see the signs?

My eyes drift over to a framed photo of Alyssa and Dylan on their wedding day. They have their arms around each other and they're grinning at the camera. Alyssa looks so young and excited, just as I was on my own wedding day. And Dylan looks like the cat that got the cream. But that's where the similarities end because Alyssa and Dylan went on to have two beautiful boys and live a charmed life. They're a happy, bustling family. Alyssa is confident and strong-willed and strikes me as the sort of person who won't take nonsense from anyone. And yet something about the photo draws me in and I can't stop looking at it.

I don't know how long I gaze at it for, but I startle at the sound of a key in the lock.

'Everything okay?' Alyssa asks as she sticks her head around the living room door.

'Fine. I didn't hear a peep out of the boys. Did you have a good evening?'

Alyssa beams. 'It was wonderful. I can't thank you enough.'

'I thought you'd be later.'

'Dylan has a long day tomorrow, so we left once we'd finished dinner.'

Dylan appears and puts his arm around Alyssa, kissing the top of her head. I stand up, aware that they probably want some privacy after their romantic evening.

'I'll be off then.'

'Wait, let me give you some money.'

'Don't be silly. It was my pleasure and I'm happy to do it any time.'

Alyssa gives me a hug. 'Thank you so much.'

It's a short stroll home and I enjoy the quiet stillness of the night. It doesn't escape me that I'm not afraid to walk home alone in the dark, I'm afraid of *being* home. But when I arrive, Benji scurries up to greet me and cheers me up. Other than that, the house is silent so Gary must still be at the pub. I remember Alyssa's advice about the fruit bowl and go over to the kitchen bin, peering inside. All I can see are empty crisp packets, half a sausage roll and some teabags. With a guilty look over my shoulder, I stick my hand in, wincing as I rummage through the rubbish. There's nothing there but household waste. I find a torch and go back outside to open the wheelie bin, peering gingerly in. There are some black bags, tied neatly, but that's it. I close the lid, feeling more than a bit idiotic about my sleuthing, when something on the ground catches my eye. I crouch down and pick it up, shining the torch on it. It's a fragment of broken china and I immediately recognise it as a piece from the fruit bowl.

I stand up, feeling both relieved and peeved. Alyssa was right after all, Gary must have broken it and tried to hide the evidence. It makes me see Gary in a new light, and one which is not favourable to him, but it means something else too. The missing fruit bowl has nothing to do with Frank and it's further proof that the only thing that's haunted is my own mind.

I throw the china into the bin. So what if the fruit bowl is broken? Our marriage was broken long ago so in a way it's symbolic. I'm letting go of the past, piece by piece. I'll buy a lovely new bowl for the coffee table, a bright and colourful one that cheers up the room. And I'll have a gentle word with Gary and tell him that honesty is the best policy. After all, we're grown-ups, not children, and he should act like one. I can't reconcile with how I feel about him now. I still think he's a decent bloke, but Alyssa's warning echoes around my head, fuelled by his lie about the bowl. Can I trust the man that I've just invited into my home? Is he the good-natured person I've painted him out to be or does he have a dark side? But I'm being silly because making a mess and breaking a bowl doesn't make him a monster. I'll give him the benefit of the doubt for now, I decide, because none of us are perfect.

I'm so lost in my thoughts as I start to head back inside that I don't notice that someone is standing a few feet away in the darkness, watching me.

I don't realise until their cold, strong hands are gripping on to my arms.

10

For a split second, I'm frozen with terror. But then I find my voice and scream. The grip immediately loosens and I spin around to find Dylan staring at me with wide eyes.

'I'm sorry,' he says quickly. 'I didn't mean to frighten you.'

'What are you doing here?' I demand.

He holds out my phone. 'You left this at our house.'

I take the phone wordlessly, my heart still thudding against my chest.

'I really am sorry,' Dylan says again. 'It was stupid of me, I should have called out.'

There's something about Dylan in the gloomy night that unnerves me. It's like I'm looking at a younger version of Frank. The chiselled jaw, his almost black hair. A slightly cocky stance. And perhaps it's because he's just scared the life out of me, but adrenaline is coursing through my body and I can't tear my eyes away from his. I'm transfixed in terror.

But then Dylan breaks eye contact and backs off slowly with his hands up, as though I'm an unpredictable wild animal, and whatever spell I was under is broken.

'I'll leave you to it,' he says, and his voice is nothing like Frank's. I blink a couple of times and hurtle back to reality.

'Thank you for bringing my phone,' I manage to say, although my voice is shrill.

'Of course. Thanks for babysitting.'

With a final glance, probably to make sure I'm okay, Dylan walks away. I hurry back inside and close the door, pulling the chain across it. Benji is hovering, looking at me anxiously and I bend down to pat him. It's late, and I should go to bed, but I'm wide awake. It was irresponsible of Dylan to sneak up on me like that. What was he thinking? Did he mean to frighten me on purpose? But that's just ridiculous, why would he do that?

No, I overreacted. He was just trying to get my attention and I got myself all worked up. And just after I had told myself that it was all in my head too.

I let Benji out into the garden, make myself a cup of tea and settle down on the sofa. But as the adrenaline seeps out of my body, a wave of exhaustion takes its place and I begin to drift off. I'm just about to plunge into a deep sleep when the sound of the door rattling wakes me again.

It takes a few disorientated and frightening seconds for me to realise that it's Gary, trying to get in. I clamber up and hurry to the door, taking the chain off.

'I'm so sorry,' I tell him. 'I put the chain on without thinking.'

'I thought I was going to have to sleep in the front garden,' Gary says good-naturedly as he comes through the door and closes it behind him.

'It won't happen again.'

'Maybe you should give me a copy of the back door key too, just in case?'

The thought of the back door key makes me shudder.

'Gary,' I begin hesitantly, eager to get to the bottom of the fruit bowl mystery so that I can move on and forget about it. 'Did you break the fruit bowl?'

'What? No, of course not.'

'I don't mind if you did. I just wish you'd tell me.'

'I didn't break the fruit bowl.'

'I found a fragment of it by the bin.'

Gary's tone is defensive. 'Maggie, I didn't break your fruit bowl, okay? I'd tell you if I did and I wouldn't sneak around trying to cover it up.'

I've never liked confrontation and even now, as I'm growing in confidence, my instinct is to shy away from it. 'Okay, I'm sorry. Forget I said anything.'

Gary shrugs, like it's already forgotten. 'You missed a great evening at the pub. It was quiz night. And Alyssa was there with her fella.'

I think of Dylan again, the way he looked at me. 'I'll come next time.'

'I bet you're good at a pub quiz, Maggie.'

I frown. 'Why do you say that?'

'Because you're really clever.'

'I'm not clever. I never even went to university.'

'You don't need to go to uni to be clever, love. You're an intelligent lady, I can tell.'

It's enough to make me blush. I wonder what Gary sees when he looks at me. The person he is describing is not the person I think I am. It's like when I look at Alyssa and see a beautiful, radiant young woman but all she sees is an exhausted mum with wrinkles and dark circles under her eyes. I like the way Gary thinks of me.

I smile. 'Thank you. Anyway, I'm shattered so I'm off to bed.'

He puts his hand over mine and my eyes widen. But he only gives it a quick squeeze and then lets go. 'Goodnight, Maggie.'

In bed, my hand still tingles from where Gary touched me. I have not been touched by a man in years. Was it a friendly squeeze? I'm certain that it was. And even if it wasn't, I'm not interested in another relationship. Even so, I suddenly feel like a young girl again and I stifle a giggle. After the twenty-four hours I've had, the triviality of wondering whether my new lodger fancies me is a blessed relief. And it's that thought that sends me into a peaceful sleep for the next seven hours.

When I wake up, I feel like a new woman. I'm singing to myself as I go downstairs to let Benji out into the back garden. Today I'm going shopping with Beth and although I need to be careful not to spend too much money, I'm really looking forward to it. I'm earning a wage now and Gary's rental payments will be a huge help. I'm excited to treat myself to a few new bits and bobs. Maybe even some nice make-up.

When I go to fill up the kettle, I notice that there are two mugs out on the counter already, with coffee granules in the bottom of each, and I frown. Gary must be up already but I haven't heard him moving about. I boil the kettle and fill the mugs with water and milk, leaving one on the side for Gary.

I'm showered and dressed by the time he finally appears, rubbing his eyes.

'Good morning,' I say. 'I made you a coffee, but it will have gone cold by now.'

'Ah thanks, Maggie, but I'm more of a tea drinker.'

'Thanks for putting the mugs out this morning.'

'I didn't put the mugs out.'

I look at Gary, my brow furrowed. 'There were two mugs out this morning.'

'Nothing to do with me, love.'

I think back to last night. Did I put the mugs out myself on autopilot? I'm sure that I didn't. But if it wasn't Gary, and it wasn't me, then who was it?

I don't like this train of thought and I certainly don't want it to ruin the day I've been looking forward to for ages. But the list of unexplained events are stacking up in my mind, creating a dossier of evidence. Of what, I'm still not sure. Or perhaps I am, but I don't want to face it. The idea of admitting that the cottage really is haunted is too frightening.

'I'm going shopping with Beth today,' I tell Gary, changing the subject.

'Need a lift somewhere?'

'Thank you, but she's picking me up.'

'I'd better get shifting myself actually, I've got a client this morning.'

I smile. 'Have a good day.'

Gary winks at me. 'You too, love.'

I feel a bit giddy as I walk outside to wait for Beth. It's silly because I don't think I even like Gary in that way, and I have no intention of ever being with another man, but the distraction is just what I need. It's as though I've gone back in time to being an innocent schoolgirl again. I can't remember the last time I had any male attention, however small, and although the idea of pursuing anything with Gary is absurd, it's also entertaining.

When Beth arrives, she raises her eyebrows. 'You look happy.'

'Oh, I just slept really well last night for the first time in ages.'

'Great, well let's hit the shops then.'

As Beth drives, she tells me all about what's going on at her work, and with her cycling club. She asks me how my shifts at the pub are going and enquires after Benji. Then, inevitably, the subject of Gary comes up.

'How's the new lodger?' she asks.

'It's taking some getting used to,' I admit. 'But he's a nice bloke. And a great cook.'

She gives me the side eye. 'Anything to do with that dreamy expression you had earlier?'

I blush. 'No.'

'Fair dos. Well, I'm glad it's working out.'

'Something a bit odd did happen though.'

I tell Beth about the fruit bowl, but she's not concerned. 'Maybe Benji broke it.'

'And put it in the bin with his paws?'

Beth laughs. 'Good point. Well even if it was Gary, I wouldn't give him too hard a time. He was probably mortified that he'd broken something when he'd only just moved in.'

'He should have told me though.'

'Well yes, he should have. But we all do things in the heat of the moment that we regret. He probably panicked and then it was too late to change his story. I wouldn't worry about it, unless it happens again.'

I think of the two mugs on the counter that morning. Then I look out of the window at the trees whizzing by and a wave of nausea hits me. But I'm not letting this spoil my day. I just hope that whatever is happening stops as quickly as it started.

Perhaps I should look into selling the cottage again so I can make a fresh start. I'm surrounded by memories and it's clouding my judgement. I could get the house valued and see how much it's worth, at least. If I can't buy anywhere, I can always rent. But what would happen to poor Gary who has only just moved in? Plus, Benji is really settled there too and I don't want to cause any more upheaval to his life. No, I'll stay put for now. Pay a bit more of the mortgage off and see where the land lies in a few years. I will not be forced out of my own home by some unexplained events that are confusing but not harmful.

And I tell myself, yet again, that Frank is gone and cannot hurt me.

After a few hours of shopping and a quick lunch, I return home laden with bags and I'm tired but happy. Beth has said we need to show off our new clothes and so we've arranged to go for dinner the following evening. I'm going to invite Gary. In fact, I realise, as I let myself into the house, I'm looking forward to seeing him.

But apart from Benji, who rushes to greet me, the house is empty, which means that Gary must still be at work. I have my shift at the pub starting in an hour, so I decide to do a quick tidy of the house before taking Benji out for a walk. As I dust the bookcase, I notice that some things have been moved around. Nothing significant, just a candlestick in the wrong place and a few books out of order. Has Gary been snooping? Or attempting to clean? But judging by the black dirt on my cloth, those shelves haven't been dusted in a while.

Why is Gary moving my things around? It must be him, because who else would it be?

No. No, I don't want to think about that.

I abandon my dusting and call out to Benji, taking his lead from the hook and hurrying out of the house. Why is this happening? Why, when I'm finally starting to feel happy, is someone trying to sabotage it? It's becoming harder to deny what's going on in the cottage, and it all started with that psychic supper. I wonder if it somehow unleashed a force which now can't be contained. And I hate that I'm even thinking this way, that I'm entertaining the idea. But what are the alternatives? I can't think of any plausible ones.

I hurry to the pub, craving the noise and chaos. It is surprisingly busy when I arrive and I immediately spot Gary, sitting on a stool at the bar. His face lights up when he sees me and it cheers me, despite my angst. It makes me feel safe. I know he'll walk me home at the end of my shift and the idea of not having to go back to the cottage alone is a tonic. But I wonder if it's becoming more than that. It's not just his mere presence, I'm actually looking forward to our conversation on the way home and laughing at Gary's stories. I push Alyssa's words to the back of my mind and smile back at Gary.

I pull him a fresh pint and then set to work, serving customers and cleaning glasses. Benji wanders around, greeting everyone. He's become a real pub mascot, and he loves the attention. A happy glow spreads over me as I watch my dog socialising with the locals, just as I'm doing too. We've both gone through hard times in our lives and just look at us now. We've been welcomed into the community like old friends. Whatever happens, I'm never going back to my old life. I'm not going to retreat from the world ever again.

As I'm wiping the surface of the bar, I overhear Gary's conversation with a friend.

'Yeah, the new digs are going great,' he's saying. 'Maggie's wonderful.'

I flush with pleasure and feel guilty for ever doubting Gary. He catches my eye and I look away, embarrassed at being caught earwigging. But when I look back, he gives me an unabashed smile. I have no idea what's going between us, if anything. I'm probably reading way more into it than I should, highlighting my inexperience around men. Poor Gary would probably be mortified if he knew I was taking his friendliness as something more. And anyway, I don't *want* something more, I remind myself, not after Frank.

But my rational thoughts are competing with something new and unexpected. Anticipation is building up inside me, butterflies dancing in my stomach. It's not like I felt when I first met

Frank. That was obsession, intoxication. This is something else, something more measured, but equally enjoyable. I shake my head and try to concentrate on polishing the glasses. I'm being naive, getting caught up in the moment. But I still can't help but steal a glance at Gary from time to time. The objects being moved and smashed fruit bowl seem trivial now and even if Gary did break it, he's done me a favour as it's forced me to get rid of it.

As the night draws to a close and the prospect of going home looms, my good humour evaporates. I wish I could stay here forever, surrounded in the warm, friendly glow of the busy pub. When Mark tells me to head off, I resist the urge to ask if I can stay.

At least Gary is coming with me. How he manages to drink all evening without getting sloshed is beyond me, but he seems perfectly sober as he tells me about the landscaping he's been doing for a client that day. He offers to tidy up my garden a bit and I gratefully accept. Despite my best intentions to do it myself, I haven't been out there since I smelled Frank's aftershave in the shed. Whenever I let Benji out, I hover in the doorway watching him, one eye on the shed. The garden is tainted for me now, an unofficial no-go area. What frightens me is that the cottage is heading that way too and it's the one place I can't avoid.

When we get home, Gary suggests a nightcap and I reason that a small splash of whisky might be just the thing to ensure I get another good night's sleep. He pours the drinks and hands me one, and we sit down on the sofa and clink our glasses together.

'Mark says you're doing a brilliant job at the pub,' he says.

I smile shyly. 'Well, I don't know about that but I'm really enjoying it.'

'He reckons you're one of the best bar staff he's ever had. You're a natural.'

'It's lovely to be working again, I forgot how much I missed it.'

Gary looks at me. 'You don't talk much about your husband.'

The change of subject surprises me. 'Excuse me?'

'It's just you were married for what? Thirty years? And yet you never talk about him.'

What is this? First Alyssa and now Gary. It seems that everyone is interested in my marriage these days. But if I was honest with Alyssa, why shouldn't I be with Gary too?

'There's not much to say,' I tell Gary. 'We weren't happy.'

'Why didn't you divorce him?'

'I had nowhere else to go.'

Gary is looking at me intently, as though he can read my thoughts. 'That's not the whole story though, is it?'

I feign ignorance, playing for time to work out how much I want to share with him. I like Gary but I don't know him well and I'm still not accustomed to talking about this.

'What do you mean?'

'There's something you're not telling me. There's a wariness about you, like you're on edge. Something happened that you don't want to talk about. I can sense it, Maggie.'

I gave Alyssa a more sanitised version of events but with a few glugs of whisky inside me and Gary's kind, inquisitive expression, I'm tempted to go for the warts and all version. I'm afraid to say the words aloud but maybe it will be good for me to confront my fears.

'He told me if I ever left him, he'd kill me.'

Gary is horrified. 'Did Frank hurt you, Maggie?'

Tears prick at my eyes and I look away. 'Yes.'

'What did he do to you?'

The words are waiting to spill out of me along with my tears. So much for a bit of harmless, minor flirtation with Gary, I'm about to bare my soul to him and it doesn't get much deeper than that. I'll just have to hope he doesn't judge me.

'At first I thought it was because he loved me. He wanted to keep me safe. After we married, he made me quit my job and didn't let me go out without him. I disobeyed him once and he started locking me in the flat after that. Sometimes he didn't come back for days.'

'He did *what*?'

But I'm not done yet. 'He played rough games with me even when I didn't want to. Tied me up, smacked me. Left me in handcuffs for hours. And then when I gained weight, he told me I was nothing. Ugly. Useless. Fat. He said no one else would have me.'

Gary is horrified. 'You should have called the police.'

'I knew they wouldn't believe me. Frank would charm his way out of it, like he always did, and punish me even more afterwards. And even when he didn't want to play with me any more because I was too disgusting, he still refused to discard me. I was his possession. The one person he could order about and get away with it. I think it made him feel powerful.'

I can tell Gary is struggling to process it all. What must he think of me? Is he seeing me like Frank did now? Useless, ugly. But then he takes my hand and I can see that his eyes are glistening. 'Maggie, I am so sorry that happened to you.'

'Well, it's my fault. I let him do it.'

'No. It's not your fault. It's his.'

'I was weak. Pathetic.'

Gary shakes his head vehemently. 'No, Maggie, you've got it wrong. He manipulated and coerced you. He abused his power. He was evil.'

Evil. Yes, Frank was evil. But with everything that's going on at the cottage, that doesn't make me feel any better. In fact, it makes me feel worse.

'I should have left him. I know that now, but I couldn't see a way out.'

'Of course you couldn't, because he made sure of it.'

Deep down, I know Gary is right. And as time goes by, I'm becoming acutely aware of how toxic my relationship with Frank was. Maybe I wasn't the best wife to him but nothing I did justifies what he did to me. He destroyed me. I became who I was *because* of him.

'I always believed it would be different if we had children. And when I failed to conceive, I blamed myself.'

'How do you know it was you who couldn't conceive?'

'Because Frank told me.'

'But how did *he* know? Did he have tests?'

I've honestly never thought about it. I doubt Frank had any tests done. It was easier to blame me instead.

'I don't know,' I admit. 'And there's no point in worrying about it now. That ship has sailed. In any case, I was kidding myself because nothing would have changed. Perhaps it was a blessing after all, saving children from having a father like Frank.'

As I say it, though, I begin to cry. Really cry. For the children I yearned for and never had. For the boy or girl who might have given me the strength to leave him and make a better life for us all.

Gary leans forward and embraces me and it feels strange to be in the arms of another man. But I'm not thinking about anything romantic right now. I'm thinking of how I finally feel safe. Safe to share my secrets and darkest thoughts. Safe to cry. I don't know how long we stay like that for but after a while, my tears subside and I begin to feel a little awkward. I pull away and force a smile.

'Thank you for listening. For not judging me.'

'Of course I don't judge you, Maggie. You didn't deserve any of it, you need to realise that. It wasn't your fault. This Frank bloke was a right bastar—'

A crashing sound makes us both jump and we look at each other before dashing into the kitchen. The teapot which was on the table is now on the floor, smashed to pieces and Benji is staring at it, snarling. I have never seen my dog snarl before.

'Oh, Benji,' Gary says, bending down to pick up the pieces.

But I'm rooted to the spot, staring at the teapot. The timing of the accident is too precise. Just as Gary and I shared an intimate moment, at the exact point when he criticised Frank, the teapot hurtled to the floor. And it didn't do it on its own.

'Are you alright, love?' Gary asks, looking at me in concern.

'How did it happen?' I splutter.

'Benji must have knocked it with his tail, silly boy.'

I look at Benji, who is still snarling, his teeth bared. He looks frightening and I instinctively take a step back. This is not the gentle, good-natured dog I've come to know. Why is Benji acting this way? Why is my teapot in pieces on the floor?

And despite everything I've told myself over the last couple of weeks, no matter how hard I've tried to reassure myself that the strange goings-on are all in my head, the physical evidence is becoming too compelling to deny. Frank is watching me. Messing with me.

And he wants me to know it.

11

I've slipped down a rabbit hole and I'm in so deep that I can't find my way out. I've googled ghosts, the afterlife, poltergeists. I've read about people, experts, who believe that spirits can be left behind after a person has died because they have unresolved business. I've scoured dozens of reports of haunted houses and strange goings-on. I've learned, with horror, of people being physically hurt by the unexplained. I've also devoured articles that suggest poltergeists symbolise psychological stress, and that the phenomenon is down to a living person's intense emotional turmoil rather than the paranormal.

And now I don't know what to think any more.

Is Frank here? Is he doing what he promised to do, to punish me for daring to be happy without him? Is that why he hasn't moved on from this world? Or am I causing these events myself, my own emotions creating this unexplained energy?

My mind is all over the place, taking me to dark places that I have never considered before, and don't want to consider. But ever since the teapot incident, Benji has been acting strangely. He's nervy and unsettled, barking at thin air. Whatever is going on in my house is ramping up, I can feel it. And I can't help but wonder if it's because Gary is here. Someone, or something, doesn't like him being in the house.

But I need Gary more than ever. He's become my rock. He knows I'm on edge and he's taking good care of me. A few times I've woken up screaming after vivid nightmares and he's been in my room in seconds, making sure I'm okay. He's been taking Benji out for me too, suggesting that maybe the dog needs some more exercise to work off his energy. He walks me home from work because he knows I don't want to be alone.

It's not enough though. I'm now frightened to be in the house. And Benji is no help because he's just as nervy as I am. Of the three of us, only Gary has remained calm and so I've come to rely on him and, slowly, I'm finding it hard to imagine him not being around.

Gary rarely goes to the pub on his own now, unless I'm working. In the evening, we eat dinner together and then watch television or play cards. Gary's taught me a few new games. At the weekend we've got into the habit of going for a walk or to the cinema. We are growing closer day by day and yet I still don't know what it means, only that I need him in my life. He has become my constant, my companion. I haven't seen much of Beth and Alyssa recently and I'm feeling guilty about it. I need to make sure I don't withdraw too much because I can't lose my friends again. And yet I want to spend all my time with Gary.

Life feels like a horrible contradiction. I want Gary in my life but the closer we get, the more afraid I become of things happening in the cottage. So what do I do about it? Do I tell Gary to leave and hope that it all stops? Or do I let him stay and wait for what happens next?

It's consuming my every thought and I'm so distracted that I don't hear Alyssa calling out to me until she's standing right in front of me.

'Earth to Maggie!' she says, waving her hand in front of my face.

I come to and focus on Alyssa's face. 'Sorry, I was miles away.'

Gary is at work today and I've taken Benji out for a long walk across the fields. He's happier when he's out of the house, just as I am, and he bounds up to Alyssa, his tail wagging and his tongue lolling, with no hint of the growling version of him I'm seeing at home.

'I haven't seen you for ages,' Alyssa says cheerfully as she pats Benji.

'I'm sorry, we should arrange a get-together,' I say absent-mindedly.

'Is everything okay, Maggie? You seem distracted.'

I look around. 'Where are the boys?'

'Dylan's got the day off and he's taken them swimming so I thought I'd go for a rare walk on my own without any buggies or grumpy toddlers. Would you like to join me?'

'Oh, I don't want to intrude if you're enjoying some time to yourself.'

'I'd love the company, actually.'

I smile. 'Great!'

We walk side by side and Benji rushes ahead, chasing squirrels.

'How are the boys?' I ask.

Alyssa rolls her eyes. 'Crazy. But lovely.'

'Are you getting more sleep now?'

'Things are better. And thanks again for babysitting, we really needed that night out.'

'Any time, honestly. It was my pleasure.'

'So how have you been, anyway?'

It's a tricky question to answer. Part of me is living in a near constant state of fear. The other is enjoying my time with Gary. One step forward, two steps back.

'Busy,' I say. 'But good.'

'How's it going with Gary?'

An even trickier question, but I can't hide my smile. 'Good, thank you.'

Alyssa looks at me quizzically. 'Are you blushing?'

I grin. 'No.'

'You are, you're blushing! Don't tell me you and Gary are a couple now?'

'No, we're not. But we're getting on very well.'

'I'm pleased for you.' But something about the way Alyssa says it tells me she doesn't mean it.

'You're still not sure about Gary?' I ask her.

She looks conflicted, before saying, 'I wasn't going to say anything, but now I know that you two have grown close, I think you need to know. I've become quite friendly with Sophie, his daughter-in-law. And she's told me some more stuff.'

My heart sinks. I don't want to hear anything bad about Gary. I want to believe that he is the lovely, genuine person I think he is. I need to believe it.

'I think maybe it's a clash of personalities,' I say diplomatically.

'It's more than that,' Alyssa replies quietly. 'Do you know why his wife left him?'

I know a little about Gary's divorce from what he's told me. Apparently, she met someone else and now lives with him in Australia, close to their daughter. From what Gary has said, it was acrimonious at first, but over time they've become civil, if not friendly.

'She had an affair,' I tell Alyssa.

'That's not what I heard. I heard she left because of his unreasonable behaviour.'

'What do you mean by "unreasonable behaviour"?'

'He wasn't very nice to her. Not very nice at all.'

No. I don't want to hear this. It's not true. 'I think Sophie's got her wires crossed.'

'I don't think so,' Alyssa says adamantly. 'And I'm worried about you.'

I stop and look at her. 'Me? Why?'

'I haven't seen you in ages and I think you're spending all your time with Gary. What if he's a bad person, like your husband was? I don't want to see you get hurt again.'

I shake my head. 'Gary's not a bad person. He's a lovely bloke.'

'Maybe that's what he wants you to think. To draw you in before he shows his true colours. Isn't that what Frank did to you?'

I'm hating this conversation and I'm trying to stem my rising frustration. I don't need this right now. With everything else going on, I don't have the capacity to deal with this too.

'Look, Alyssa, I appreciate your concern, but it's unfounded. Gary has been nothing but a gentleman and what you've heard is rumour and gossip. Nothing more.'

Alyssa blanches. 'I didn't mean to upset you.'

I soften. 'I know you mean well. But trust me, you have nothing to worry about.'

She looks like she wants to say more but changes her mind. 'Fine. Okay. But just be careful, that's all I'm saying. Keep your wits about you.'

Oh, my wits are more than about me. My wits are on 24-7 duty. I can't turn the damn things off.

'Did you ever get to the bottom of the missing fruit bowl?' Alyssa asks me.

'Yes, you were right,' I say. 'I found a fragment of it by the bin.'

'Did Gary apologise?'

'He insisted it wasn't him.'

I'm more than aware that this does not paint my lodger, who is fast becoming more than that, in a good light and I'm not surprised when Alyssa's eyebrows raise in suspicion.

'What is he, five years old?'

'Maybe it wasn't him,' I say quietly.

'Who else would it be?'

'A ghost?'

Alyssa looks incredulous. 'Are you serious?'

'Other things have been happening around the house recently. Objects being moved around, things breaking. Benji's out of sorts too. It's really freaking me out. I don't know what I would do if Gary wasn't there, keeping me sane.'

Alyssa is frowning, her brow furrowed in concentration.

'Do you really believe in the paranormal?' she asks me.

'I never used to but now I'm not so sure. Remember the psychic supper, when Zara told me about the back door key? Well, it was exactly where she said it would be. How would she know that? And I can feel him, Alyssa, I can even smell him sometimes.'

'Frank?'

'Yes.'

Alyssa now looks like she wants to stage an intervention. 'Are you getting enough sleep, Maggie?'

'Not really.'

'You look tired. Perhaps you should see a doctor?'

I realise, with a sinking heart, that there's no point in continuing this conversation. Alyssa is a cynic and nothing I say will change her mind. In fairness, I was too until not long ago. I want to cling on to her scepticism, to let it infect me, but I'm in too deep for that now. Alyssa hasn't seen what've I've seen. If she had, perhaps she wouldn't be so quick to dismiss it. But Gary's living with it too and he doesn't believe it. He thinks it's the dog being clumsy, and me being paranoid. I'm the only one who's affected by this.

'You're right, I should see a doctor,' I say, eager to end the conversation and move on.

'Did all this strange stuff you're talking about start happening when Gary moved in?'

'No.' I shake my head with certainty. 'It started before that.'

'Just before?'

I think of the smashed window, which had revived my conversation with Gary about moving in. 'Yes.'

'Hmm.'

'What is it, Alyssa?' I ask, a touch impatiently. I'm not enjoying this at all.

'Nothing. Never mind.'

I'm tempted to prise it out of her, but the truth is that I don't want to hear it. She doesn't like Gary any more, that much is clear. And I really don't like the idea of our foursome breaking up when we've only just come together. I need to make her see Gary for who he really is, rather than what his daughter-in-law has made him out to be.

'Why don't we go out, the four of us?' I suggest. 'We haven't done it in ages.'

'What about a girls' night instead?' Alyssa suggests. 'You, me and Beth?'

My goodness, she doesn't even want to socialise with him any more. This Sophie has really turned her against Gary, and I wonder if she has an agenda. Why would Gary's daughter-in-law be so spiteful about him? And why is Alyssa so quick to believe her?

'Gary might feel left out,' I say. 'We've always invited him before.'

'I know, but I haven't had a girls' night in ages and I'd really love one.'

I back down, aware that pushing the issue any further might turn this conversation into a row. 'Okay, sure. I'll send Beth a message.'

'Maybe we could make a proper night of it? Get the train into London or something?'

My eyes light up at the prospect of going back to London with my new friends. Of experiencing the city like I should do again, rather than as I failed to do when I was married to Frank. But that makes me think of my husband, of the things that happened in our small South London flat, and I'm overcome by a wave of nausea.

'Or St Albans,' I suggest hopefully.

'Sure, why not. As long as it's a Saturday, so I don't have to wait for Dylan to get back from work.'

The mention of Alyssa's husband reminds me of that strange night, when Dylan returned my phone and scared the life out of me. With everything else that's been going on in my life, I haven't given him a thought until now.

'Everything okay with you and Dylan?' I ask.

'Great, thanks. We're talking more and he's taking a bit of time off to spend with the boys. Our date night really benefited us both, so thank you again for babysitting.'

'As I said before, I'm happy to do it any time.'

'You're such a good person, Maggie.'

I turn to her with a smile, ready to thank her for her kind

words. But she's looking over my shoulder with a scowl. I follow her gaze and see Gary striding towards us.

'There you are!' he says with a grin when he reaches us. 'I finished work early and wondered if you fancied a spot of lunch?'

'I'd love to,' I enthuse. 'Alyssa, will you join us?'

'I'm sorry, I've got to get back to give the boys their lunch. Another time.'

Her smile doesn't reach her eyes as she says goodbye and hurries away.

'Everything okay?' Gary asks, his face open and friendly.

'Fine,' I say. 'Pub or cafe?'

'Pub. I'd kill for a pint.'

We begin heading towards the pub but my conversation with Alyssa is still on my mind. And although I shouldn't need reassurance, I can't stop myself from seeking it.

'Gary, do your children know that your wife had an affair?'

He looks at me quizzically, but he answers the question. 'No. They were just kids when it happened and anyway, I didn't want them to hate their mum.'

'So what did you tell them?'

'Just that Mummy and Daddy still loved each other but that we were going to live apart. The usual stuff you tell children. They were upset of course, but they got used to it over time. My ex and I made sure that we kept the routine and consistency for them.'

'Did you see a lot of them?'

'Once a week and every other weekend. It doesn't seem like much, but things were different then. I worked and she didn't. They were closer to their mum, and although it made me angry after what she did, I knew it was best for them.'

I release a breath I didn't even know I was holding. Gary's

son has no idea that his mum cheated and that's why Sophie doesn't know either. And given that both the children lived with their mum after the divorce, she probably had a few choice things to say about her ex. After all, Gary has openly admitted his failures in the past. It's all becoming clear to me now. Sophie isn't being cruel, she's just giving Alyssa an unreliable version of events based on what her husband remembers from his childhood. This is all a misunderstanding.

I'm so relieved that I link my arm through Gary's, and he tenses for a second, before relaxing into me. It's a small gesture but it's an uncharacteristically bold one for me, and I'm not sure what possessed me to do it. But for the first time I'm starting to seriously consider the prospect of falling for someone again. I don't fancy Gary in the way that I fancied Frank when I first met him. My body is not overcome with lust, my mind is not consumed with thoughts about how I will die if I can't be with him. But I'm older now, and wiser too. Perhaps this is what the start of a normal, healthy relationship should feel like. And I'm not going to let anyone ruin it. Not Alyssa, and not Frank.

But it's still there at the back of my mind. A lingering thought that has become so ingrained in my mind over the years that it refuses to go away. That torments me every day. And no matter how hard I try to free myself from it, it keeps yanking me back again.

I've been a naughty girl. And I will be punished for it.

12

A few months after Frank turned forty, he lost his job and our relationship shifted again. He never told me what had happened but it was like the wind had been taken from his sails. He was no longer the suit-wearing high-flying charmer he prided himself on being and he couldn't cope with it. He sat around all day, drinking, smoking and scowling at me. He found fault with everything I did, so that even my breathing offended him. He needed to berate me even more to feed his dwindling ego.

One day I found him crying in the bedroom. I stopped in the doorway, torn between seeing if he was okay and fleeing in the opposite direction. I didn't want to get into trouble for witnessing him in a vulnerable state. But he looked up and saw me watching. For a moment my heart stopped and I wondered what my punishment would be. But he held his hand out to me and I reluctantly went to him. I breathed in the scent of his aftershave, which evoked such a conflict of emotions in me that I couldn't reconcile with them.

'I don't know what I'd do without you,' he said.

It was the closest he had ever come to telling me that he

loved me. For a brief moment I wondered if this was the turning point. If Frank and I would find each other again. But then he stood up and walked out. I heard the front door slam. He returned half an hour later with beer and cigarettes and sat in his chair all evening, drinking, smoking and staring into nothing. The appearance of Vulnerable Frank had been fleeting and I knew then that I'd probably never see it again. So instead, I lived for the moments when he went out to stock up on more supplies. I dreaded the moment when he came home. And I wondered if he'd ever get another job or if he'd devote himself fully to finding fault with everything I did.

For six months Frank sat around, ordering me about. Fetch this, fetch that. Clean this, hoover that. He gained two stone and his fingers were stained yellow from chain-smoking. But then one day, he squeezed himself into an ill-fitting suit and told me that he had a job interview. Hope surged through me at the prospect of him being out of the house again.

But Frank didn't get that job. He didn't get the one after either. And each time he became angrier and more paranoid. He didn't want to blame himself for his failures and so he blamed me. I could do no right. Once, when we were at the supermarket, he accused me of staring at a man. I had barely glanced at him, and I tried to protest my innocence but it fell on deaf ears. He brought up Juan again, saying I couldn't be trusted. That he wouldn't be a cuckold. After that, he started locking me in the flat again when he went out. He was terrified of being made to look a fool, but he was the one acting it because by then, I didn't need to be locked in to stay at home. I wasn't going anywhere.

Finally, after countless interviews, Frank was offered a new position. The salary was lower, but he had no choice but to take it because our money was running out. I thanked my lucky stars and hoped that things would shift again but they didn't. Frank hated that job. He was a no one and he knew it. He wanted to schmooze with the executive team as he had done before and feel powerful and important. But he was not the man he once was. Now he was just an ageing worker bee competing with the bright young graduates who were willing to step on any toes to climb the career ladder. He could no longer charm his way to the top. He felt emasculated and that's when he really let himself go.

He smoked more, drank more and gained even more weight, but I didn't say anything. I didn't want to risk his wrath, or his punishment, for speaking out of turn. And, in all honestly, I no longer cared. In some ways it was a relief because Frank stopped chastising me for not cooking healthy food. He craved the junk and the ready meals as much as I did. We ate them, in silence, every evening. He became breathless just walking up the stairs to our flat. His father had died of a heart condition and I wondered if Frank was heading for the same fate.

I thought about it often. Wondered where the man I'd fallen in love with had gone, or if he was ever even there. If I hadn't made him up in my head. I watched him suffer with an almost scientific fascination. Sometimes I fantasised about him dying and then I felt so worried about my dark thoughts that I tried to bury them, as though somehow he might be able to read my mind and punish me. I was even afraid to *think* around him.

I went to the doctor with Frank and the GP warned him that his cholesterol was sky-high. Told him to eat better and stop smoking. Prescribed exercise and statins that Frank refused to take. The doctor, an old-fashioned family man who had seen Frank for years, turned to me and told me I should look after my husband better. But I didn't listen.

Frank was sending himself to an early grave.

And still I did nothing.

Guilt is a strange thing. It's not always rational or reasonable.

But that doesn't mean it doesn't grip you by the throat and squeeze tightly until you can hardly breathe.

Until it takes over your life, constantly reminding you that you really are a bad girl.

* * *

I awake with a start. What disturbed me? Then I hear it. A low, rumbling growl. I turn on the light and Benji is by the door, snarling.

'Benji,' I say quietly. 'Come back to bed.'

But he ignores me. He's growling at nothing, as far as I can see. There is no shadow lurking in the darkness like the one I saw previously. Then I hear a crash coming from downstairs. In an instant, Benji is off like a shot, a frenzy of fur and legs.

By the time I've put my dressing gown on and got downstairs, Gary is already there. He is looking down at the floor and I follow his gaze and see the new bowl I bought for the coffee table smashed to pieces. Benji is circling the table, his haunches up.

'Benji's been up to his old tricks again,' Gary says.

'But Benji was upstairs with me. It wasn't him.'

I can't believe this is happening again. I look around the empty, still room and I shiver, wrapping my arms around my body. I'm freezing, even though the room is warm.

'I think you're confused,' Gary tells me. 'You've just woken up. It must have been Benji. Who else could it have been?'

I know who else it could have been, and the thought makes me burst into tears. I can't take it any more, it's all become too much. The emotion I've been holding on to pours out of me as I sob uncontrollably. Gary looks at me in shock before wrapping his arms around me.

'There, there, it's okay,' he says. I'm embarrassed that I'm crying on him again. How can I make this stop? What do I need to do to make Frank go away and leave me alone? I'll do anything in this moment, absolutely *anything*.

As my tears slowly begin to subside, Gary releases his grip. 'I'll go and put the kettle on,' he says, as he disappears into the kitchen. I follow him because I don't want to be alone and hover just behind him, watching him make us both a brew and spooning sugar that I no longer take into mine. He hands me a steaming mug and we sit down at the table.

'Feeling better?' he asks.

'No.'

'What's up, Maggie? Why are you so upset?'

'I know you think it's Benji who's breaking things, but I don't. I think... the house is haunted.'

I remember my conversation with Gary weeks ago in the pub, when I told him about the smashed window and my wisp of a theory about it being the ghost of Frank. That wisp has now become a solid, undeniable fact in my mind. Gary hadn't laughed at me then and I hope he won't now because I can't handle his mirth.

'That psychic really did a number on you,' he says, shaking his head.

'She may have set the wheels in motion, but she's got nothing to do with what's happened since,' I argue. 'All the unexplained events.'

'Which *can* be explained by the presence of an overexcited dog.'

'No. Benji was upstairs,' I insist.

'You really think that the ghost of your husband is here?'

'Yes.'

Gary is thoughtful. At least he's not laughing at me or calling the emergency services to have me sectioned. 'Where did your husband die?'

'In our bed.' I think back to the day when I woke up to find Frank dead in bed next to me. When I touched his cold, clammy skin and realised he was gone. Grief, guilt, horror, relief all mingled into one. And, above all, a terrible fear of what would happen next.

'Okay.' Gary looks around, almost as if he's looking for Frank. But if he was here, he's not any more. 'Have you done any research on ghosts?'

'Yes. A little.' A lot.

'What did you find?'

I tell Gary about the various explanations I've read online, and his eyebrows rise when I mention that poltergeist activity has been linked to a person's psychological stress.

'So a living person can cause these things to happen?'

'That's what some people believe.'

'Let me get this right. Somehow, *you* could be making these events happen?'

'Apparently.'

'How?'

'I don't really know. Something to do with energy.'

'And why does it happen?'

'Usually because the person is in some sort of emotional turmoil.'

'Are you in emotional turmoil?'

'Well, I am now!' I say, and laugh, despite my distress.

'What about before? How did you feel when Frank died?'

'I was all over the place. I felt free, and guilty for feeling free. I felt elated, and terrified to be on my own. And I felt angry, but I wasn't entirely sure who at.'

'Well, that sounds like emotional turmoil to me.'

'So you think the theory might be true?'

'I mean, it's better than an actual poltergeist, right?'

I'm relieved and grateful that Gary is taking me seriously. 'I guess so.'

'How do you make it stop?'

'I don't know.'

'Do you need to see a counsellor or something?'

I can't afford a counsellor. Or maybe that's just my excuse because I'm not ready to unpack thirty years of my life. 'Maybe,' I concede.

'Well, until you work it out, how about I sleep in your room? So you're not alone.'

I'm stunned into silence. Is he suggesting what I think he's suggesting?

'No funny business,' he adds quickly, sensing my unease. 'Just to keep you company.'

I'm conflicted. I crave Gary's presence. I like the idea of him being in my bed. I'm anxious about being that close to a man and at the prospect of anything happening between us because my experience of being intimate has been Frank and only Frank. It's easier to live in a fantasy of Gary and I becoming romantic than actually living in the reality of it. And, more than that, I'm afraid of my dead husband's wrath if I let another man into my bed.

I really do need to see a counsellor.

'It was a bad idea,' Gary says, when I remain silent. 'Forget I said it.'

'No,' I say slowly, defiantly. 'I'd like that. Thank you.'

'Okay. Well, erm, great.'

We sip our tea in awkward silence, but I'm so pleased that he's here. I think I would have lost my mind if I was on my own to deal with all this strange stuff. I love Benji but he's of little comfort to me given how uptight he's acting. Even now, he's pacing the room agitatedly. Gary must notice too because he stands up.

'I'll let Benji out the back for a few minutes.'

They head towards the back door and I follow them. Gary and I stand, side by side, squeezed into the doorway, as Benji darts around the back garden.

'You need to let it go,' Gary says quietly.

I turn to him. 'What do you mean?'

'The turmoil you're in. You need to let it go.'

'That's easier said than done though, isn't it.'

'You were in an abusive relationship, Maggie. I know you didn't acknowledge it at the time, but you do now. And the man who hurt you is gone. Let him go and move on.'

Gary sees things in black and white, not in the various shades of grey that have dominated my life for so long. To him, it's simple. Forget about Frank and get on with my life. But it's way more complicated than that, a messy tangle that I'm yet to unravel.

When Benji comes back inside, he's much calmer. Perhaps he just needed to let off some steam. I give him a stroke and then we turn the lights off and head up to bed. Gary gets in on Frank's side and it feels surreal, and wrong, and right all at the same time. I'm acutely aware of his presence and when Benji jumps up and nestles between us, I'm glad that he's acting as chaperone because I'm intensely nervous, even though Gary and I aren't even touching. We lie, side by side, and I wonder if Gary is as self-conscious as I am, until I hear his breathing become steadier. Within minutes, he is fast asleep and I wish I was too.

I know I will not sleep. I have a man in my bed. A dog who is acting like he's seen a ghost, and quite possibly has. I'm not sure I'll ever sleep again.

I contemplate my conversation with Gary. If this really is in my head, then I have the power to stop it. I just need to make peace with my disastrous marriage and then I can move on. But when I close my eyes, all I can see is Frank staring back at me, hostile and angry.

'Why are you doing this, Frank?' I whisper.

But there is no reply. Because, as always, he refuses to listen.

13

It's been five days since the second smashed bowl incident and Gary is still sharing my bed. We haven't discussed the sleeping arrangements, it's more of an unspoken agreement between us which is fast becoming a habit. And I'm not sure what to think, or feel, about it.

Gary hasn't so much as moved a toe into my side of the bed. I'm getting used to his presence but I'm obsessing over what it means. Surely two friends don't share a bed for days on end. But if Gary likes me romantically, why hasn't he tried to kiss me? Do I want him to kiss me? Do I even remember how to kiss? Would it be callous to move on from Frank so quickly? And what will Frank do if something happens between us?

My mind is swimming with unanswered questions. And at the top of the pile is the most puzzling and distressing of all. What the hell is happening in this house?

There have been no more strange events since the broken bowl and I'm daring to hope that my conversation with Gary has put an end to the madness and proved that somehow it was my own emotions causing the disturbances. That I've had an epiphany moment.

Benji seems happier too, although he still paces around the house sometimes, sniffing each corner. Gary and I are taking him out for lots of walks to burn off some energy and I've noticed how much fitter I am. I no longer crave four slices of toast and a packet of biscuits every morning. I don't work my way through a family-sized portion of chocolate in the evening. Yesterday I went to a Pilates class in the village hall and although it nearly killed me, I felt such a sense of achievement afterwards. I've just signed up for a six-week block of sessions and I'm already looking forward to the following week.

I feel like I've turned a corner, and the house is peaceful once again. I'm daring to hope that my troubles are now behind me, if only I could work out this business with Gary.

It's a heady mix of emotions. Trepidation, excitement, confusion. Beth says I deserve to be happy but I'm not sure whether it's appropriate to move on yet, or ever. I worry about what people will think of me. What Frank would think. He still invades my thoughts, every day. I sense his judgement and his disapproval. And I still hear his words, as if they were spoken yesterday. *No one would have you anyway*.

It's hard to let go, even when the thing you're clinging on to hurts you over and over.

But there's no rush. Gary isn't putting any pressure on me. In fact, he's so relaxed that sometimes I wonder if he's just being a good friend. I fret that he feels sorry for me and pity is the last thing I want. I yearn to talk to someone about it, but Alyssa doesn't approve of Gary and Beth has been busy with a work deadline.

I'm polishing glasses behind the bar when Sophie walks in, pushing a pram. She's chatting to another new mum with a baby and I take a moment to appraise her. I know who she is because I've seen her out and about, but we've never been formally introduced and I'm not sure she knows who I am. When she catches my eye, I realise immediately that she does.

She comes over to the bar and I smile. 'Hi, what can I get you?'

'Two coffees, please.'

I nod and turn my back to switch on the coffee machine and prepare the drinks. I can feel her gaze on me, burning a hole. When I swivel around, she's still watching me.

'You're Maggie,' she says.

'Yes, that's right. And you must be Sophie.' I peer over the bar at the sleeping baby in the pram. She looks so peaceful, with her head turned to the side and her arms thrown up above her. But this time, I don't experience a searing pain of jealousy. I simply see another woman's very lovely baby and the detachment I feel surprises me.

'She's beautiful,' I say. 'Congratulations.'

'Thank you.' Sophie pays for the drinks, but she doesn't move away. 'How's it going living with Gary?'

'Great, thank you. And I bet you're enjoying having the place to yourself.'

'Yes.' Sophie looks around, as though making sure no one is listening, and then she leans in. 'You know, if you want to kick him out, you have every right.'

I try to keep my voice neutral. 'I have no intention of kicking him out.'

'Sure, but if you did, I'm just saying that would be fine.'

I frown. 'Why would I do that?'

'Come on, Maggie, we all know he's a useless alcoholic. I'm pleased that he's out of our house, but I feel guilty that we've sent him your way.'

Anger surges through me. This woman is so ungrateful. Gary has moved out of his own house so that she can have the run of it and she's still bad-mouthing him.

'Gary likes a drink, but he's not an alcoholic,' I say, thinking of how nasty Frank used to get when he'd had a few. Gary has never been visibly drunk in my presence and nor has he once been aggressive or critical.

'He's been a drinker for years. That's why his wife left him.'

I want to tell Sophie the real reason why Gary and his ex-wife separated but I know it's not my place to do so. It's clear that Gary's ex made up lies about him to cover up her own infidelity and get her children on side. It's horribly sad, but it's not my business.

'Just be careful,' Sophie says. 'I don't want you to get hurt.'

She takes the pram over to her friend and returns for the coffees without saying another word. Our conversation has upset me and I feel outraged on Gary's behalf. But I also can't stop a tiny seed of doubt from embedding itself in the pit of my stomach. Why do Alyssa and Sophie have it in for him so much? Can they see something that I can't?

It's still playing on my mind when the lunch rush ends and soon the bar is empty, with just a few regulars scattered around the pub. When Mark comes over to check the tills, I watch him work for a few moments, trying to summon up the courage to ask him about Gary. He's known him for a long time, and he can set the record straight. But will asking Mark be a betrayal of Gary's trust? I was so wrong about Frank and look how that turned out. Perhaps it would be sensible to find out more about the man who is sharing my bed because I don't want to make the same mistake twice.

'Mark?' I say tentatively.

'Mmmmm?'

'How long have you known Gary?'

'Oh, donkey's years. We went to secondary school together.' Mark chuckles. 'We used to get up to all sorts of trouble, me and Gary.'

'What sort of trouble?'

'Oh, just the usual teenage stuff. Skipping school, smoking behind the bike shed.'

I never did those things but then I was about as well behaved as it was possible to get. Well, until I ran away to London with Frank.

I brace myself. 'He's a good bloke, right?'

Mark gives me a curious look. 'Yeah. Why?'

I lose my nerve. 'Nothing, don't worry.'

'What's on your mind, Maggie?'

I hesitate. 'It's just that his daughter-in-law doesn't seem to like him very much and, well, he's living with me and I just want to know if I have anything to worry about.'

'Sophie's stuck-up,' Mark retorts. 'Thinks she's better than everyone else.'

'She warned me to be careful.'

Mark rolls his eyes. 'Of what? Does she think he's going to murder you in your bed while you sleep?' He sees my look of horror. 'Sorry, Maggie, that was meant to be a joke. Look, Gary's not perfect, but no one is. And he'd be the first to put his hand up and admit his faults.'

'Which are?'

'He was never one for commitment when he was younger. He was a job here, a job there kind of guy, not settling to anything. And he's always liked a drink. His wife got fed up with him in the end and when she left, I don't think he blamed her. He spent more time at the pub than at home. But he's not the same person he was back then.'

'He's not?'

'Of course not. He grew up. We all do, in the end. Well, most of us, anyway.' Mark chuckles and closes the till. 'I think he's pretty fond of you.'

I can't stop the blush from creeping up my neck. 'We're just friends.'

'Well, you could do a lot worse than Gary, that's all I'm saying.'

Mark touches me gently on the shoulder then heads out to the back. I consider his assessment of Gary against Sophie's. Mark has known Gary since they were kids and so I'm inclined to go with his. Especially as it's the one I want to hear.

Sophie and Alyssa are wrong. They're judging Gary by his previous crimes. But we all have a past, things we're ashamed of or wish we could go back and change. If I deserve a clean slate, so does Gary. It's time to put my faith, and my trust, in a man again.

When I get home from work, Gary is sitting on the sofa, staring at the television screen. Except it's blank.

'Watching something good?' I joke.

'The set's playing up,' he tells me. 'It keeps turning off.'

'That's strange.'

'Every time I turn it on, it switches off again.'

Suddenly the room feels cold. Very cold, as though someone has put the air conditioning on. Except I don't have air conditioning. I shiver, rubbing my arms vigorously. I look at Gary, but he doesn't seem to have noticed. Surely it can't just be me who feels it? It's as though the cold is wrapping itself around me and squeezing my heart.

'Are you cold?' I ask.

'A bit. Shall we put the heating on?'

'I'll do it.' I go to the kitchen and turn up the thermostat. And then I hear Gary say something. I rush in, thinking that he's talking to me but then I realise it's Benji.

'Calm down, boy,' he's saying. I look at Benji who is standing near the window, snarling. It's like he's been transformed from a docile family pet into a wild animal again.

A blaring noise breaks through Benji's snarls and I turn to see that the television is back on, and the sound is on full blast.

'It's working again,' Gary says, stating the obvious.

I put my hands to my ears. 'Can you turn it down?'

Gary does as he's asked and I look at the screen again and recoil in horror.

'Did you put this on?' I demand.

'No. What is it?'

I stare at the screen. 'It's a film called *Unfaithful*.'

'Never seen it. Is it any good?'

But I can't answer because I've just been plunged back twenty years in time. To when Frank and I were watching that very film, about a wife having an extramarital affair and the husband killing her lover. *If you ever cheat on me, I'll kill you both*.

I look at Gary, my eyes wide, and I'm about to warn him he's not safe when I hear a loud smashing noise, and the next thing I know, I'm lying on the floor.

14

Someone has wrapped a blanket around me. I'm clutching a cup of tea but I have no memory of who gave it to me. I'm staring, unseeing, at the now blank TV screen.

'She's in shock,' I hear Gary say. 'She fainted. Don't worry, I'll look after her.'

The window has been smashed to pieces. Among the shards of glass littering the carpet, Gary found a cricket ball. He called the police because he said that I might need a crime reference number to make a claim on the home insurance.

'It's kids,' he reassured me. 'Just like I told you it was the last time.'

But kids didn't make the television flicker on and off. Kids didn't put *Unfaithful* on.

A dog barks and I blink and turn to see Benji, being petted by a police officer. He's back to his old self now, as if nothing ever happened. Gary seems perfectly at ease as well as he hands out mugs of tea. I'm the only one who knows what really happened.

I am not safe in this house. And neither is Gary.

It's all my fault. I should never have asked him to move in

with me. I should never have let him into my bed. What was I thinking?

I'm aware of how irrational I'm being. I'm terrified of a dead person. But my fear is not rational, and I can't control it. No, it's Frank who is still controlling me. He's exerting his power, his authority on this house and he's trying to intimidate me. It's working.

The police officers leave and Gary closes the door quietly and comes to sit next to me.

'How are you holding up, love?'

'I can't stay here,' I say. 'I can't be here.'

'There's nothing to be afraid of. It was just kids playing games on the street, the little blighters. They've run back home to their mummies and are hiding under their Batman duvets as we speak.'

'It wasn't kids. It was him.'

'Who?'

'*Him*.'

Gary cottons on. 'Your husband?'

'Yes,' I whisper.

'Maggie, he's dead. He can't frighten you any more.'

But he is frightening me. And it's never going to stop. 'I can't stay here,' I repeat.

'Okay. Give me five minutes.'

Gary leaves the room and I hear him talking quietly in the kitchen. He returns a few minutes later, clutching his phone.

'I've just spoken to an old friend, Paula, who runs a small hotel in Harpenden. She's got a spare room tonight and she says we're welcome to it. There's only one though, if you don't mind sharing?'

We're already sharing a bed and all I want to do is get out of this cottage and never come back. 'That's fine. Can Benji come too?'

'She said that's no problem.'

I look at Gary gratefully. 'Thank you so much.'

'Come on then, pack a bag and I'll find something to cover up the broken window.'

I do as I'm told and within fifteen minutes, we're in Gary's Jeep, on the short drive to Harpenden. It's where Beth lives but I'm in no mood to socialise. All I want to do is get into bed and hide under the covers. I never want to come out again.

I know this is a quick fix, a temporary solution, because I can't live in a hotel forever. For one, I can't afford it. But I'll deal with that tomorrow. Tonight, I just want to feel safe.

We park outside the hotel, which is more of a pub with rooms, and we're greeted by a cheerful lady who hugs Gary and shakes my hand. She shows us up to our room, which is small but cosy and, mercifully, has an en suite bathroom.

'Fancy something to eat?' Gary asks.

I'm not hungry but it's only eight o'clock, too early for bed, and I haven't eaten since midday. 'Sure, okay.'

We go downstairs to the pub and Gary orders a bottle of wine, which he brings over along with some menus. He orders fish and chips and I go for a salad which, when it arrives, I pick at without really digesting any of it.

'What are we going to do with you?' Gary says, looking at me fondly.

'I don't know. I'm sorry, Gary.'

'You've got nothing to be sorry for.' Gary looks around. 'Although it feels a bit cheeky, doesn't it? Stealing away for a night in a hotel.'

I hadn't thought of it that way. All I'd thought about was

getting out of that godforsaken house as quickly as possible. 'I suppose so.'

'Listen, I still think you've got nothing to worry about. Everything that's happened can be explained. Benji broke the bowls, kids smashed the windows.'

'And the TV?'

'A technical glitch. These things happen.'

Maybe they do. But not all at once and not to the same person. Gary's trying to be reassuring but he doesn't understand. He doesn't believe in the paranormal and up until recently, I didn't either. But there's no going back for me now, I'm in too deep.

'I'll have to sell the cottage,' I say. But my words are empty because I know I can't afford to move. I've already done some research and the housing market has stagnated because of interest rates, making mortgages unappealing. I doubt my pub job and solo income would be enough to persuade a lender and rents seem even more expensive than a mortgage these days. Anyway, where would I go?

'Steady on, Maggie, don't go overboard. Everything will seem better in the morning.'

I want him to be right, but I know that he's not. Because it will happen again, and again, until someone gets hurt. Me. Gary. Or both of us.

Benji yawns and rests his chin on his paws. He's exhausted from all the excitement. What did he see in the room that we couldn't? His reaction only fuels my paranoia.

Gary tries to make small talk and I pretend to listen until his plate is empty and the bottle of wine is finished. Then we take Benji out for a walk and return to our room. I'm suddenly self-conscious, despite living with Gary for weeks. Something about being in a hotel makes everything seem more intimate and when I go into the bathroom to change, I wonder what on earth I'm doing there. But when I emerge again, Gary is propped up in bed, reading a tatty paperback he'd found on a shelf downstairs and Benji is curled up on an armchair, and for the first time in weeks I feel protected. Nothing can happen to us here.

I climb into bed next to Gary, light-headed. It hits me that I've just drunk half a bottle of wine with very little food to accompany it. I look at Gary's bare arms and imagine them wrapped around me. I want to feel warm and secure in his hold. I want to forget about everything that happened this evening and become lost in the moment.

I push my body up against Gary's and start stroking his chest. He freezes and I wonder if I've made a mistake. What possessed me to be so forward? I've never done anything like this before, and clearly for good reason. Shame and humiliation are already building up inside me, my body getting ready to flee. But then he slowly puts the book down and turns towards me, putting his arm around me. We gaze at each other and then he kisses me.

It's nothing like I'm used to. This kiss is gentle, respectful. It's hesitant at first but it becomes more passionate and it's glorious. It's escapism at its finest. And the day melts away from me as I fall into the kiss and forget about everything else.

But then Gary pulls away and it's like someone's turned the heating off and plunged me into a pool of freezing cold water.

'I'm sorry, Maggie.'

I'm mortified. I was a fool to think that a man might want me. How many times did Frank tell me that I was nothing, no one?

'No, it's my fault, I'm sorry.'

Gary looks distinctly uncomfortable as he shuffles around and I'm embarrassed for myself and for him. 'I just don't want to take advantage of you,' he says. 'You're upset.'

A chink of hope opens. 'Is that why? Not because you don't want me?'

'Of course I want you, Maggie. I've wanted you since we first met.'

His words are music to my ears. This man wants me. He admires me. I want to bathe in his affection, to bask in it. I am not no one, I am someone.

'It's not because I'm upset,' I say quietly. 'That's not why I did it. I wanted to.'

'Are you sure?'

I look at him straight in the eye. Hold my chin up. 'Yes.'

He looks conflicted but a glorious and unexpected feeling of confidence has come over me and I decide to ride high on it and take the initiative. I lean in and kiss him again.

'Are you sure, Maggie?' he murmurs.

'I've never been surer of anything in my life.'

It's like I've spoken the secret password because Gary throws his arms around me again and kisses me as though his life depends on it. And for the first time I'm not apprehensive, or scared of what might happen next. I'm not even embarrassed about my wobbly bits or the fact that I've only ever been with one man in my life.

For the first time, I discover what making love really is.

* * *

The following morning, I wake up with a fuzzy head and a dry mouth. For a moment I'm disorientated as I try to work out where I am. Then it all comes rushing back to me.

I'm in a hotel room with Gary. And last night we slept together. I turn my head to the side and see that he's still fast asleep. I'm relieved because I need a few minutes to myself to get my head around what's happened.

It feels like a dream, but the adrenaline coursing through my body tells me that it's real. It really happened. And although it was strange and unfamiliar, it was so good. Gentle, yet passionate. Mutual and respectful. Like it's supposed to be. Afterwards, I fell into a deep sleep, secure in Gary's arms and the safe bubble of the hotel room. I realise now that I never want to leave this bed, I want to stay in it forever.

Benji wakes up and starts pacing around the room and I know that he needs to go to the toilet. Reluctantly, I slip out of bed and dress quietly, but Gary stirs and opens one eye.

'What time is it?' he asks croakily.

'Just after seven. I'm taking Benji out for a walk.'

'Wait, I'll come with you.'

'No, don't worry, you sleep.'

Gary sits up. 'We'll go together.'

I try to suppress my smile, but I can't. Gary still wants me. He wants to spend time with me. I go into the bathroom to freshen up and when I come out, Gary is dressed.

It's freezing outside and I zip up my coat as we walk along the road that Gary says leads to an open space. I'm holding Benji's lead in one hand and Gary takes my other in his and squeezes it. I feel like a teenager again and I can barely stop grinning. We're only a few miles away from home but we could be on the other side of the world because it's like we're on holiday, all the stresses of everyday life forgotten.

I wonder if Gary will bring up what happened last night but he doesn't. We walk in companionable silence and after Benji's had a run about, Gary suggests we go back to the hotel for breakfast. When we arrive, Paula's laid a table in the pub and the smell of freshly brewed coffee wafts up my nose and makes my stomach rumble. She gives us a knowing look as we walk in but doesn't say anything. She's being discreet and I have to remind myself that we're not doing anything wrong. There is no reason to feel guilty. We're two single people in later life, searching for companionship. For love.

Love. Am I in love? It's too early to tell. But I'm growing very fond of Gary and it feels healthy, not like the obsession I had with Frank. But as I think about Frank, unease builds up inside me again because I know that at some point I have to go home.

Gary must sense it because he says, 'When are we going back to the cottage?'

I fuss with my coffee cup. 'I don't know.'

'I mean, this is lovely, don't get me wrong, but we have to return to real life eventually.'

'Are you working today?'

'No. You?'

'Not until tomorrow.'

We look at each other, a silent acknowledgement. 'One more night then?' Gary suggests.

'Yes please,' I say quietly.

We have the most amazing day. We go for another long walk, have a mooch in the shops and afterwards we return to the pub and sit by the fire to enjoy a long lunch. Then Gary suggests we go to the cinema, so we leave Benji with Paula and drive to the nearest one. We watch a comedy which makes Gary guffaw and I'm laughing too but not because of the film. I'm laughing because I'm happy.

We have dinner at the hotel and then go up to our room and the second time we make love it's even better than the first because there are no more doubts in either of our minds. This is what we want. We know that we both feel the same way.

But I don't sleep deeply that night. I lie awake, the sheen of my perfect day rubbing off as I realise that tomorrow we must go back to the cottage. I can't hide here forever, no matter how much I want to. And I'm petrified of walking through that door again.

He'll be waiting for me. And if he knows what I've done here in Harpenden, if he knows that I've been with another man, he'll be angrier than ever.

The realisation is brutal and sobering. But it also makes me indignant. How dare Frank continue to intimidate me? What right does he have to destroy my happiness and drive me out of my own home? I've come a long way in the last few months and I'm stronger than I've ever been. I need to fight back, to reclaim my space. I can't let him win.

Once of us must go. And I need to make sure that it's him. I just don't know how yet.

15

I haven't been inside a church since Frank's funeral, and before that it was probably my wedding day. So it feels strange as I push the heavy wooden door open, step inside and look around anxiously. I feel like an imposter in this holy place.

The village church is empty and I stare in wonder at the stained-glass windows, mesmerised by the beautiful depictions of saints and angels. I breathe in the scent of incense and feel a sense of calm tentatively creeping under my skin, not removing my anguish but numbing it. And then I close my eyes and breathe. In and out. In and out.

When I open them, I'm still alone and I walk quietly down the aisle, stopping about halfway to sit on a wooden pew. I'm not sure what I'm doing here. It's like my feet took control of my mind and led me to this place. We returned to the village this morning and Gary had to head straight off to work so I dumped my bags in the hallway and immediately left again. I'm still determined not to let Frank win, but I need time to gather my thoughts and work out what to do. And as I walked and mulled it over, I found myself in the churchyard, wondering if subconsciously this was my plan all along, if it was why I left Benji behind.

I sit in silence for a few minutes, not really sure what to do with myself. At school we had prayed all the time but it seems like a lifetime ago now and I was never sure that I believed in it anyway. My parents had sent me there for the academic results, not the religious attachment. But something about the church feels pure and inherently good, a stark contrast to the evil that inhabits my cottage. It's like I want some of it to rub off on me, so I can take it home and unleash it on the demon that haunts my house.

A noise startles me and I turn to see the vicar, Steven, approaching. He's about my age and I spoke to him a few times when I was organising Frank's funeral. When Frank died, I wasn't sure what to do at first because he wasn't a religious man and he left no list of wishes. In the end, I came to this church seeking advice and Steven was incredibly helpful.

He smiles kindly at me now.

'Hello, Maggie, how lovely to see you here.'

'Hi, Reverend.'

'Steven, please. Would you like some company or are you looking for solitude?'

I don't answer but I shuffle up the pew and he sits beside me.

'Is something on your mind, Maggie?'

I'm quiet for a moment and then I say, 'Do you believe in ghosts?'

I look sideways at him, curious to see his reaction, and his expression is contemplative. 'The Bible is clear that once a person dies, they cannot return from the dead without divine intervention. But I think it's a bit more complicated than that.'

'How so?'

'Well, firstly there are mentions of spiritual beings in the

Bible, angels and demons, for example. Some people believe that there can be a delay between death and judgement so we might ask ourselves what happens in this interim period? But one thing the Bible tells us is that we should not seek out mediums to try to communicate with spirits.'

I think of the physic supper and suppress a shudder.

'Are you thinking about your husband?' Steven's eyes are sympathetic.

I am, but not in the way that he thinks. He probably assumes that I'm asking these questions because I miss Frank and I'm seeking comfort. He couldn't be more wrong.

'Do you perform exorcisms?' I ask him, my voice tinged with desperation.

The poor man looks at me in alarm. 'Why do you ask?'

'I think my house is haunted.'

'Ah.' He nods solemnly. 'And why do you think that?'

I tell him about the shadows, the TV and broken windows, the smell of Frank's aftershave and Benji's snarling. I don't mention the back door key because I don't want him to judge me for going to a psychic supper. As I speak, I realise that if someone else was telling me this story, I would agree that their house was haunted because there's no other explanation. But I'm talking to a vicar and I have no idea what his reaction will be. Will he order me out of the church for some sort of blasphemy? Call an ambulance because he thinks I'm ill? Or will he do what I yearn for and come to my house to get rid of this ghost? When I'm finished talking, he's silent, digesting everything I've just told him, and I hold my breath and wait. To see if he'll tell me I'm doomed to all eternity.

When he finally speaks, his words are not what I was expecting. 'You seek answers to the unexplained, Maggie, but perhaps you're looking for them in the wrong place.'

What the heck does that mean? I stare at him, searching for answers.

He hesitates, before saying. 'You are looking to the dead. But maybe you should be looking to the living. In life, most things can be explained.'

'But Frank *is* dead,' I exclaim. I saw his lifeless body with my own eyes. I watched them take him away in a body bag. I witnessed the man being cremated. There's no way he can be alive. Unless he's talking about me? Is he saying I should be looking inside myself? Perhaps this is a nice way of telling me that I've lost it.

The vicar doesn't answer and his reaction frustrates me. He's trying to communicate something, but I don't know what it is. Why is he being so cryptic? Or am I just turning into a total, paranoid mess? Maybe his words are simply meant to comfort me.

'So you won't come?' I ask, the last shred of hoping draining away.

He puts his hand over mine. 'I'm sorry, but I don't perform exorcisms. And in any case, I'm not sure it would help. Look to the rational, Maggie, not the irrational, and you will find the answers you seek. And God will be with you, to guide you.'

The man is talking in riddles and I've had enough. It was a mistake to come here, it hasn't given me the comfort I crave; if anything, it's made me feel worse. God is not guiding me in this moment, He's making me even more confused.

I stand up abruptly, brushing my trousers. 'Thank you for your time,' I say.

'You're welcome any time, Maggie. My door is always open.'

I nod and make my way outside. I need to get back to Benji because he doesn't like being left alone for too long. My shift doesn't start for a few hours, but I'll pick him up, take him out for a walk and get to the pub early. I need to keep busy.

When I reach the cottage and call out Benji's name, there is no response. I frown. It's unusual because Benji normally comes rushing to the door to greet me, his tail wagging furiously. I force myself to step inside the house, taking deep breaths as I call Benji's name again. Where is he? I glance in the living room but it's empty and so I go to the kitchen and see that the back door is wide open. Why is the back door open?

I look for Benji in the garden but there's no sign of him and panic takes hold. He's gone. My beautiful dog has gone. I should never have left him alone, not in this place. As I run upstairs and rush from room to room, the panic fills my body and spills out of every pore.

'Benji,' I scream frantically. 'Benji!'

But it's pointless. He's not there.

I find my phone and call Gary, my voice hysterical as I tell him what's happened.

'I'll be there in fifteen minutes,' he promises.

While I wait for Gary I search the back garden again, forcing myself to walk behind the shed. I don't want to go anywhere near it but this is an emergency and Benji is more important. There is no smell of aftershave, thank goodness, but I discover a hole under the fence. One I hadn't noticed before, unless it's new. And I realise that's how Benji got out. He could easily have dug the hole himself, but he can't have opened the back door. So who did?

By the time Gary arrives I'm beside myself. I show him the hole and he crouches down and nods gravely. 'You're right, Maggie, he's done a runner.'

'What if he's been hit by a car?' I ask, tears pooling in my eyes.

'We don't know that, love. Come on, Benji's a sensible boy, he won't have gone far.'

'Did you leave the back door open?'

'I barely stepped inside the house, remember? I left to go to work as soon as we got back.'

'So why was it open? It wasn't open when we left the other night.'

Gary scratches his head. 'I don't know. Has anything been taken?'

'Not that I noticed but I was more worried about Benji.'

We do a quick scan of the cottage, which shows that it hasn't been burgled and then we set out, walking around the village calling Benji's name and asking passers-by if they've seen him. By the time we reach the pub, I'm in tears.

I step inside and feel a momentary surge of hope that Benji might have made his way there and is lying by someone's feet, having a fuss made of him. But a quick glance around tells me that my dog is not there.

Gary goes over to talk to Mark, explaining what's happened and I watch as the landlord shakes his head. My heart sinks even lower. He's gone forever, I know he is.

Mark comes over and puts a hand on my shoulder. 'He'll turn up, Maggie. Is he microchipped?'

'Yes,' I whisper, barely able to speak.

'Maybe call around the vets.' Mark sees the alarm on my face. 'Someone might have taken him there if they found him loose, that's all. I'm sure he's fine.'

A few of the locals have been listening in and within minutes, half a dozen people have offered to help find Benji. We set off in pairs, scouring the village and nearby fields for Benji. If I wasn't so upset, I'd be chuffed that so many people are offering to help me. But with each minute that passes, despair embeds itself deeper inside me.

This is my punishment. Frank hasn't hurt me, or Gary. He's hurt my dog. He's showing me that he knows what I've done. I've disobeyed him and I must pay for it. In my panic, my earlier resolve is slipping away. Frank *is* winning and there's nothing I can do about it.

Suddenly I remember that in my haste to find Benji, I didn't close the back door before we left.

'I need to go home,' I tell Gary urgently. 'The back door's still wide open.'

He nods. 'Let's go.'

When we reach the cottage, I want to smash the windows myself. I want to keep smashing until everything inside it is broken. I'm angry and I'm scared. And now I'm worried that while we've been looking for Benji, someone has taken advantage of the unsecured house too.

The first thing I see when I open the front door is my dog. He's sitting there, waiting for me.

'Benji!' I say, throwing myself at him and burying my face in his fur.

Gary laughs with relief. 'You gave us quite a fright there, mate.'

Benji seems nonplussed as he turns and nuzzles me. He's a little bit dirty but other than that, he's just how I left him. I cling on to him, never wanting to let go.

Gary wanders into the kitchen and then comes back out. 'The back door's shut.'

'It can't be. It was wide open when we left.'

'Well, it's shut now. It must have blown closed in the wind.'

'But how did Benji get in then?'

Gary shrugs. 'Maybe it closed after he got back? But it doesn't look like anyone's been inside anyway. I'll call Mark now and tell him the search is off.'

As Gary phones Mark, I stand up and go to the back door myself. Gary's right, it's not only closed, it's locked too. Which means it wasn't down to the wind. But no one else has a key to this cottage. No one could have got in while we were in Harpenden. Apart from Frank.

Ghosts don't smash windows. That's what Gary said to me weeks ago. And he'll probably say that they don't open and close back doors either. But I know what's happened here. It's so clear to me that there can be no other explanation.

And the thought that overcomes me is this. *Is he done punishing me now, or is there more to come? And just how far is he willing to go?*

16

I look out of the window to see a taxi pulling up outside and Alyssa waving at me from the back seat. We're meeting Beth for dinner at an Italian restaurant in St Albans and I'm looking forward to catching up with my friends. I haven't seen either of them for ages.

Gary and I spend almost every waking minute together. We're what you might call joined at the hip and whenever he goes to work, I feel like I'm missing a limb. It's so easy, so effortless, like we've always been together. But I've neglected my friends and it's time to re-engage again. I will not make Gary the centre of my world like I did with Frank. I have to keep hold of my new-found independence and cherish my friendships too.

Since Benji disappeared a couple of weeks ago, I've been waiting for the next thing to happen. But the cottage is still and quiet again and with each day that passes I feel a fraction calmer. I got the front and back door locks changed, just for peace of mind, and Gary and I are the only ones who have the keys. I don't know if it will make any difference, not if it's all down to Frank, but at least I'm doing something to try and stop this madness. I need to take back control, of the house and my life. Gary and I have been doing some work in the garden, filling up the hole that Benji escaped through, tidying up the lawn, pulling weeds from the patio and planting bulbs. We ordered a new outdoor table and chairs in the sale so that we can sit outside. With winter fast approaching it's the wrong time of year for al fresco dining, but it gives me hope. I like imagining us sitting there together next spring, in our garden. Not Frank's. *Ours.* New beginnings. And a future I'm starting to imagine with Gary.

As I climb into the taxi and greet Alyssa, I want to gush about my new romance but I hold my tongue because of Alyssa's feelings about Gary. Instead, we talk about her two boys and catch up on village gossip. She doesn't ask about Gary and I don't tell her about what's been going on in the house because I want to forget about it all for the evening.

A rush of pleasure runs through me when I see Beth waiting for us in the restaurant. A ladies' night with good wine, food and company is just what I need.

'I've ordered a bottle of white,' she says as she hugs us. 'I hope that's okay.'

We peruse the menu, order and then share our news. If Beth is offended that I haven't been in touch with her lately, she doesn't show it. Anyway, I'm sure she has a busier social life than me. She's talking about booking a holiday to Vietnam in the spring.

'You should come, Maggie,' she says.

'Oh, I don't know,' I say automatically.

'What's stopping you?'

I think about it. Money. Work. Benji. And, above all, Gary.

'Gary and I have been talking about going away on a dog-friendly UK break,' I say, a little shyly.

'Oooh!' Beth leans forward, her eyes lighting up. 'And is this a friendship thing or something else?'

I don't meet Alyssa's eye as I say, 'Something else.'

'Is this why we haven't seen you for weeks?'

'Kind of. I'm sorry.'

Beth waves away my concerns. 'Oh, no need to apologise. I'm so happy for you, Maggie. When did it happen?'

I give Beth an abridged version and then risk a glance at Alyssa. She looks like a bulldog chewing a wasp. By now I'm on my second glass of wine and I'm tired of Alyssa's disapproval. If she really is my friend, then she should be happy for me.

'I know you don't like him, Alyssa, but he's really been there for me these past few weeks when I needed it,' I say stubbornly.

'What do you mean?'

I wasn't going to say anything to them but it all comes spilling out. I tell them about what's been going on in the cottage and how the unexplained events seem to be coming more frequently. Beth listens, rapt, but Alyssa maintains a stony expression.

When I'm finished, Beth takes my hand. 'I can't believe you've been going through all of this. You should have told me. But I'm so glad that Gary's been looking after you.'

We both turn to Alyssa. I tell myself that I don't need her approval, I'm my own woman and I make my own decisions. But I also know that I yearn for it anyway.

'He's looking after you.' She repeats Beth's words, but they don't sound so positive.

'Yes.'

'He walks you to and from work.'

'Yes.'

'You don't know what you'd do without him.'

'Yes,' I say again, a little uncertainly this time.

'He's like your husband.'

Her words hit me like a train. 'That's not true,' I exclaim, my voice carrying across the restaurant. A few diners turn to look at me and I redden.

'You told me that your husband controlled you until you no longer knew how to look after yourself. That's what Gary's doing to you.'

'Alyssa,' Beth says in a low voice. 'I don't think that's fair.'

'I'm only saying it because I care about Maggie. I don't want her to get hurt.'

'And I don't want her to get hurt either. But maybe you're wrong about Gary.'

They're talking about me like I'm not here. Like I'm a passenger in my own life and I've worked so hard not to be that person any more.

'Do I get a say?' I demand.

They both turn to look at me. 'Of course,' Beth replies.

'Gary couldn't be any more different to Frank. He is kind and respectful, and he listens to me. He's been a huge support through this awful business in the cottage.'

'The awful business that started *just* before he moved in,' Alyssa interjects.

I'm fast losing patience with Alyssa. 'What's that supposed to mean?'

'I've been thinking about it,' she says. 'What if he's doing it on purpose?'

'Doing what?'

'Messing with you to scare you. He knew you were unsettled by what the psychic said, right? And you told him you were worried that the house was haunted. So he saw an in with you. He found your weakness and manipulated it.'

I'm incredulous. 'You're honestly suggesting that Gary made

it seem like my house was haunted so that I'd get scared and ask him to move in?'

Alyssa nods. 'Maybe.'

'But it hasn't stopped since he moved in. In fact, it's got even worse.'

'Exactly!' Alyssa says triumphantly. 'Because once he was in your house, it was even easier for him to trick you.'

My voice is rising again. 'And why would he do that?'

'So that he could sweep in, your knight in shining armour, and you would fall straight into his arms. Which, to be fair, is exactly what you've done.'

I feel sick. And angry. Who is this woman? She's certainly not the person I thought she was. She doesn't have my best interests at heart, she's meddling in my life, and I want to stand up and storm out of the restaurant.

But I hold my ground. 'Gary was with me when the window got smashed the second time, so it can't have been him.'

'He could easily have paid someone else to do it. How was the window smashed?'

'A cricket ball.'

'Sophie told me once that Gary's obsessed with cricket.'

'Come on, that's hardly damning evidence! Half the village is obsessed with cricket.'

Alyssa folds her arms defensively. 'Well, it's more likely than your dead husband haunting you, isn't it?'

We stare at each other furiously, in a stand-off that neither of us intends to back down from. I loathe confrontation and I can't remember the last time I argued with anyone but this time I'm not giving in. Gary doesn't deserve this and I don't either.

Beth finally breaks the silence. 'Ladies, let's not fall out. We're supposed to be supporting each other, not attacking one another.'

Alyssa has the good grace to look guilty. 'I'm sorry. I'm not trying to be mean. I genuinely care about you, Maggie, and I'm worried about you, that's all.'

My resolve softens a millimetre. 'I know you mean well, but you're wrong about this, I'm certain of it.'

'And what if I'm not?'

It doesn't bear thinking about if she's not. But she's so far off the mark that there's no point in even considering it.

'You know, it could be a ghost,' Beth says and we both turn to stare at her.

'Not you too,' Alyssa scoffs.

'Why not? There's so much evidence that the paranormal exists and how do you explain the psychic knowing where Maggie's back door key was?'

'Lucky guess?'

'But it was so specific. Much too specific to be a lucky guess.'

'I still think my Gary theory is more plausible.'

The walls of the restaurant are closing in on me. I was looking forward to this dinner but instead it's turning into a nightmare. The two people I considered to be my friends are dissecting my life like I'm a specimen rather than someone they care about and none of their so-called theories are making me feel better. They're making me a million times worse.

'Has anything specific happened that makes you think it's Frank rather than another ghost you inherited with the house?' Beth asks me.

'I smelled his aftershave. And when the TV came on the other week, it was showing a film that we'd watched together years ago.'

Beth's eyes widen. 'Fascinating. What film was it?'

I don't want to tell them, especially not the way I'm feeling right now. 'It doesn't matter. The point is that the incidents haven't been random.'

'Maybe he's just trying to reach out to you. To show you that he misses you?'

'No chance,' I say forcefully without even thinking. When they both stare at me, I feel compelled to elaborate. 'You already know that our marriage wasn't a happy one. If he's haunting me, it's to make my life a misery not because he misses me.'

'And it's got worse since you got together with Gary? Like he's angry with you?'

Alyssa rolls her eyes at Beth's comment, but she's just voiced my biggest fear and hearing someone else say it aloud makes it even more real.

'That's what I'm worried about,' I say.

'All the more reason to end it with Gary then,' Alyssa says and we both ignore her. Beth and I are looking at each other, caught up in the same moment. We both believe that it's Frank. The difference is that she's intrigued and I'm terrified.

'Have you asked him to go away?' Beth asks me.

'Excuse me?'

'I read once that if you ask a spirit to go away, sometimes they do. If they're good.'

I already know that Frank is not good, but I'll try anything right now.

Alyssa is watching us with disapproval. 'You're both off your rockers.'

I'm still cross with her but my rage is beginning to pass and I don't want to end the evening in a blazing row. 'Can we just change the subject please?'

We move on to other topics but the easiness between us is gone and the conversation feels more polite than intimate. By the time we've paid the bill I think we're all relieved to be going home. Beth says goodbye outside and Alyssa gets her phone out to order a taxi.

'I'm really sorry I upset you,' she says. 'I come on a little strong sometimes.'

I swallow my hurt. 'It's okay,' I lie.

'Dylan's always telling me off for it. Warning me to mind my own business. But you're such a kind, gentle soul and I just don't want to see you being taken advantage of. Oh, speak of the devil, he's calling me.'

She answers the phone, tells Dylan where we are and then thanks him.

'Dylan's going to pick us up,' she says. 'He'll be here in ten minutes.'

'What about the boys?'

'His mum's staying with us at the moment. Shall we wait inside?'

We go back into the warmth, but our conversation is stilted and when Dylan pulls up outside, we can't leave fast enough. Alyssa climbs into the front and I get into the back.

'Thanks for the lift,' I say.

He glances at me in the rear-view mirror. 'No problem.'

He pulls out and as the car moves away from the glare of the streetlight his eyes disappear into the darkness. But I'm still staring at the mirror, transfixed. Dread creeps into my body, making my skin tingle. Maybe it's my already frayed nerves, or the argument with Alyssa, or the wine that's made me feel this way. I have no idea what to think any more.

But for a split second, I could have sworn I was looking right at Frank.

17

I don't see Alyssa for a fortnight. It's cold and wet, and she's not at the playground with the boys any more when I pass with Benji. And although Beth has sent a couple of funny GIFs and memes on our group WhatsApp, Alyssa and I haven't reached out to each other directly.

I'm smarting at the loss of someone I considered to be a true friend. When you have as few friends as me, you can't afford to lose one. But maybe keeping a distance from her is the right thing to do for now. For a start, she clearly loathes Gary so we can hardly meet up for a friendly lunch or dinner at the pub like we had just started to do. And anyway, I'm becoming increasingly uncomfortable about Dylan.

His likeness to Frank is unsettling me. I don't see it all the time, but it's been there more than once, fleeting but real. It's in his eyes, the same hardness, and I'm beginning to wonder if Alyssa is really okay or if she's in the same position that I was in, only she's too afraid to tell me. Is Dylan controlling her? I see her out and about on her own so it's not like he's got her under lock and key. And she's certainly got plenty of strong opinions, so she's hardly living in Dylan's shadow, like I was with Frank. But it's still niggling at me.

I've mentioned it to Gary, but he thinks I'm projecting. He says I'm wound up like a coil and looking for things that aren't there. Maybe he's right. I haven't told him what Alyssa accused him of, because I don't want to upset him or create tension between them. So I'm lying to him now and that makes me feel terrible too, even though it's for his own good.

At least things between us are going well. More than well. He's now a permanent fixture in my bedroom, and I'm beginning to wonder how I ever lived without him. I finally know what a healthy, normal relationship feels like. We may be in our fifties, lacking the energy and vigour of our youth, but we're content. And the more time I spend with Gary, the more I recognise how dysfunctional my relationship with Frank really was. I can't believe I put up with it for so long, but when you're lost in the darkness, it's hard to see the light.

Gary has the opposite effect, filling my world with a warm glow. He makes me feel special and safe. He compliments me, he admires me. Did Frank do that at the beginning too? I can barely remember. But I know that Gary is different and sometimes I wonder what my life would have been like if I'd married a Gary and not a Frank. Although I still wouldn't have been able to have children. So perhaps any man, no matter how kind and patient, would have eventually found another woman who could give them a family.

Maybe I'm still a failure after all.

But I don't want to think about that. Gary and I are beyond the age of considering children and anyway, he has his own family. He's a granddad. There is no pressure for me to be a good wife, the perfect mother. We are simply two people enjoying the pleasure of each other's company and it's perfect. Well, almost perfect.

At least I've stopped feeling guilty about Frank. It's come easier than I thought it would. If people want to judge me for moving on so quickly then that's up to them but I know that I deserve to be happy. My worry isn't that I'm betraying Frank, it's Frank himself.

All is still well in the house, though. Benji is relaxed. Nothing unusual has happened. I'm constantly trying to find an explanation for it. I'm hoping it's my new steely resolve not to be intimidated in my own home. Although I don't want to, I've also analysed Alyssa's theory and considered whether the incidents have stopped now that Gary and I are a couple. If he's got what he wanted. But I've dismissed it again. That train of thought doesn't even warrant space in my mind. It's easier to deflect and obsess over Alyssa and Dylan instead and I wonder if she's doing the same. Is she fixating on my life because she's unhappy in her own? Is Dylan a threat? If he is then I must find a way to help her.

I'm contemplating this one Saturday afternoon, while absent-mindedly polishing glasses, when Alyssa walks into the pub. She's on her own and she heads straight over to me.

'Hi,' she says and I can tell she's nervous. We haven't spoken since that awful dinner.

'Hi. Where are the boys?'

'Dylan's taken them swimming. How are you?'

'Fine.' I eye her warily, still not sure where we stand. 'Can I get you a drink?'

Alyssa orders a glass of wine and then sits on a stool and watches me pour.

'I want to apologise,' she says. 'For the other week.'

I look at her and see genuine remorse in her eyes. 'It's okay.'

The Widow's Husband

'No, it's not. I came on far too strong. I was just worried about you, but I went about it the wrong way and it was out of order.'

I glance over to the corner of the pub, where Gary is sitting with Mark. They're too far away to hear our conversation. 'Thank you, Alyssa. And I'm sorry I snapped at you too.'

She smiles and it lights up her beautiful face. 'I deserved it. I'm so glad we've cleared the air, it's been on my mind ever since. I've wanted to call you so many times, but I was worried you were upset with me. I was a wimp and I'm sorry.'

'I should have called you too. So let's call it even.'

We shake on it and a weight eases from my shoulders.

Alyssa takes a sip of her wine. 'Ah, that's good. So how are things really going?'

'Good. Great.' I look at Gary again. 'The strange goings-on seem to have stopped.'

'Thank goodness. I'm so pleased to hear it. So you think Frank's given up the ghost?'

I suppress a smile at her joke. 'Maybe.'

'Well hopefully that's the end of it all.'

We fall into an easy conversation but I'm watching her carefully, looking for any signs of distress. I can't see anything. Her face is an open book and she talks about her family with nothing but love and affectionate frustration at her mischievous sons.

'How's Dylan?' I ask, keeping my tone neutral.

'Busy. He's on track for a promotion at work so he's in the office all hours.'

I remember Frank's constant quest for promotion. 'He must be tired when he gets home.'

'He's exhausted. And so am I from looking after the boys. But we muddle through.'

She's not giving anything away. Perhaps Gary was right and

I'm looking for things that aren't there. But I can't resist probing a little deeper.

'Is he close to his family?'

'He never knew his dad, but he gets on well with his mum.'

'He never knew his dad? That must be hard for him.'

Alyssa shrugs. 'I think it has been at times in his life. But his mum is amazing and he says his childhood was happy. He's determined to be a good, hands-on dad, and he tries so hard with the boys. But it's difficult when he's also building a successful career.'

'Has he ever tried to find his father?'

'No. His mum doesn't know what happened to him or even if he's alive.' Alyssa leans in. 'It was a one-night stand. Of course, he didn't know that until he was much older, but he has an honest relationship with his mum. They're very close.'

I wonder how knowing that he was a one-night stand made Dylan feel. Angry, probably. Bitter. Rageful. And no matter how wonderful his mum is, I can't imagine those feelings are easy to let go of. They must have stayed with him all his life.

'But you two are happy, right?'

'As happy as we can be with two demanding little monsters.'

'He's good to you, though?'

Alyssa looks at me curiously. 'Yes, he is. Why do you ask?'

I quickly backtrack. 'Oh, don't mind me, I'm just making conversation.'

Alyssa finishes her drink and stands up. 'I'd better go. Dylan and the boys will be home soon. It was lovely to see you, Maggie. Let's arrange lunch or dinner with Beth soon.'

'I'd love that.'

She gives me a smile and leaves, and I turn to serve another customer. I'm feeling so much better already. My friendship with Alyssa is back on track and she didn't mention Gary once so perhaps she's decided to keep her opinions to herself. I can't make her like Gary but I don't need to hear all the reasons why she doesn't. Or her ridiculous accusations.

When my shift finishes, Gary's still at the pub and he gets up to walk me home. I've noticed that he nursed one pint all afternoon and it's so unlike him that I bring it up.

'I've decided to cut down on my drinking,' he tells me.

'Why?'

He pats his tummy. 'Well, I've got a beautiful woman to impress now, haven't I?'

'You know I don't mind about that.'

'I know, but I do. And anyway, if I'm going to be running around after my granddaughter soon, I could do with getting a bit fitter.'

'Gary, you're a gardener. You're pretty fit.'

'Well, that's the other thing. I've had a few more potential clients get in touch and I'd like to take on the work.' He smiles at me. 'You're inspiring me, Maggie.'

I look at him incredulously. '*I'm* inspiring you?'

'Yeah. You're making me want to be a better version of myself.'

It's one of the loveliest things anyone's ever said to me. And there's still a part of me that doesn't understand how someone like me could have this kind of effect on Gary. I'm so used to being the one who drags people down, not the one who lifts them up. But I channel my new inner confidence and take the compliment with a smile. I feel like I'm blooming, inside and out. I make so much more effort with my appearance these days, even though I know Gary doesn't care about that kind of thing. It's for me, not him, and that's what I love about it. I feel like a new woman and I'm proud to walk with my head held high. I take Gary's hand and squeeze it as we walk back to the cottage, with Benji at our heel.

This is all I want. This easiness, this simple happiness, for the rest of my life. Perhaps Gary will move in permanently. We could refurbish the cottage and put our own stamp on it, banish any last traces of Frank. I'm jumping ahead of myself as Gary and I haven't been together long but at our age, time is not on our side. And Gary has made it clear that he feels the same way about me, so why can't I be optimistic about our future?

The minute we reach the front door, Benji begins to snarl. I look down at him in surprise, my heart sinking. Please no, not again.

'Benji, what is it?'

But the dog ignores me, he gaze fixed firmly on the door. Gary fishes out his keys and opens it and as soon as I step into the hallway I'm enveloped in Frank's scent.

'Can you smell that?' I ask Gary.

He sniffs. 'Smells like aftershave.'

At least it's not in my head. 'Is it yours?'

'I don't wear aftershave.'

I walk tentatively down the hallway, shivering. The heating should have come on automatically by now but it's freezing. I go into the kitchen to check the boiler and stop short. There are three cups of coffee sitting on the kitchen counter. One is black, just like Frank used to drink it. The other two are milky, except the coffee has gone cold and the milk has formed a kind of scummy foam at the top.

One, two three. Me, Gary, Frank.

I put my hand to my thumping chest as I stagger backwards. Frank has not gone after all. He's still here, watching, waiting. Playing with me.

I feel Gary behind me. 'Are you okay, love?'

I point to the coffee cups and he goes over to study them.

'Where have these come from?'

'I don't know, I didn't make them.'

'Well, I didn't make them either.'

My voice shakes as I say, 'No one else could have got inside. We changed the locks.'

We stare at each other until Benji's frantic barking draws our attention and we follow the noise up the stairs and into my bedroom. He's at the foot of the bed and he's got the edge of the duvet in his jaws. I've never seen him act like this before.

I look at the duvet, trying to work out what's troubling him. And then my heart jumps out of my chest as I hear a door slam downstairs. Gary turns and runs back down the stairs but Benji's too distracted by the bedsheets to follow him.

And then I feel it. Goosebumps on my arms. My hands become clammy.

'Frank,' I whisper. 'Frank, stop this now. Go away.'

But the feeling doesn't pass. If anything it becomes more intense. And I can't take it any more. I flee the bedroom in a mindless panic, racing for the stairs. I have to get out of this house, I'm not safe here.

I stumble as I reach the first step and I'm in too much of a hurry to stop myself from falling. I reach out for the banister desperately trying to grasp it. My life flashes before my eyes, fleeting moments blinking on and off in a split second. Meeting Frank. Getting married. Bleak hopelessness. Then Gary. Light. Happiness. Relief.

The banister is centimetres away, but I'm too late to reach it. I'm falling, down, down into the darkness. And I can hear him, his cruel, mocking voice. He's laughing at me.

18

The memories of my last ten years of marriage are a blur. Every day merged into the next, the same routine, the same nothingness. Get up, make coffee. Read the newspaper. Tidy up. Wait for Frank if he was coming home that day. Go to bed early if he wasn't.

Frank no longer needed to lock the door to keep me in the house because I had no desire to go anywhere. There was nothing left of me, I was an empty shell.

I dreaded the moment that Frank came home but I no longer feared him, not in the same way that I used to. He had no interest in me sexually, much to my immense relief. And his little digs and not so little criticisms now fell on deaf ears. I'd become so accustomed to them that I hardly registered them any more. *Do this, do that*, he'd say and I'd obey willingly, like a mute servant, while he sat in his armchair, drinking, eating, smoking and watching me.

When he was away with work, I should have been pleased. I had the house to myself, I could do whatever I wanted. Go wherever I wanted. But I still didn't do anything.

The Widow's Husband

In the months leading up to Frank's death, he was away more. I didn't care where he was or what he was doing. If he was with was another woman, or women, then more fool them. I doubted that he had the energy for it anyway, or the power to charm ladies like he used to. He was not the handsome, charismatic man he once was.

A few weeks before he died, he had a health check-up. The doctor told him his cholesterol and blood pressure were off the chart.

'You have to take statins,' the GP ordered, turning to me and handing me the prescription. 'Make sure your husband takes his medication. He needs your support.'

My support. Did I not do enough to stop my awful husband from dying? Is this why he's haunting me now? Because he was a narcissist who refuses to shoulder any of the blame?

Or has he just spent so much of his life belittling and threatening me that he no longer knows how to exist, even when dead, without me?

* * *

Beth and I walk, side by side, along the edge of the muddy field. My wellies squelch beneath me and the grey sky mirrors my mood. Benji has disappeared into the hedge, sniffing out rabbits and all I can see of him is his wagging tail.

'I'm so sorry this is happening to you,' Beth says.

'I did what you suggested. I asked Frank to leave. But he didn't.'

Beth is quiet and we walk in silence for a few minutes. I'm lucky that I'm walking at all. My fall down the stairs knocked me unconscious and I didn't wake up until the paramedics had arrived. I was whizzed off to hospital in an ambulance where I was diagnosed with concussion and a fractured rib. The doctor told me I was lucky that nothing else was broken. It could have been my arm, or my leg. It could have been my neck.

He almost killed me. Or I almost killed myself. I'm not sure what's worse.

I haven't been back to the cottage since. Gary and I have moved back in with his son, Chris, and Sophie, and it's pretty awful. Sophie clearly doesn't want us there and Chris is stuck in the middle. Poor Benji is often shut in the kitchen because Sophie doesn't want him around the baby. I offered them the cottage, telling them they were welcome to it while secretly hoping that a house swap might solve all our problems, but Sophie said she's not moving her baby into a haunted house. I can't say I blame her.

We're tiptoeing around each other and I'm doing my best to stay out of Sophie's way. But it's a small house and there's only so much hiding in Gary's bedroom I can do. At night, it's no longer my fear of ghosts that's keeping me awake, it's the sounds of a very much alive baby wailing at all hours. I've offered to help out with Emilia, but Sophie says I don't have any experience with children, her words rubbing salt into my already-raw wounds.

Christmas is only a few weeks away but I'm struggling to feel festive. It's difficult to get into the holiday spirit when the people we're sharing a house with don't want us there and I'm too afraid to go back to the cottage. If changing the locks and trying to stand up to Frank didn't keep me safe, then I don't know what will. It's my first Christmas without Frank and I'd had dreams of it being a good one. Taking Benji for a long walk with Gary in the morning, followed by a drink at the pub. Returning to the cottage to make lunch together, then perhaps a festive film with some chocolates. It was meant to be perfect and now it's tainted, just like everything else. Despite my efforts, Frank has managed to ruin it again.

It can't go on much longer, but we can't afford to stay at the hotel. And I can't bring myself to go back to the cottage yet, so we're at a stalemate. We've considered all the options. Gary doesn't want to sell the house from under Chris and Sophie's feet, so until they move on, he can't buy anywhere new. And we can't rent a place unless I can do the same with the cottage. But word has got out about what's been going on there. It's a small community where people talk and the cottage has now gained a reputation for being haunted.

Gary is being so considerate, but I know he's getting frustrated. He wants to go back to the cottage. He's furious that we've been driven out. At first, he was happy to stay with Chris and Sophie until I had recovered from my fall. But now I'm almost back to full strength and we're still there. I wonder who will lose their temper first, Sophie or Gary. And I hate that I've put Gary back in this position. It's all my fault and I don't know what to do about it.

I'm angry too. With the situation. With myself for not fighting back harder. I tried, I really did. I stood my ground, but Frank kept going, taunting me, tormenting me. And he has always been my weakness, even now as I'm finding my inner strength. He is the thorn in my side that refuses to budge, his control still embedded deeply inside me. I've been hoping that some time away will help me heal, physically and psychologically. But I'm just not there yet.

'Okay,' Beth finally says. 'This might sound a bit wacky but have you considered going back to the cottage without Gary?'

I couldn't think of anything worse. 'How would that help?'

'Well, if Frank is upset that you've moved on with another man, maybe he'll leave you alone if you're single.'

I hate this idea for many reasons. Firstly, even if Frank leaves me alone, which I doubt he will, I don't want to live in a house knowing he's there. To spend every second of my life thinking that he's watching me. I'll go mad. And secondly, why should I end things with Gary? Frank has no claim to me any more and I've wasted enough of my life obeying him. I don't want to continue even after he's gone. I will not let him win. He's already taken my home from me, but he will not take my chance of a fresh start with a good man. Anyway, if it wasn't for Gary, I would have been lying unconscious at the bottom of the stairs for who knows how long. Hours? Days? He probably saved my life.

'It's not an option,' I say simply.

'Okay,' Beth replies. 'Maybe you should try talking to him again.'

'Gary?'

'Frank.'

'And what do I say? I've asked him to leave me alone and he ignored me. I doubt a polite conversation's going to do any good, is it?'

'I'm just trying to help.' Beth sounds offended.

I place my hand on her arm. 'I know and I'm really grateful. I think you're the only person who actually believes me about all this.'

'I do believe you, and I know how frightening it must be. I just wish I could do something.'

'Thank you. But you know what? Frank's taken up enough space in my head already. Let's change the subject. What are your plans for Christmas?'

'I don't know yet. My parents are going on a cruise, lucky them. I've had an invite from a friend but I don't want to gatecrash her family festivities. What about you?'

'Same,' I admit. 'I don't think Chris and Sophie want us there.'

'Why don't we book lunch at the pub? You, me and Gary?'

My face lights up. 'I love that idea! Let's ask Mark if there's any space for us.'

I'm feeling so much better already. Perhaps Christmas can be saved after all and I can't believe I didn't think of it before. I imagine the pub all decked out for Christmas. Sitting with Gary and Beth by the fire while carols play in the background. It's perfect.

I'm interrupted from my reverie by the sound of Beth's phone ringing. 'It's Alyssa,' she says, answering. 'Yes, I'm with her now. Are you alright? Okay, we'll see you shortly.'

Beth puts the phone down. 'Alyssa wants to see us now. She says it's urgent.'

'She wants to see us both?'

'Well, she wanted to see me but when I told her I was with you, she said we should both come. We're meeting in the cafe in ten minutes.'

Scenarios flash before my eyes. If it's urgent then something must be wrong. Perhaps Alyssa plans to leave her husband and needs our help. I'll do whatever it takes to get her out of a toxic situation. I knew there was something off about Dylan, I just knew it. Could I offer her the cottage? Alyssa doesn't believe in ghosts so she's probably the only person who wouldn't be frightened off. But it might be too close to Dylan, if she's in danger. My mind is whirring at a million miles per hour and all I want to do is make sure Alyssa is okay.

'Come on then,' I say, picking up the pace and wincing as my rib protests. I call to Benji and he races after us as we stride towards the cafe.

Alyssa and the boys are already there when we arrive. The

boys are eating cake and playing with cars and I look down at Alyssa's feet to see if there are any suitcases or hastily packed bags, but all I see is the small rucksack she always carries around with her.

'What's happened, is everything okay?' I ask as I sit down next to her.

'No, everything is not okay.' Alyssa looks furious and my brow furrows with concern. Perhaps I'm wrong and it's something else, like she's caught Dylan cheating.

'What's Dylan done?' I ask in hushed tones in case the boys are listening.

Alyssa pulls a face. 'What? Dylan hasn't done anything.'

'Then what is it?'

Alyssa takes a deep breath. 'I was hoping to talk to Beth about it first. I wanted to get her take on it before I came to you. But when I heard that the two of you were together, I couldn't wait any longer.'

My heart plummets as I realise that this isn't about Alyssa and Dylan at all. It's about me. Am I about to be subjected to more of Alyssa's vitriol about Gary?

'Go on,' Beth urges.

'I was chatting to a mum at preschool pick-up. I asked her if she fancied a coffee but she said she had to go home because she's having a nightmare with her older son, who's twelve.'

I listen defensively, with absolutely no idea where she's going with this.

'He's been having nightmares for weeks, crying in the night, but refusing to tell his mum what they're about. Anyway, she finally prised it out of him last night. He said he was scared the police were going to come and put him in prison. When she asked him why, he said he smashed a window of a cottage and ran away without telling anyone.'

My eyes are as wide as saucers. Is she talking about my window? Was Gary right and it was down to a kid mucking about outside? And if a child smashed the window, then does that mean that I'm wrong about everything else too? Oh, how much I want it to be true.

'But here's the thing.' Alyssa looks directly at me and my heart sinks further. 'The boy said that someone paid him to do it. Someone named Gary.'

Beth's gasp is audible. I stare at Alyssa in disbelief. Surely this must be a mistake? Why would Gary pay a child to smash my window? Unless he wanted to scare me. To make me turn to him for support. To make me rely on him.

No, this can't be happening again. Please tell me I haven't been manipulated by another man? Surely Gary wouldn't be so cruel, or so calculating?

My mind is hurtling towards a horrible conclusion and I can't make it stop. I think about the past few months and everything that's happened. Gary whisking me off to the hotel after the smashed window. It was the night we finally got together. I think about how he accompanies me everywhere. Hangs out in the pub when I'm on shift. Oh my God. Alyssa's right. It's like me and Frank in the early years all over again.

I feel sick. Betrayed. Angry. And I don't want it to be true. I make one last attempt to disprove Alyssa's theory. 'Do we know for sure it was my cottage?'

She nods. 'Yes, the boy gave his mum the address. She said she was planning to visit you so that she could apologise and offer to pay for the damage, but I told her you're not living there at the moment.'

I'm not living there because I'm staying with Gary. *Gary.*

I try to hold back my tears but I can't and they spill down my cheeks. 'How could he do this to me?' I cry.

'He's a bastard,' Alyssa snaps, before looking at her sons to make sure they're engrossed in their game. 'I knew it from the start.'

How could I have been so wrong about Gary? Why am I such a terrible judge of character? I bet he's responsible for everything else that has happened at the cottage too. While I've been losing my mind, thinking that I've summoned a poltergeist, Gary's probably been laughing at me behind my back. Thinking about how gullible I am. How stupid.

You stupid cow. That's what Frank used to call me. And I bet Gary's thinking the same thing. It makes me want to retch.

'What are you going to do?' Beth asks me gently.

I have two choices now. Do I slink back into the shadows, hide myself away from the world and drown in self-pity and loathing like I've done all my life? Or do I do what I should have done years ago and take control. Face my fears and stand up for myself.

I get up. 'I'm going to go round to Gary's right now, pack my bags and tell him I know what he's done. And then I'm going home.'

Beth gets up too. 'I'll come with you.'

I want her to come. I know it will give me the strength to do what I'm absolutely dreading. But I also know that I need to do this on my own.

'Thank you, but I'll be okay.'

I pick up my bag, and Benji gets up and follows me.

'Good luck,' Alyssa shouts, as Beth calls out, 'I'll ring you later.'

I step out into the cold, frosty air. My blood is boiling, my hands shaking with indignation. How dare he? How *dare* he? I refuse to blame myself this time. No, this is all Gary's fault. I march straight round to his house, not even bothering to say hello to the locals I pass on the way. Benji jogs to keep up with me but I don't slow the pace.

I should have listened to Alyssa weeks ago. I should have trusted my friend, but instead I went with my instinct and previous experience tells me that it's not to be relied on. It's what sent me to London to be with Frank. And it's let me down a second time.

When I reach the house, I'm still raging. I stride into the living room and see Sophie on the floor, playing with the baby. She looks up at me and takes in my expression.

'Maggie, are you okay?'

'Where's Gary?' I demand.

'God knows, probably at the pub.'

My entire body trembles with adrenaline and with Gary absent, I don't know what to do with it. I was prepared for a row, finally ready to tackle a confrontation.

'What's happened?' Sophie asks curiously.

'I'm leaving him.'

I turn and walk back out of the room to go upstairs and pack my things. But just before I'm out of earshot, I hear Sophie mutter under her breath. 'About bloody time.'

Fifteen minutes later, I'm packed up and heading down the stairs when Gary arrives. His face lights up when he sees me and then he clocks the bags.

'Maggie, love, are we moving back to the cottage?'

'I am. You're not.'

Gary's face falls. 'What?'

I take the last few steps slowly, not wanting a repeat of what happened at the cottage. When I'm on firm ground again, I drop my bags, put my hands on my hips and prepare to face Gary. I sense Sophie's presence in the living room and guess that she's eavesdropping, but I don't care. Everyone should know what a lying creep Gary is.

'I know what you did.'

Gary stares at me in surprise. 'What did I do?'

'I know about the smashed window.'

I've got to hand it to him, he's a good actor because he looks completely confused. 'Maggie, love, I have no idea what you're talking about.'

'Don't call me "love",' I snap. 'After everything I went through with Frank, how could you treat me like this? How could you take advantage of me?'

Gary reaches out to me, but I take a step back. 'I'd never take advantage of you. I don't understand what's going on.'

'You paid a child to smash my windows. What else did you pay him to do?'

'Now hang on, I never—'

'I don't want to hear it, Gary. I thought you were different. I thought I'd finally found someone who respected me as an equal. But what you did was even worse than Frank.'

Gary's guilt makes him defensive. 'Don't you dare compare me to that man.'

'Oh, I will. I'll do whatever I like because you can't control me. You don't own me.'

'Of course I don't own you, what the hell are you—'

I hold my hand up. 'We're over. If you contact me again, I'll call the police and tell them what you did.'

I push past him and he makes no move to stop me. He knows he's been caught and there's nothing he can do about it. Hopefully my threat will be enough to ensure he leaves me alone. I never want to see him again, even though I know that in a small village that's unrealistic. But I don't have to speak to him and I don't have to serve him at the pub. He's dead to me. From now on, Gary does not exist in my world.

It's not a dignified exit as I'm laden with bags, while also trying to hold on to Benji's lead. Tears are streaming down my face. As I walk back to the cottage, I keep my head down, wishing I was invisible. I don't want anyone to see me like this and I desperately want to avoid people in the village gossiping about me. But I suspect that they will anyway. In fact, I wouldn't be surprised if word is out by the end of the day, thanks to Sophie.

And suddenly all my fight evaporates as quickly as it arrived. The adrenaline that has fuelled me for the past hour vanishes, leaving me drained and miserable as the reality of my situation settles in. Yet again, I allowed myself to fall for someone without realising he was manipulating me. I dared to dream of a better life, a happier one, but it was all a lie.

I will never be happy because I'm a stupid, stupid woman.

My fleeting fantasy of a happy Christmas disappears before my eyes. Maybe Beth will still want to meet at the pub but I'm not sure I'm up for it any more. I can't think of anything worse than being cheery and festive. No, I'll be spending it alone this year, and probably for every year to come. I'm sinking deeper into melancholy but I can't stop myself.

I've been afraid of the cottage for weeks but now I yearn for it. The silence and the solitude. I want to lock the door and hide away from everyone, from the whispers and the stares, the mirth and the pity. I want to eat and sleep for days on end. Now I know that the house isn't haunted I have nothing to fear from it. It's the rest of the world that I'm afraid of. It's a terrible place, a cruel one. Perhaps it's karma, for dreaming of a better life, for believing that I deserve to be happy again. It doesn't matter any more because I give up.

Frank may be dead, but I'm the one with nothing left to live for.

19

I stare out of the window, watching the world go by. The dog walker with the toned arms walks past, wrapped up in a trendy black aviator coat. It suits her. Children scurry along the pavement, as skittish as the fallen leaves blowing across the ground. I eat a packet of biscuits, and then rip open another, as I vacantly observe everyone else living their lives.

I haven't left the house in ten days. Poor Benji's only exercise has been in the back garden, the lawn and plants neglected again since I found out about Gary. Gary. I don't want to think about him. I wish I'd listened to Alyssa sooner. I wish I'd never met him.

I've quit my job at the pub and although Mark sounded upset when I called to tell him, he didn't give me a hard time for leaving him in the lurch. I suspect he knows what's been going on, although I do wonder what Gary has been telling everyone. He's probably painting me out to be a total madwoman and he's lived in the village long enough to have good friends who will believe whatever he says. Who will trust him over me.

I didn't bother decorating the house for Christmas and I

don't put the radio on any more because all the seasonal songs just make me feel more depressed. As far as I'm concerned, Christmas is cancelled. Apart from the piles of chocolates and other sweet treats I added to my online grocery shop, which are rapidly depleting already.

Benji is staring at me forlornly. I'll have to give him up soon because it's not fair to impose this life on him. I want to do better, to be better, for my dog if not for myself but I have no energy or motivation left in me. I am nothing. No one.

I am the ghost of this house now. It's almost comical that I thought it was ever haunted. But that's me. Stupid. Gullible. Someone to be laughed at. For a while I honestly thought I'd been given another chance, that I'd even been brave and bold enough to create these chances myself, and I was so proud of how far I'd come. I should have known better.

Alyssa and Beth have called, but I haven't answered the phone. Alyssa came round yesterday and I ignored the doorbell. I haven't heard from Gary and although that's supposed to be what I want, I feel strangely disappointed. He's not even trying to fight for me and it's the final proof I need of who he really is. And, in turn, of who I really am.

Benji jumps up onto the sofa and I stroke him absent-mindedly. I know I should take him out but I just don't want to see anyone. As I look at him, I consider my options. Should I call the shelter and ask if they'll have him back? No, I can't, it would break my heart.

Maybe Alyssa would have him? Or Beth? The thought of losing my beloved dog crushes me but it's the right thing to do. I can't drag him down with me, he deserves so much more than that. And so I force myself to lift up my phone and type a message on our group WhatsApp chat. I'm doing this for Benji, I tell myself with an aching heart.

> Do either of you want to have Benji? I can't look after him any more.

I put my phone down again and close my eyes. Just the effort of sending a message has exhausted me, but at least I've done it now. I'm too sad to cry.

Alyssa replies within minutes.

> I'm coming over now.

I can't believe how quick that was. Alyssa must really want Benji. I ignore the anguish which threatens to overcome me. Numbness is better. Easier. I wonder if she'll take him straight away. Better to rip the plaster off rather than prolong the agony. I heave myself off the sofa and start gathering Benji's things. He follows me around, his eyes sad and questioning. I ignore him because there's no point in pretending everything will be okay. There's a little voice inside me that's desperate to be heard. That is screaming and shouting at me not to do this, but I force myself to block out the noise. When I'm done packing his things, I sit by the window and wait for Alyssa to arrive, nibbling on another biscuit.

A few minutes later, I see Alyssa marching up the footpath. She's alone and I immediately wonder where the boys are. Then I remember that it's Saturday, so they'll be with their dad. I've lost track of days, they've all merged into one. Just like it used to be before, when Frank was still alive. When my life was an endless cycle of sleep, eat, exist.

I open the door and hand Benji's lead over wordlessly. I don't want to talk to Alyssa or invite her in, I just want to get this over and done with. But she ignores the lead and barges past me into the house before I can stop her. I turn and stare at her, wide-eyed.

'I'm not taking Benji,' she says.

'Then why are you here?'

'To talk some sense into you.'

I walk into the living room and sink down onto the sofa. I don't have the energy for this. Why won't she just take the dog and leave? Why is everything so hard?

'You're being pathetic,' Alyssa says matter-of-factly. She's blunt, I'll give her that.

I don't even bother to answer.

'I'm sorry about what happened with Gary, I really am. It must have been awful for you, especially after what you went through with Frank. But you need to stop wallowing in self-pity. And are you seriously about to give up your dog?'

'It's for his own good.'

'No, Maggie, it's not. What would be best for Benji is if you got up, dusted yourself off, took him for a nice long walk and went back to work. Mark says you've quit.'

'That's right.'

'Why?'

'Because I don't want to be around people.'

Alyssa's expression softens. 'No one's talking about you, you know.'

'Really?'

'Okay, they're talking about you a bit. But it's because they're worried about you. They care, Maggie. Everyone just wants to know you're okay.'

'What about Gary?'

'I haven't seen him at all, he's disappeared.'

Disappeared? Where has he gone? Is he coming back? My

mind is swimming with questions, but I don't ask Alyssa any of them. Instead, I look at her strong, beautiful, determined face and wonder if I was ever like her once.

'I don't think so,' I say morosely.

Alyssa rolls her eyes, as though I'm one of her children in a strop. 'I'm not taking no for an answer. Get your shoes on, we're going for a walk.'

At the mention of the word walk, Benji's tail starts wagging and he makes a dash for the door. The sight of him waiting expectantly ignites something inside me. It's a small flame, a flicker, but it's enough to make me stand up and look for my shoes. Perhaps a short stroll would do us both good and I'll feel more confident with Alyssa by my side. I can broach the subject of her taking Benji while we walk, persuade her it's the right thing to do.

Alyssa smiles with satisfaction. I get my coat, clip Benji's lead on and make my first, tentative steps back out into the world. It's freezing and I shiver but the fresh air is like a blast of energy. Within a couple of minutes, I'm already a little more alert. I gaze at the houses we pass, the Christmas wreaths, light-up reindeers and blow-up Santas.

'So what exactly are people saying about me?' I ask Alyssa.

'They've heard about the whole Gary debacle, and they feel awful for you.'

'But hasn't Gary tried to deny it?'

'No, no one's seen him. It's like he's vanished. The spineless bastard probably didn't want to face the music. Sophie said he left the morning after you broke up with him.'

'What does Sophie make of it all?'

'She's fuming. And she said he's never welcome in her house again.'

'Well, to be fair, it's actually Gary's house.'

Alyssa snorts. 'Not if Sophie has anything to do with it. I think everyone's just hoping that he's crawled under a rock and never comes back out.'

'What has Beth said?'

'She's worried about you too.'

We pass an elderly couple coming in the opposite direction and I keep my eyes averted. Alyssa says good morning but doesn't chastise me for my rudeness. Fortunately we don't see anyone else. But the more we walk, the better I begin to feel. The cold, biting weather has woken me up from my self-imposed coma. I can see the world in all its colour again and the fog is clearing in my mind. Alyssa's right, I can't let myself spiral because I'm not sure I'll be able to claw my way back out again. I've been wallowing in self-pity and it *is* pathetic. I can do better than this and I'm not going to let all my hard work go to waste.

Perhaps this was a temporary blip after all, I think with a surge of hope. Maybe all is not lost. After all, the house isn't haunted. I still have my friends. Gary isn't around so I don't have to worry about bumping into him. And it sounds like most of the village is on my side, for now at least. I can re-engage again, if I want to. Do I want to?

Yes. I do. More than anything.

'Thank you,' I say to Alyssa quietly.

'What for?'

'For getting me out. For making me realise how silly I was being.'

She links her arm through mine. 'That's what friends are for.'

'And I'm sorry too for not believing you when you warned me about Gary.'

'Well, they do say love is blind.'

Love was certainly blind when I met Frank. And again with Gary. I am never trusting another man, for as long as I live. But that doesn't mean I need to be alone forever. I look down at Benji, who is wagging his tail with delight. Thank goodness I didn't give him up. I'm overwhelmed with relief that I've finally seen sense.

But as we reach the pub, a stab of anxiety winds me. I feel terrible for quitting on Mark with no notice, especially at what is one of the busiest times of year in the hospitality industry. He must be furious with me and I'm not sure that I'll ever be able to set foot inside there again. I'm too embarrassed and ashamed.

'I want to go home now,' I say, desperate to get away before anyone sees me.

'Not yet,' Alyssa urges, taking my hand. 'Come on. Let's have a drink.'

As she gently guides me towards the pub, I resist. 'I don't want to go in.'

'The sooner you do it, the better you'll feel.'

I know she's right but I'm still terrified. Then Benji starts pulling me too, eager to go inside and greet his human friends. This is it, I think. The turning point. Whatever decision I make right now will have an impact on the rest of my life, and I finally listen to that small, determined voice inside me.

'Okay, let's do it,' I say, taking a deep breath.

As we reach the entrance, a regular on his way out holds the door open and smiles.

'Hi, Maggie, love, it's good to see you again.'

I muster a smile and Alyssa looks at me smugly. 'See, that wasn't so bad, was it?'

'No,' I agree.

Mercifully, Mark is not behind the bar, it's another staff

member who I barely know as we were never on shift together. I cast my eyes around the pub and can't see him anywhere but then my gaze rests on Beth, sitting in a corner and looking at us expectantly.

'Is this an intervention?' I ask Alyssa.

'Kind of,' she admits.

Beth stands up and gives me a hug. 'I'm so pleased to see you.'

I hug her back, squeezing her tightly. I've missed my friends dearly. I shouldn't have shut them out like I did but they've come through for me now and I'm eternally grateful.

Beth pulls away and gives me a long, hard look. 'What's this about you giving up Benji?'

I gaze at Benji as I unclip his lead and he wanders off to greet some regulars.

'Ignore me, I was being pathetic,' I say, smiling at Alyssa.

'And are you done with that?' Beth asks.

'Yes.' I look at my friends. 'I'm done with that now.'

She gives me a high five and whoops, and it makes me laugh. The sound is unfamiliar after so many days of silence. The camaraderie of being around people emboldens me and I realise how much Alyssa and Beth are rooting for me. I'm not alone, and I never was. I've still got people in my life who care about me and who are looking out for me. Screw Gary, I think angrily. And screw Frank too. I'll show them what I'm made of.

Alyssa orders our drinks and then she and Beth fill me in on their news. They avoid talking about Gary and I'm pleased because I'm enjoying the distraction of other people's lives. I keep glancing around the room to see if anyone is looking at me. A couple of regulars give me a nod and return to their drinks, but no one gawps. No one is judging me.

I still can't relax completely, though. I'm on tenterhooks

about seeing Mark again. He could appear at any moment and I'm ashamed of how I behaved.

Sensing my unease, Beth gives me an encouraging look. 'You're doing great, Maggie.'

'What if Mark hates me?'

'Mark doesn't hate you.'

As if on cue, Mark appears from the door behind the bar. He catches my eye and I gulp.

'Go on,' Beth urges. 'Go and talk to him.'

Rip the plaster off. 'Right,' I say, standing up before I can change my mind. I walk over to him and sit on a bar stool. 'Hi, Mark.'

'Hi, Maggie. How's it going?'

'Better, thank you. Mark, I'm so sorry.'

He nods. 'I know you are.'

'I take it you've heard what happened.'

Mark looks over my head to where Beth and Alyssa are sitting. 'I've heard some of it through the grapevine. But I can't get my head around it.'

'Have you spoken to Gary?'

'No, he's taken off. But listen, Maggie, I've known Gary for a long time and I'm finding it hard to believe it's true. Why would he do something like that?'

'I have no idea.'

Mark shakes his head. 'There's more to it. You need to speak to Gary.'

I frown. 'I never want to speak to that man again.'

Mark looks sad. 'Fair enough, I understand. So, are you here to ask for your job back?'

I stare at him in surprise. I assumed that I'd burned that bridge by quitting so unexpectedly. Do I want my job back? Yes, I do. I've missed being behind the bar, and chatting to the locals, and watching Benji curled up by the fire. I've missed the routine and the busyness that comes with having a job. And I damn well need the money.

'Yes,' I say, and this time my voice is steady.

'I need someone reliable, Maggie.'

'I know. I'll never let you down again, I promise.'

He nods. 'I believe you. And if I'm being honest, I haven't found anyone to replace you yet and I could really do with an extra pair of hands. Can you work this evening?'

Joy washes over me. 'Yes. Thank you so much, Mark.'

He gives me a wink. 'See you at five, then. I'll add you back on to the rota. By the way, Beth mentioned earlier that you might want a table on Christmas Day?'

I look at Beth, who is stroking Benji and then back at Mark. Perhaps I won't be alone after all. 'Unless you want me to work?'

'No, you're alright. Take the day off and enjoy yourself. I've reserved you a table. But if you could work on New Year's Eve, I'd be grateful.'

'Of course, that's no problem.'

With a grin plastered across my face, I walk over to Alyssa and Beth.

'I've got my job back,' I declare.

They both beam at me. 'That's wonderful,' Beth says. 'We should have a drink to celebrate.'

'Just a coffee for me,' I say proudly. 'I'm on shift tonight. Mark says he's reserved us a table on Christmas Day too.'

Beth smiles knowingly. 'I had a feeling we'd need it.'

I look at Alyssa. 'You should join us.'

'Thanks, but we've got Dylan's mum and my parents coming to stay and I think they'd prefer to eat at home. We might pop in for a drink though.'

We discuss our Christmas plans for a while and then Beth

leaves as she's meeting a friend. As Alyssa and I walk out together I put my hand on her arm.

'Thank you so much. I'm not sure I could have done it without you.'

'Yes, you could. You just needed a kick up the bum.'

I laugh. 'I want to repay you. Maybe I could babysit for you again?'

'You don't need to repay me.'

'I know, but I want to.'

'Well then, babysitting is always welcome.'

As I walk back to the cottage, I keep my head held high, nodding and saying hello to all the villagers I recognise. I vow then and there never to shut myself away again. I was given a second chance after Frank died and it would be ludicrous to pass that up. What happened with Gary was horrible and heartbreaking, and it will take time to get over it. But I just need to take it slowly, day by day, starting with walking Benji again and going back to work. After that we'll see. Gary shattered my already fragile confidence but he didn't destroy it beyond repair and I'm daring to hope again.

By the time I reach my front door, I'm exhausted from all the excitement of the morning but my mind is occupied, drowning out my vicious cycle of negative thoughts. I need to feed Benji, do some washing, iron a top before work. I let myself in and decide to start with a cup of tea. Immediately I wonder if Gary is home and if he fancies a cuppa, and a wave of sadness comes over me as I remember that I'm alone. I miss him, despite everything. But then I square my shoulders and head into the kitchen, filling the kettle with water and turning it on. I reach for one mug and slam it purposefully on the counter, trying to ignore the tears that have come from nowhere and are threatening to spill out of me.

One walk isn't going to heal me, I know that. I must be patient with myself. And for a brief moment I allow myself to think of what could have been. Walking hand in hand with Gary, chatting about everything and anything. Laughing together over a film. Cuddling up to him in bed. A future of companionship and contentment. I sink down onto a kitchen chair and listen to the kettle clicking off but make no move to finish preparing my tea.

I had thought Gary was different, I'd felt it in my bones. And yet he ended up being exactly the same as Frank. Manipulative. Cruel. A wolf dressed in sheep's clothing. What is it about me? Why do I attract these kinds of men? Why do I let people walk all over me?

Alyssa wants me to call the police and report Gary, but I know that I won't. What would I say to them? Is pretending to be a ghost even a crime? And anyway, Gary has gone AWOL. I hope he doesn't come back, at least not for a while. I need him out of the picture as I make my tentative steps back into the land of the living again. It reminds me, though, that Gary still has my keys and some of his belongings are here too. I'll need to get his things packed up and the locks changed again, but at least this time I know it will make a difference. It will protect me from the person who has been messing with me.

Benji wanders in and looks pointedly at his bowl. His hopeful expression is enough to make me get up again. I feed him and then finish making my tea, taking it into the living room. As I put my drink down on the coffee table, I see one of Gary's books about garden maintenance is still on there. Without thinking, I pick it up and hurl it across the room. It feels good. Anger is so much better than sadness because at least it makes me feel alive. I decide there and then to box up the rest of his things and keep them out of sight.

A few hours later, I walk to the pub for my shift. Despite my earlier determination, I'm nervous again. An afternoon of solitude has given my mind too much time to wander. What if Gary's come back and he's there when I arrive? What if people treat me differently?

But I quickly realise that I have nothing to fear. There's no sign of Gary and the regulars act as though I've never been away. Being busy is a glorious distraction and I barely have time to think about Gary, or Frank, or anything for the next six hours. I make a mental note to ask Mark for more shifts. The more the better as far as I'm concerned.

At the end of the evening, Mark says he's thrilled that I'm back and I glow with pride. I call to Benji and we make our way home in the darkness. I left some lights on in the cottage so that it would be welcoming when we got back late, and the heating should still be on too. For the first time in ages, I'm actually looking forward to getting home.

But when I reach the path, the house is shrouded in darkness and my blood runs cold. I'm certain that I left the lights on. Has Gary been here? Would he really have the gall to return? And if he has, am I safe? What if he's in there, waiting for me?

I make a mental note to call the locksmith first thing tomorrow, but it doesn't solve my immediate problem. I reach for my phone with trembling fingers and call Beth. Alyssa is closer but she's got two young children and I don't want to disturb her this late at night.

Beth answers quickly so at least I don't have to worry that I've woken her up.

'Are you okay, Maggie?'

'I'm so sorry to ask, but can you come over?'

'What's happened?'

'I think someone's in the house.'

I hear her shuffling around. 'I'm leaving now. Call the police.'

By the time Beth arrives in her car, I've moved to the end of the street, out of sight of the cottage and I'm shivering. She sees me and pulls up.

'Are the police here yet?'

'I haven't called them.'

'Why not?'

'Because I might be wrong. I might just have turned the lights off when I left without thinking. I don't want to waste their time if I'm just going senile.'

'Okay.' Beth cuts the engine and gets out. 'Talk me through what happened.'

I explain it to her and she agrees that we should go into the house first and see what's what. She takes the key from me and strides ahead, opening the door and stepping inside.

'It's freezing in here,' she says, wrapping her arms around her.

I know for sure then that something is wrong because I definitely left the heating on. I want to turn around and run. To get as far away from the cottage as I possibly can. But Beth is inside and I can't leave her alone. I follow her tentatively and Beth's right, it's icy cold. I shiver and not just because of the plunging temperature.

'He's here,' I whisper.

'Who? Gary? Hold on.' Beth turns on the lights and bravely searches the entire house, throwing doors open and making plenty of noise. It's then that I realise Benji hasn't come inside. I turn and see him, standing on the doorstep.

'Come on, boy,' I say, but he sits down on the step and refuses to move.

Something is not right here. All my old fears are rushing

back to me, as though they'd never gone away. But now I don't know who or what I'm afraid of, Frank or Gary.

Beth returns. 'There's no one here. Everything is as it should be. Are you sure that you didn't just turn off the lights and the heating?'

'I'm sure,' I say with certainty because this sensation I have is familiar. It's not senility that's making my entire body pulsate with fear, it's something else.

'Do you think Gary might have come back?'

'I don't know. He has a key but why continue to mess with me when I know the truth?'

'I agree. I don't see why he'd do that.'

'But if it wasn't Gary, then who was it?'

Beth looks at me and I know we're both thinking the same thing.

'I'll stay here tonight,' she says. 'Just in case.'

I don't try to argue with her. I'm beyond worrying about putting people out.

'Where's Benji?' she asks.

'He won't come in.'

Beth goes to the door and Benji snarls, making her step backwards again.

'What's going on? I've never seen him act like that.'

'He's been doing it quite often,' I admit.

'Do you know much about his past? Any behavioural difficulties?'

'Not that I know of.'

Beth is looking at Benji with caution. 'The thing with rescue dogs is that you never really know. Maybe he's had a traumatic past and there's something that sets him off.'

'Like what?'

'I don't know, it could be anything. A smell, a sound we can't hear.'

'A ghost?'

Beth doesn't laugh. 'Maybe,' she says. 'Animals are very intuitive.'

It must be Gary. All the evidence points to it being him. And yet Benji adores Gary. I've never once seen my dog snarl at him. None of this makes sense and I'm confused and scared. Beth's presence reassures me but it's not enough to calm my nerves. Why has this started again? And just as I was beginning to feel better, too. It's not fair.

We finally coax Benji in with a treat but he's on edge, refusing to settle. Beth makes us both a cup of tea and I show her to the spare room, grateful that I've changed the sheets since Gary moved out of there. I can't stop thinking about Gary. Why he's doing this again? If it is even him. What is this all about? And what the hell am I going to do about it?

'Thank you so much for coming,' I say to Beth. 'I really appreciate it.'

'Of course.' She gives me a hug. 'Try to get some sleep.'

I get ready for bed and crawl under the duvet. I can hear Beth moving about in the spare room and Benji pacing around downstairs. I close my eyes and try to think peaceful thoughts but I'm too anxious to drift off. I've turned the heating back on and so the cottage is warming up, but it doesn't stave off the chill that's taken hold of my body and I can't get warm, no matter how deeply I bury myself under the duvet.

The lights flicker on and my eyes snap open. Within seconds they've gone back off but soon they're back on again. And then off. Someone is messing with the lights. Benji starts barking and I hear movement coming from the room beneath mine.

'Beth!' I scream, too afraid to get out of bed.

She appears a minute later, breathless. 'The lights!' she gasps.

'I know!'

'Stay here.'

She runs downstairs and I hold my breath, waiting for something to happen without knowing what it is I'm waiting for. Then I hear a crash, followed by a blood-curdling scream.

20

Every instinct tells me to stay where I am. I fight it. If Beth is hurt, I have to help her. I'm the reason why she's here, the one who brought her into this godforsaken house.

I rush downstairs, gripping on to the banister so I don't fall again, and find Beth in the kitchen. Her body is rigid, but at least she doesn't look hurt.

'Beth, are you okay?'

On closer inspection she looks awful. Her face is pale, her eyes glassy. She looks... well, she looks like she's just seen a ghost. *Oh no. Please no.*

'Beth!' I repeat, my voice pleading. I need her to snap out of this, she's scaring me.

'The vase,' she gasps. 'It just fell off the table onto the floor. I didn't touch it.'

I look down and see a vase in pieces on the floor. I can't believe this is happening. I thought it was all over. I grip on to Beth's hand, which is as cold as mine. 'Are you hurt?'

'No. I'm just in shock.' She turns to me, her eyes wide.

'Could it have been Benji?'

'Maybe, I don't know. I was distracted by the lights.'

But I know deep down that it wasn't my dog. 'It was Frank,' I say quietly.

I want to run out into the road in my flimsy nightdress. I don't care if it's cold or if the neighbours think I've lost my mind or if I have nowhere to go. But then Benji comes and sits at my feet, looking up at me expectantly. He's calm and relaxed, and I exhale with relief, sensing that we are safe again, for now at least.

But I'm still all over the place. Petrified, confused, distressed. If it was Frank all along then that means I'm wrong about Gary. I've blamed an innocent man. But what about the smashed window and the boy mentioning Gary's name? He must have had some part in all this, I just don't know what, or why. Is he in cahoots with Frank?

But how could a living man be working with a dead one? Unless they knew each other before Frank died. Unless Gary is finishing what Frank started.

'Why is this happening?' I say hopelessly.

'Come and sit down.' Beth seems to have composed herself as she takes the lead. She helps me into a chair and then goes to fill the kettle up.

'Now that I've calmed down, I think you're right. It must have been Benji. He was running around when the vase fell. He probably bashed into the kitchen table and wobbled it.'

I'm not sure which one of us she's trying to reassure.

'Perhaps,' I concede.

Beth looks at me and I know she doesn't believe her own words.

'Are you okay?' we both ask each other at the same time and then laugh weakly.

'I'm fine now,' Beth answers. 'For a moment I was peeing my pants.'

'I don't blame you.'

'Have the lights ever done that before?'

'No,' I admit. 'It's a first. But the TV has flickered on and off.'

Beth is quiet for a moment. Then she looks at me intently. 'If it is Frank, and I'm not saying it is, perhaps you're going about this the wrong way.'

I frown. 'How do you mean?'

'Instead of trying to ignore him, or banish him, perhaps you should embrace him.'

'*Embrace* him?' I'm aghast.

Beth brings two cups of tea over and sits down, before saying tentatively, 'I'd do anything to speak to David again. To feel his presence and know that he was near me. I was so gutted when the medium didn't have a message from him at the psychic supper.'

Beth looks away and wipes her eyes. My heart goes out to her. She should have received a message that night, not me. It would have given her the comfort she deserves. Unfortunately, it had the opposite effect on me.

'I'm sorry,' I say, putting a hand on her arm.

'It's not your fault.' Beth looks back at me and smiles through watery eyes. 'I just miss him so much.'

'I know you do.'

'And sometimes I still struggle to believe it really happened. I wake up and for a brief moment, I think about what the two of us will do that day. And then I remember.'

Now I'm in tears too as I squeeze Beth's arm gently. 'It will get easier,' I tell her.

'I know. It already is. But I still have bad days.' Beth picks up her phone and scrolls until she finds what she's looking for. She turns the phone around to face me and I see a lovely, tanned-looking man smiling back at the camera. He's exactly as I had pictured him.

'David,' she whispers.

'He was very handsome.'

Beth smiles, almost proudly. 'He was.'

We sit in silence for a while and then Beth puts her phone down, signalling the change in conversation. 'I don't want to be insensitive, Maggie. I guess I'm just trying to figure out why you're so closed off to the idea of communicating with Frank. Why you're so afraid.'

'Ten minutes ago, you were afraid too,' I say accusingly.

Beth nods. 'Yes, I was. I get it. It's really freaky. But if you think about it as being Frank, rather than a creepy ghost, doesn't that change things for you a bit?'

I snort. 'It makes it even worse.'

Beth frowns, confused, and it occurs to me that while I've divulged details about my marriage to Alyssa and Gary, I've only given the basics to Beth. It's not that I don't trust her, it's just that we always seem to talk about other things and I've enjoyed the innocence of our friendship. Maybe I don't want to taint it. But given what's just happened, I think she deserves to know the truth. Some of it, anyway.

'I've mentioned before that our marriage wasn't happy,' I say and Beth nods at me to continue. 'I think he wants to punish me.'

'What for?'

'For moving on. For being happy now.'

Beth looks at me quizzically. 'But why wouldn't he want you to be happy?'

I look away. 'I don't know.'

'I think it's more likely that he wants to tell you something.

You need to find a way to communicate with him, discover what it is, and then you can both be at peace. Why don't we go and see a medium again? They can find out what's keeping Frank here.'

I hate the idea immediately. After all, it was the psychic supper that started this in the first place. And I don't want to hear what Frank has to say to me.

'I'm not sure,' I say hesitantly.

But Beth is already scrolling on her phone. 'That medium at the psychic supper said she spoke to Frank, so let's start with her. Can you remember her name?'

'Zara something. Mark will probably know as he'll have booked her.'

'Okay, let me see what I can find, otherwise we can ask Mark.'

As Beth does some research, I sip my tea and glance around the kitchen. Benji has dozed off at my feet, which takes the edge off my anxiety, but the darkness of the hallway beyond the door still scares me. I shudder and turn my attention back to Beth.

'I've found her Facebook page,' Beth says triumphantly, holding up her phone to show me a photograph of a woman who is undoubtably the psychic who had that strange message for me all those months ago. 'She's based in Cambridge. Oh, and she's doing another psychic supper in Harpenden in three weeks! Well, that must be fate, right? Just round the corner from my place. I'll book us tickets.'

I open my mouth to say no. But then I close it again. This might be a terrible idea but it's the only one I've got. And I'm so desperate that it's a risk I'm going to have to take. I will do anything to make Frank go away once and for all, even if that means being shamed or humiliated in front of Beth and a room full of strangers. Let him say what he needs to say to me and maybe, with Zara's help, he will finally leave my life forever.

Deep down, I know that this is a shot in the dark. It's riddled with problems, not least that up until recently I didn't even believe in psychics. The vicar's warning about not using mediums to communicate with spirits echoes in my head. But desperate times call for desperate measures.

'Okay,' I say. 'And maybe Zara will have a message for you too this time.'

Beth looks up at me hopefully and it hits me again how stark the differences between us are. One of us dreading a message from their partner, the other dreaming of one.

As Beth books the tickets, I think about Gary again. I wonder where he is and how he got involved in this. It's a puzzle that I can't solve and no matter how hard I try to think of how the two men might be connected, I can't. Frank and Gary may have lived in the same village, but they were worlds apart. Unless they met by chance. Frank rarely socialised in the local area, but it's possible that their paths crossed at some point. Did Frank pay Gary to do this? But that would mean that he planned it and how did he know he was going to die? No, it doesn't make any sense. I rub my head in frustration. What is the link? What am I missing?

Beth puts her phone down. 'All booked. We'll get to the bottom of this, Maggie.'

'And until then?'

'I can stay with you for a couple of nights, if that would help?'

'Aren't you frightened to stay here?'

'Not really. If anything, now that I'm over the shock, I'm quite intrigued about it all. And let's face it, if it is a ghost, I don't think it's interested in me.'

She's right, Frank's not interested in her. It's me he's trying to intimidate.

'I'm not sure I want to stay here,' I admit.

'I'd invite you to come to mine but I live in a one-bedroom flat that's still crowded with bikes and David's other stuff – I have started bagging things up, but I can't quite bring myself to get rid of anything yet. So it'll be pretty tight. And no garden for Benji either. I think we're better here.'

I know she's right but I'm still disappointed. I'd take Beth's sofa over the cottage any day, but the mention of Benji makes me feel guilty. Beth's right, he needs some outside space. 'And you really don't mind?'

'Not at all.' Beth beams. 'It'll be an adventure.'

She's making light of it, trying to cheer me up and I appreciate it. But I'm too upset by the events of the evening to even smile.

'What I still don't understand,' I say, 'is how Gary's involved.'

Beth considers this. 'Maybe he's not.'

'But what about the smashed window and the kid who said Gary paid him to do it?'

'Kids lie all the time.'

'Alyssa seemed pretty certain that it was Gary.'

'Well, it's all very odd, I'll give you that. I would get your key back off Gary anyway, just to be safe.'

'I'm getting the locks changed again tomorrow.'

We sip our teas in silence. When our mugs are empty, Beth gets up, preparing to go back to bed. I look at Benji, who's snoring. I have no choice, I have to go back to my room and try to get some sleep. There's nowhere else to go.

'If you need me, just shout,' Beth says, putting a hand on my shoulder. As soon as she's gone, I call to Benji and go upstairs too. I climb into bed and Benji nestles at my side, keeping me warm.

But I don't sleep a wink that night. I'm not sure I ever will again.

* * *

The next morning, I'm shattered. I hear Beth moving around downstairs and shortly afterwards she pokes her head around the door to say she's going home for the day to do some work and pack a few things. She promises to be back in the evening.

I thank her and then haul myself out of bed. In the daylight, the house doesn't seem as ominous but I'm still nervy, looking over my shoulder constantly. I have some breakfast and then get dressed and take Benji out for a walk. When I return, the house is exactly as I left it but that does nothing to alleviate my nerves which have taken up permanent residence. I put the radio on to drown out the silence, no longer resentful of Christmas songs but grateful for the cheery background noise, and I do a few chores and then head to work early.

The pub is empty when I arrive and I get to work, emptying the dishwasher and wiping the tables. Benji curls up in his usual spot and dozes off. When it's time for my break, I brave the chilly air and take a cup of coffee outside, sitting down on a bench and playing with my phone. I find Zara's Facebook page and scroll through her posts. They don't give me any insight into who she is as a person. Most of them are advertising her upcoming events. I'm nervous about going to another psychic supper and I'm still not convinced that it's a good idea, but I'll take any help I can get because I can't go on like this. Somehow, this has to end.

When I can no longer feel my hands, I go back inside and slip behind the bar. Mark is doing the rota and I ask him to add me on to as many shifts as possible. He raises his eyebrows but doesn't say anything. My plan for the next few weeks is to stay out of the house as much as possible. And at least Beth will be there in the evenings.

'Have you heard from Gary?' Mark asks me.

I try, and fail, to hide my disgust. 'No.'

'Do you have any idea where he's gone?'

'No, and I don't care.'

'I've messaged him a few times, but he hasn't replied.'

I turn away from Mark. 'Probably because he's got nothing to say.'

'Maggie...' Mark begins but I keep my back to him and go to serve a couple who are approaching the bar. I'm thankful when Mark doesn't mention him again.

Just before I'm due to finish my shift, Beth comes in and suggests that we stay for dinner. We order a bottle of wine and some food. In the end, it's nearly nine o'clock by the time we leave and as the cold air hits me, so does my trepidation.

'I really don't want to go home,' I admit to Beth.

'Don't worry. I'm here.'

'I know, but what if *he's* there? Frank, I mean.'

'Well then I'll put my hands on my hips and tell him, quite politely, to eff off.'

I laugh, glad that Beth is with me. 'Are you sure you don't mind staying?'

'Not at all. Actually, I thought I might take advantage of it to get the flat repainted. I've been meaning to do it for ages and it's so much easier if I'm not there, so the decorator doesn't have to tidy up at the end of each day. Do you mind if I stay a little longer?'

I'm not sure how much of this is true. I suspect Beth knows that I don't want to be alone, and this is an excuse so that I don't feel guilty or insist I'm fine on my own. But I'm so grateful at the prospect of having company that I don't question it.

'Not at all. It'll be lovely to have you. Stay as long as you need.'

'Great, I'll call around and see if anyone has any last-minute availability.'

I reach into my bag and pull out a set of keys. 'Here, these are the new ones. I got two sets, so you keep hold of one while you're staying with me.'

When we reach the cottage, Beth moves ahead of me to open the door. She knows I don't want to go in first. She steps inside and calls out.

'Hello! Anyone here, human or ghost?'

I know she's trying to make me laugh but I lost my sense of humour when we arrived at the cottage. I step tentatively inside as Beth walks around turning on all the lights.

'We're alone,' she says. 'No ghosts tonight.'

I force a smile. 'I'm going to go straight to bed.'

'Okay, I'll stay up for a bit longer, it's too early for me. Sleep well.'

I head up the stairs, with Benji at my heels, and get ready for bed. Once I'm tucked up under my duvet, I take a tatty paperback from my bedside table and start reading. It's a book I've read a hundred times before and I find the familiarity of it soothing. After a while I hear Beth coming up the stairs and using the bathroom and I realise I've been reading for well over an hour. I'm putting off turning the lights out because I know I won't be able to sleep.

Benji, on the other hand, has no such qualms. He's snoring peacefully and I take that as my cue to try and get some shut-eye. If Benji's relaxed, then it means I have nothing to fear. I turn my bedside lamp off and close my eyes. They immediately snap open again.

There's something in the bed next to me. I can feel it but I'm too afraid to look. Too afraid to even move. Instead, I open my mouth and scream. 'Beth!'

She's in my room in seconds, wearing shorts and a vest. 'What is it?'

I scramble to a sitting position and turn on the lamp, looking at the empty spot next to me in bed. Benji, who has woken up, is looking at me with his ears up. But he's not growling. Because, I realise, there's nothing to growl at. There's nothing here.

'False alarm, I'm sorry,' I say.

Beth looks uncertain. 'Are you sure?'

'Just a bad dream,' I lie.

'Okay. Well don't hesitate to call again if you need me.'

She gives me one last worried look and then goes. I leave the bedside light on and reach for my book again. It's going to be a long night. I glance at the empty space next to me.

'I won't give up,' I hiss. 'Not until you're gone for good.'

The only response is Benji, who grunts as he repositions himself and rests his head on his paws. I curl up next to him and start reading.

But the dark night brings dark thoughts. And no matter how hard I try to distract myself with a good book, I struggle to concentrate. I jump at every creak, wondering how much longer my heart can take the strain for. I keep glancing around the room, thinking I can hear whispers and I no longer know whether they're real or not.

I'm falling deeper into the abyss and I'm losing hope that I'll ever escape.

21

I muddle through the next couple of weeks, surviving on adrenaline to make up for the lack of sleep. Beth and I have a gorgeous Christmas lunch at the pub and I'm glad that I changed my mind about spending it alone. Alyssa and her family join us for a drink and it's so delightful to be surrounded by people that for a while I forget about my problems.

But they soon come flooding back. I'm exhausted and paranoid but I put on a brave face at work as I'm desperate to prove myself to Mark again. I do a double shift on New Year's Eve, earning myself some brownie points with him. And I enjoy it too, the noise and the chaos. Watching everyone get increasingly tipsy and joining in with the singing. But it also reminds me that it's a new year and yet I'm still saddled with my old demons.

Beth stays with me at the cottage every night, never complaining about missing her own space. She's found a student, home from university and looking for some extra cash, to repaint her flat and I helped her pick the colours. We watch television together in the evenings and sometimes we have dinner at the pub. Alyssa joins us when she can. Gary is still AWOL and I'm getting used to life without him, but it hurts. I miss him, even though I know that I shouldn't. And while I'm enjoying Beth's company, she's no substitute for Gary. I hadn't realised how much I was falling for him until he was gone. And I have to keep reminding myself what he did to me. Telling myself that he's a bad person.

I still don't know why he did it and I don't think I can rest until I do. But I can't bring myself to contact him. Every time I pick up my phone to call him and demand answers, I stop myself. I've spoken to Alyssa about it and she thinks I should give him a wide berth. She's probably right. But a small part of me yearns to talk to him again.

I'm so paranoid now that I'm convinced every small thing happening in the cottage is Frank. A newspaper I left on the coffee table appeared in the kitchen and I called Beth in a panic, only to discover that she had taken it to read over breakfast. A book I was looking for disappeared off the shelf and I almost ransacked the house in my desperation to locate it. I eventually found it on my bedside table and remembered that I had moved it weeks ago.

Beth has gently suggested that I'm looking for things that aren't there. She's trying to reassure me, but it only makes me feel more isolated. I spend most of my days out of the cottage. I've started visiting the church more, sitting on one of the pews in quiet contemplation, which helps to calm my tattered nerves. The church makes me feel safe. Sometimes the vicar comes and sits with me, trying to draw me into conversation but I never go beyond polite chit-chat. I already know he can't help me.

Eventually, in the New Year, I summon up the courage to call Gary. But the ringtone is different and I realise that he must be abroad. I'm half expecting him to ignore my call, so I'm surprised when he answers quickly.

'Maggie? How are you?'

'Fine,' I say curtly. 'Where are you?'

'In Australia. I'm visiting my daughter.'

'What time is it over there?'

'A little after midnight. I was hoping to hear from you.'

I close my eyes. If Gary's on the other side of the world, then he has nothing to do with what's been happening in the house. Still, I'm glad I changed the locks, just to be safe.

'How long are you staying for?'

'I'm not sure yet. I booked a last-minute one-way flight and figured I'd work it out when I got here. I'm always quiet with work during the winter so I thought I'd take advantage of it to have an extended holiday. And I needed a change of scene after, well, you know. Although, I think my daughter's getting sick of the sight of me.'

I picture Gary, sitting around in his shorts, drinking beer. Getting underfoot. But the vision is accompanied by affection, not annoyance, and I can't reconcile with my feelings.

'Why did you do it, Gary?'

'I didn't do anything.'

'You paid a child to smash my window.'

'I didn't. I would never do that.'

'So why did he say that you did?'

'I have no idea. I was so upset when you accused me that I just upped and left.'

'You ran away, you mean.'

I can almost hear his self-deprecating smile. 'I'm quite good at running from my problems. Ask my ex-wife. I'm not proud of it, Maggie.'

'Did you ever care about me?'

'How can you even ask me that? I adore you. I was happier than I've ever been in my life with you. I thought we had a real future together.'

Tears threaten. 'I did too. That's why I'm struggling to understand why you would do what you did. Did Frank make you do it?'

'What? What are you talking about. I never met Frank.'

'Then why? Please just tell me. I'm going mad trying to work it out.'

'There's nothing to tell you, that's the problem. I don't know what's been going on, or how I've ended up getting involved. And I'm sorry that I legged it, but I knew you didn't want to talk to me and I felt so wretched about our argument and the constant hostility with Sophie that I needed to get away. I should have stayed and tried to fix this.'

I don't think he can fix it though. It's too broken.

'The strange things are still happening,' I tell him.

'Well at least you know it wasn't me, then.'

'I'm really scared.'

'Listen, why don't you come out here for a bit? Book a flight this evening. We can talk and try to work out what's going on together.'

It's tempting. More than tempting. But I don't trust Gary any more and there's no way I can leave Mark in the lurch again so soon. Anyway, without Gary's rental income, I can't afford to spend thousands of pounds on a plane ticket.

'I don't think so. But can we talk when you're back?'

The hope in his voice splinters my heart. 'I'd really like that. Listen, look after yourself, okay? I'm worried about you. Why don't you stay at mine? I can clear it with Sophie.'

I picture Sophie's horrified face at the sight of me standing on her doorstep with Benji and a suitcase. 'I appreciate the offer, but I'm okay here.'

'Are you on your own?'

'Beth's staying with me.'

'Good. That's good.'

'Okay, well, I guess I'll see you soon.'

'See you, Maggie.'

I hang up and stare at my phone. I'm even more perplexed. I want to believe that Gary is a good person who unwittingly got mixed up in this, but something just isn't adding up and I need to run it past someone. With Beth at work, I decide to call Alyssa.

She's tidying up when I arrive at her house twenty minutes later. The boys are watching a film and she's looking harried.

'I'm exhausted,' she confesses.

'I'll make us a cuppa.'

I go into Alyssa's kitchen and put the kettle on, looking at the photos stuck to the fridge while I wait for it to boil. They're largely of the kids at various stages in their lives, from babies to toddlers to preschoolers. There's one of Alyssa and Dylan and I gaze at Dylan's face, searching for whatever it was that I saw in him so many weeks ago.

'That was taken on our honeymoon,' Alyssa says, interrupting my thoughts.

'It's a lovely shot.'

'Thank you. We went to the south of France, it was incredible.'

I busy myself making the drinks, but I have no idea where everything is and soon Alyssa takes over.

'I spoke to Gary,' I tell her.

'And what did he have to say for himself?'

'He's in Australia. And he still insists he had nothing to do with the smashed window.'

'Innocent people don't flee the country.'

'I'm not sure he's fled the country. He's gone to see his daughter.'

'At the last minute?'

'Why not? He's not busy with work during the winter and he knew he wasn't welcome in his own home, or mine. I think he just needed to get away from it all.'

Alyssa scrunches up her face. She's still not convinced, just as she's not convinced that there's a ghost in the cottage. Alyssa's a pragmatist, always looking for a logical answer. But even she has to admit that there doesn't seem to be one in this case.

'I just don't buy it,' she says, handing me a tea. 'Gary has to be involved.'

'I still have feelings for him.'

'Of course you do. We can't turn our feelings on and off like a tap. It'll ease, over time. And you're far better off without him. You don't want to end up with another Frank.'

I want to argue that Gary is nothing like Frank, but I've already tried that and she didn't believe me. Alyssa is refusing to budge from the negative perception she has of Gary. Instead I tell her about the psychic supper that Beth and I are going to and ask if she wants to come.

'No thanks. I'm done with psychic suppers and I'm surprised you want to go after what happened last time.'

'I don't really want to go,' I admit. 'But I'm clutching at straws.'

Alyssa's phone rings and she gives me a look of apology before answering. I can tell it's Dylan she's speaking to and when she hangs up, she looks miserable.

'Dylan's got a client dinner tonight so he's staying over in London.'

'Does he do that often?'

'It's becoming a habit, since we moved here. I get it, because it's a bit of a trek to come home late at night and then go back into the office in the morning but I'm lonely, Maggie.'

'Have you tried talking to him about it?'

'I don't want to nag him. He's so busy with work and he's really stressed.'

'When the boys start school, you'll make plenty of new friends.'

Alyssa wipes away a tear. 'I know. And I have started to make friends already. Sophie and I hang out a bit and she's introduced me to a few other mums. I'm just tired today, that's all. And I sometimes wonder if moving here was the best thing for us.'

'Why did you move?'

'It was Dylan's idea. He said that he'd had a drive around after playing golf nearby and the village was perfect. He wanted the boys to grow up with fresh air and fields to run around in. I was shocked at first because he always loved London and I thought we'd be there forever. Then he drove me out here to have a look at some properties and that was that.'

'But did you want to come?'

'Not really,' Alyssa admits. 'But Dylan was adamant. I've never seen him so determined about anything. I never really got it, why he was so insistent on coming here.'

'Do you think there was something he wasn't telling you?'

Alyssa scrunches up her nose. 'I can't think what.'

I can't think of a reason either. Maybe he was just like a dog with a bone. Frank was the same when we moved here. He came home one day and said he was putting the flat on the market. At first, I thought he was leaving me. But then he'd said, 'We're moving to Hertfordshire,' and when I asked why, he'd just said 'Because I want to.'

And that was that. Five months later, we'd sold the flat and bought the cottage and to this day, I still don't know why. That was the thing with Frank, I never questioned him. I just went along with whatever he wanted and it seems that Alyssa has done the same thing. I can't help but see similarities between our relationships and I wonder again if Dylan really is the perfect husband she makes him out to be.

'Just make sure that you talk to him,' I say. 'Tell him you're not happy. It's your life too.'

'We agreed to give it two years, so we've got a while to go yet. Anyway, I'm sure I'll feel better after a good night's sleep. Not that it's going to happen, of course.'

I consider offering to have the boys for the night but I'm reluctant to invite young children into the cottage. I can't guarantee their safety and I'd never forgive myself if they got scared or, worse, something terrible happened to them. Then I have an idea.

'Why don't you stay at the cottage with Beth tonight and I'll sleep here with the boys?'

'Are you serious?'

'Yes. You and Beth can have a couple of drinks and then you can get a good night's sleep in my room. And if I need you, you're only down the road.'

'Oh my goodness, that would be amazing, but only if you're sure.'

'I'm quite sure. As long as you don't mind a sleepover in a haunted house.'

Alyssa pulls a face. 'I'm so knackered that if a ghost tries to stand in the way of me and my sleep, it'll wish it had never died.'

I smile. 'You might not be saying that tomorrow morning.

But you can always come home if you need to. And I'll leave Benji there to keep guard.'

'Oh thank you so much, Maggie, you have no idea how exciting the prospect of some uninterrupted sleep is.'

I stand up. 'I'll go home and change the bedsheets in my room for you. Then I'll come back around five?'

'Are you sure you're okay putting the boys to bed? They can play up. And you might get a few middle of the night visits too. They'll probably ask for me.'

'We'll muddle through.'

I'm doing this as much for myself as Alyssa. I'm excited about spending a night away from the cottage. I'd much rather be woken up by a crying child than a sinister presence.

On my way home I message Beth to tell her the plan and then I give the cottage a quick tidy, with the radio on full blast. Then I take Benji for a walk, pack a small bag and head back over to Alyssa's. She opens the door wearing a tracksuit and a grin.

'I'm so excited,' she says, letting me in. 'I've written down some information for you about the boys' bedtime routine and so on. And call me if you need anything at all.'

'We'll be fine, go on, off you go.'

Alyssa kisses the boys goodbye and legs it before they have a chance to cry. I see their little lips wobbling and decide to distract them.

'Who wants some ice cream?'

By eight o'clock the boys are fast asleep and I'm shattered. How Alyssa does it every day is beyond me. I've only been looking after them for three hours and my whole body aches. But they were well behaved really, with only a few tears when we couldn't find a missing teddy. Fortunately, it turned up under the sofa and harmony was restored. Now I can't wait to put my feet up and relax, safe in the knowledge that Frank can't reach me here.

Alyssa has left me some lasagne and I heat it up in the microwave and decide to have a glass of wine from the open bottle in the fridge. Then I take my dinner into the living room and put the television on. As I'm sitting down on the sofa I drop my fork, and I lean down to pick it up, my eyes falling on an envelope underneath the coffee table. It's addressed to Dylan and I'm about to pick it up and put it on the table when I see the company logo stamped on the crisp white envelope.

I recoil, as though the envelope contains a bomb. The letter is from a solicitor and I recognise the name as it's the same one who looked after Frank's affairs. I pick up the envelope and study it carefully, in case I've made a mistake. But it's definitely the same firm. What does this mean? Is it just a coincidence? I hold the envelope up to the light to see what's inside but I can't make anything out. I want to open it but there's no way I could make it look like an accident. Dylan and Alyssa would know I was snooping and they'd be right. But I'm perturbed by this revelation and I remember the odd feeling I've previously had around Dylan. How he scared me when he grabbed me outside the cottage. Why was he so insistent that they move to this village? Is there a connection between him and Frank?

Thank goodness he's staying in London tonight. I'm too freaked out to see him now, but I'll ask Alyssa about it tomorrow and, with any luck, she'll tell me that it's simply a coincidence. Then I'll be able to relax again.

I put the letter on the coffee table, pick up my dinner and attempt to eat it, but I've lost my appetite. I keep glancing at the envelope, trying to work out what it means. I've completely zoned out of the television programme I put on and I can barely hear it. Something is telling me that this is not a coincidence, that it's somehow important.

Then I hear a car outside, tyres crunching on gravel. A door slamming. I peer out of the window and my heart plummets at what I see. But before I have time to work out what to do, the unmistakeable sound of a key turning in the lock makes me freeze. Dylan is home.

22

Dylan walks into the living room and does a double take when he sees me.

'Where's Alyssa?' he asks, without even bothering to say hello.

'She's staying at mine tonight with Beth. I offered to babysit because she was exhausted and needed a night off. They're having a girls' night in. She'll be back in the morning.' I try to act normal, but nerves are making me babble.

'The boys?'

'They're asleep upstairs. I thought you were staying in London tonight?'

Dylan sits down and takes off his shoes. 'The dinner was cancelled at the last minute, so I decided to come home and surprise Alyssa.'

He seems annoyed and I can understand why. Alyssa clearly hasn't told him that she's staying out tonight and he's probably tired and a bit ratty. But now I've seen that envelope I'm suspicious of everything Dylan says and does. Especially when he looks at me, those piercing eyes boring into me. I came here tonight to feel safe and now I feel the opposite.

Should I call Alyssa and tell her what's happened? She'd be over like a shot. But I don't want to ruin her night away, not when she was so excited for it. And if Dylan is angry with her, I don't want her to get into trouble either. Perhaps Dylan will take the matter out of my hands and call her himself. But instead he stands up, looks at my glass of wine and disappears into the kitchen. When he returns, he's got his own glass.

'You can go home,' he says. 'There's no need to stay now that I'm back.'

'Have you told Alyssa you're here?'

'No. Tell her she's welcome to stay with you tonight. I know she needs a break.'

'Okay.' I exhale as I gather my things. Dylan wants me to leave and that's fine by me. I need to get to the bottom of that letter but there's no way I'm asking him outright. Not until I've worked out whether he's got something to do with Frank because I'm vulnerable here on my own and I'm increasingly afraid of Dylan. I pick up my barely eaten lasagne to take it back to the kitchen, my eyes involuntarily resting on the envelope for a second. Dylan follows my gaze and snatches up the envelope. That's when I know for certain that I need to get out. I'm beginning to feel claustrophobic. Trapped.

I hurry into the kitchen, empty the lasagne into the bin and put the plate in the dishwasher. Then I stick my head around the door.

'I'll be off then.'

To my surprise, Dylan is holding his head in his hands. This is my moment to get away while he's distracted, but something about his body language makes me stop. I hesitate and then step tentatively into the room.

'Dylan, are you okay?'

He doesn't move. I take another cautious step into the living room, still unsure if I'm doing the right thing. I'm wary but Dylan seems really upset. Defeated almost. I see the envelope on the coffee table and realise that it's been opened. There's a letter beside it.

'Dylan?' I ask.

When he finally looks at me his eyes are bloodshot. 'I've messed up,' he says simply.

I stare at him, trying to read his expression, to see into his mind. Nothing about his stance is aggressive or menacing. He's slumped on the sofa, looking like a man who has lost everything. But why, when he has a good job, a beautiful wife and two adorable children? Curiosity, and concern, get the better of me and I sit down on the sofa opposite him.

'What's happened, Dylan?'

'I put a load of money into an investment and it went bad. I've lost everything.'

I glance at the letter and things start to add up horribly. 'Is that what the letter is about?'

'Yes. It's from a solicitor representing the company, which went into liquidation. They were dodgy as hell and I've got no rights at all. I've been pursuing it for months but I keep reaching dead ends and I think I have to accept that the money is well and truly gone.'

'Are you in debt?'

'Yes,' he whispers. 'And I don't know how to tell Alyssa.'

'When did this happen?'

'Last year. That's why we moved. I needed to release some equity from our London house and I couldn't bring myself to tell Alyssa why. I can hardly bear to look at her.'

I watch Dylan as he takes a bracing glug of wine. His hands

are shaking. 'You need to talk to her, Dylan. She'll understand, I know she will.'

'No, she won't. She gave up her career to be a mother, but I haven't kept up my side of the bargain. I'm supposed to be providing for her and the boys. I'm a failure.'

'No.' I shake my head vigorously. 'You're not a failure. These things happen.'

'I'm such an idiot. I got sucked in by this man, he promised me huge returns on a new investment and I fell for it hook, line and sinker. I thought I had more intelligence than that. The company was a bloody fraud, I'm telling you. What the hell was I thinking?'

My eyes widen as my heart starts racing. There is a sinking feeling brewing in my gut and I want to be wrong but I know that I'm not.

'This man, what was his name?'

Dylan doesn't even look at me when he says in a clear voice, 'Frank Rossi.'

* * *

I feel sick. And exposed. Does Dylan know who I am? Is that why he puts me on edge, because he's been watching me? I have no idea how much Alyssa has told him about me but the fact that we've all ended up living in the same village can't be a fluke. I do the maths in my head and realise that Frank died at around the same time Dylan and Alyssa came to live here. And soon afterwards, the strange things started happening in the cottage.

My head is swimming with thoughts. Dylan has every reason to hate Frank. Perhaps if he couldn't get revenge on my husband for ruining his life, he decided to come after me instead. Is that what this has been about the whole time? Dylan trying to scare me, to intimidate me? And how much does Alyssa know about it? For a horrifying moment I wonder if she's been pretending to be my friend to get close to me, but then I remember that she doesn't know anything about what her husband has been up to. A shiver runs up my spine as I remember how frightened I'd been when Dylan returned my phone that night. But he could have hurt me then and he walked away, so what are his intentions now?

There's one thing I know for certain. Dylan detests Frank, so that rules out the possibility that he's acting on my husband's behalf in any way. And although I'm still wary of Dylan, I make no move to leave. I want answers. I need to unravel this mess.

If Dylan can sense my turmoil, he doesn't show it. In fact, he seems lost in his own.

'Frank was all charm,' he explains. 'He told me my money was as safe as houses. Showed me testimonials from other happy clients. And I wanted enough cash to send the boys to private school. To give them the best possible education. I was so *stupid*.'

'How much trouble are you in?' I ask. I'm clutching my phone in one hand, ready to dial for help. Dylan could turn on me at any second and he could easily overpower me. He's young and fit. And very, very angry. I think of the boys asleep upstairs. Surely Dylan wouldn't hurt me with them in the house? Would he believe me, if I told him I had no idea what my husband got up to? Or is he beyond reason?

'I've got no savings left and unpaid credit cards,' he tells me. 'I can afford the mortgage on this place, but I don't know how I'll be able to pay off the debts too. If I don't find a way, we might default on the mortgage. We might be homeless.'

Oh my goodness. Despite my suspicions about Dylan, my heart softens. No wonder he hates Frank so much. I wonder how many other people my husband has swindled over the years.

How he's got away with it for so long. Unless he genuinely believed his own hype? Is that why all our money disappeared too? I wouldn't put it past Frank to think that he was invincible, even when he kept losing money. To refuse to see any weakness in himself.

I'm torn between making an excuse to leave, comforting Dylan and finding out if he realises who I am. But then he looks at me and I know the answer without needing to ask. And a jolt of apprehension surges through me.

'You know I'm his wife.'

He nods. 'Yes.'

'Does Alyssa?'

'No. She doesn't know any of this.'

'I'm so sorry,' I whisper.

I've left it too late to run away. Dylan's focus is now firmly on me and physically I'm no match for him. He is faster and stronger. I have to find a way to make him understand that I am not responsible for what happened to him, that Frank ruined my life as well.

I force myself to look Dylan in the eye. 'I knew nothing about what Frank got up to. He didn't tell me anything about his work or his clients. Perhaps I should have asked more questions, but I didn't. And even if I had, I doubt I'd have been able to stop him.'

He studies me carefully before looking away. 'I know.'

His response surprises me. 'You do?'

'Yes. Alyssa's told me all about your marriage to Frank. It seems he was ruthless at home as well as at work. I'm sorry that you had to go through that.'

I exhale slowly, my breathing jagged. Is Dylan really giving me an out here? Or is he trying to lull me into a false sense of security before he pounces?

'It's not your fault,' he says simply.

As I study him carefully, I begin to relax. This is not a man who wants to hurt me. He's upset, yes, but not with me. He's angry with Frank and, most of all, himself. But I have to be sure. So I brace myself to ask him the question that's been nagging at me.

'Have you been trying to scare me?'

Dylan's head snaps up. 'What? No.'

'I haven't got any money,' I say quickly, 'Frank lost all of ours too. But I'll give you whatever I have. I'll keep working, I'll pay you in instalments...'

'Stop it, Maggie!' The harshness of Dylan's tone stuns me into silence but then his face softens. 'I don't want anything from you.'

'But Frank stole all your money.'

'Yes, Frank did. You didn't.'

Is he genuinely just seeking a listening ear? I'm struggling to believe it. Perhaps I was just in the wrong place at the wrong time. I caught Dylan at a vulnerable moment and he opened up to the next person he spoke to. Who just so happened to be the wife of the man who potentially defrauded him. It still seems too odd to be a coincidence.

'Why did you move here?' I ask him. 'Why come to this particular village?'

Dylan gives a humourless laugh. 'When Frank was schmoozing me, he invited me here to play golf and told me it would be a great place for a family to raise kids. I took a drive around and I liked it. It stayed on my mind, so when I needed cash fast, I decided to sell the London house and move here where properties are a bit cheaper.'

'Did you know Frank lived here too?'

'He told me he had a flat in London and a big country pile nearby.'

Another thing he lied about. 'He had neither of those things.'

'Well, I know that now.'

'When did you realise I was his wife?'

'When Alyssa mentioned your husband's name. But Maggie, I never wanted to scare you, I promise.'

'Has Alyssa told you what's been going on at the cottage?'

'Yes. And it's got nothing to do with me, if that's what you think. She reckons it's Gary.'

'I'm not sure it is Gary any more,' I admit.

'She says you think it's a ghost. If it is Frank, can you tell him to piss off from me?'

Join the queue, I think bitterly.

'I'm so sorry, Dylan,' I tell him earnestly. 'I'm devastated about what Frank did to you and I want to make amends in some way.'

'They're not your amends to make.'

'Still, I feel responsible. I'll do anything to help.'

'Short of giving me seventy-five grand, there's not much you can do.'

Seventy-five thousand pounds? Oh no, it's even worse than I thought.

'You need to tell Alyssa,' I repeat. 'Trust me, she'll understand.'

'And if she doesn't?'

'Well then, at least it's all out in the open. Frank and I never really talked to each other. Our marriage was a disaster. Don't be like us, Dylan, be better than that. Do the right thing.'

He nods. 'You're right. I know you're right.'

'This wasn't your fault, okay? You were taken in by a conman.'

'It *was* my fault. I work in finance for goodness' sake. What's wrong with me?'

'You wanted to do right by your family and sometimes that can make us do foolish things we wouldn't usually do. Frank told you this was an easy win, and I can see why you were tempted.'

'I was an idiot. A stupid, stupid idiot.'

'You'll fix this, I know you will.'

He shakes his head. 'I really don't know how.'

If I had any money, I'd gladly hand it over to him. Anything to stop Alyssa and the boys losing their home. But, just like Dylan, I've got nothing to spare. And he's already made it clear that he doesn't want my money anyway. Knowing what Frank did to that family makes my blood boil. And it also makes me wonder again who else out there is angry. Who might want revenge on Frank and, in his absence, his widow.

A thought occurs to me. Did Frank convince Gary to invest in his corrupt funds too? Is that why Gary's got it in for me? I've been racking my brains trying to find a link and now I wonder if I've finally discovered it. Perhaps Gary charmed himself into my life, and my bed, in order to steal from me. To get back the money he was owed by Frank.

It's a crazy theory but given everything else that's been going on recently, I no longer doubt anything. Is it possible that there really is no ghost? That it was Gary all along? But then I remember that he's in Australia and so he can't be responsible for what's been happening over the past few weeks. Unless there's a group of people who are all working together to destroy me. To get their revenge on Frank.

I'm spiralling and it's not going to help me. Nor is sitting here with Dylan because it's Alyssa he needs to talk to right now, not me.

I stand up. 'I'm going to go home and tell Alyssa to come back here. When she does, you're going to tell her everything you just told me. The whole story.'

He winces. 'Tonight?'

'Yes, Dylan, tonight.'

He slumps but he gives me a nod.

'It'll be okay,' I assure him, even though I have no idea if it will. I love Alyssa but I know she can be unforgiving. And she is going to be furious with Dylan. I don't know if they will be able to get past that, but I hope they will. I've only spent a short amount of time with Dylan, but I've realised that he's nothing like Frank after all. He's devastated because he's let his family down. Frank didn't care one bit about letting me down, he only cared about himself. Would it have been different if we'd had children? Could I have prevented this all happening if only I'd been able to conceive? Maybe Frank would have softened, settled into being a family man. Perhaps he wouldn't have been hell-bent on destroying other people's lives for his own gratification, or to feed his arrogance.

As I let myself out of the house, I'm all over the place. I've been living on adrenaline for so long now that it's almost become habitual. But the fear I felt tonight when I initially thought Dylan wanted to hurt me ramped it up a notch. Now it's been replaced with a heavy sadness for Dylan and Alyssa. And worry that once she knows the truth about Frank, she'll want nothing to do with me. But I put my own selfishness to the side because Alyssa deserves to know what's going on, even if that means she turns against me.

It's only when I reach the cottage, comforted by the fact that Beth, Alyssa and Benji are inside and it's not cold and empty, that I realise I forgot to ask Dylan something important.

I didn't ask him how he met Frank in the first place.

23

It's been two days since Dylan's revelations and I haven't heard from Alyssa. I've texted her a couple of times, but she hasn't replied and I'm worried about her.

I don't think Dylan would do anything to harm her. Our conversation has changed my opinion of him and I sense he's not a threat to anyone but himself. He feels guilty because he thinks he's failed his family, but his rage is inwards. No, my worry is that Alyssa has kicked him out and she's alone and afraid, with two small children to look after.

Beth told me to give Alyssa some space but after forty-eight hours, I decide to go and see her. I need to know if she's okay. I'm certainly not. Beth has been acting strangely for the past couple of days and this morning she said she was going to work from the flat all day. I asked her if she was okay and she said she'd had a bad dream but wouldn't divulge any more details. Now I'm wondering if something has happened in the cottage and she doesn't want to tell me. I have the date of the psychic supper etched in my mind, as though it will all be over after that. The problem is, I fear it's a false hope.

When I arrive at Alyssa's house, the curtains are closed, blocking out the world. Dylan's car isn't in the driveway. I ring the bell and she answers, looking awful. Her face is blotchy and her usually shiny hair is dull and greasy. She stares at me and for a second, I wonder if she is going to close the door in my face. I brace myself for the slam or to be told in no uncertain terms to leave. But then she throws herself into my arms and starts sobbing.

'It's okay,' I tell her, hugging her tightly. 'It's okay.'

I help her inside and peek my head around the living room door. The boys are in there, playing with cars. I make sure they're alright and then guide Alyssa into the kitchen.

'Is Dylan at work?' I ask.

'Yes,' she sniffs, putting the kettle on.

'I take it he's told you everything.'

'He has. Because of you.'

I can't tell from her tone whether she's upset with me or not. But when she looks at me, I see gratitude, not fury, on her face.

'If it wasn't for you, I don't know how long he would have kept it a secret for.'

'Did he tell you who persuaded him to invest the money?'

'Yes. I couldn't believe it. I mean, what a strange coincidence. But given what you've told me about Frank, it makes sense. You're not his only victim.'

'I'm so sorry, Alyssa.'

'Stop that.' She scowls at me. 'It wasn't your fault. I'm not angry with you.'

'What about Dylan?'

'Oh, I'm fuming with him. How could he have been so naive?'

'He wanted to do right by you and the kids.'

'By losing all our money? For goodness' sake, he's the one

always telling me that if something seems too good to be true, it usually is. And then he went and did this.'

'He is genuinely sorry.'

'I know he is and that's why I haven't kicked him out. Well, that and the fact that we can't afford the rent on another property anyway.' She laughs bitterly. 'We're screwed.'

'I have an idea,' I say tentatively.

'You do?'

'Yes. You've been talking about feeling lonely and isolated for ages. Why don't you get a job? The extra income could help to pay off the debts.'

'Yes, but the cost of childcare is extortionate.'

'That's where I come in. I can look after the boys.'

Alyssa looks at me in surprise. 'But I can't afford to pay you.'

'I don't want to be paid.'

'Maggie, I know you feel bad about what Frank did, but it's not up to you to fix his mistakes.'

'That's not why I'm doing it,' I insist. It's a half-truth because I do want to make amends to Dylan and Alyssa. But I also want to help my friend and, to be honest, experience the joy of looking after children, something that I never got to do, having never had my own.

'But what about your job at the pub?'

'I can work around that. I'll do evening and weekend shifts at the pub and I'll be here for the boys during the day.'

Alyssa shakes her head. 'I can't ask you do to that.'

'I want to do it.'

'But why?'

'Because I want to help,' I say simply.

She looks at me and her face crumples. 'I've never met anyone as generous as you. I really don't know what I would do without you, Maggie.'

My face flushes with pleasure. To know that I mean so much to someone leaves me speechless. It's all I've ever wanted, to be part of a family. To have people in my life who I care about and who care about me. And I've learned over the past few months that you don't need to be biologically related to someone for them to feel like family. I feel closer to Alyssa and Beth than I ever did to anyone else in my life. And for a while I felt closer to Gary too.

I push away the melancholy that threatens and return to the matter at hand. 'So, it's agreed then. You'll start job hunting and I'm ready to step in whenever you find something.'

'How will I ever repay you?'

I think about it, knowing that Alyssa needs something to give me in return. 'You can look after Benji whenever I'm away,' I say, knowing that I'm not going anywhere soon.

It's a small gesture but Alyssa seizes upon it. 'Any time,' she says.

'And don't be too hard on Dylan. You have every right to be angry with him but remember that he was trying to do the right thing. At least he was honest with you.'

'In the end.'

'Better late than never.'

She narrows her eyes. 'I suppose so.'

'By the way, did Dylan tell you how he met Frank?'

'No, why?'

'No reason,' I say. 'I was just wondering.'

'Probably through work. Can you believe that my husband works in finance and he still invested in a dodgy deal? I mean, talk about ridiculous.'

She's off again, ranting about Dylan, and I let her talk because she needs to get it out of her system. She doesn't see what I see. That Dylan adores Alyssa and the boys so much he'd do anything for them. He was blinkered by a macho instinct to provide for his family and it made him do a stupid thing. If they can claw their way out of this, and I desperately hope that they will, I know he won't make the same mistake again.

When I leave Alyssa, she seems in better spirits and she's already talking about sprucing up her CV that evening. She thanks me again and I walk home satisfied that I've done the right thing. I decide to take Benji for another walk and then head straight to the pub for my shift. That means I'll only need to be home for about five minutes.

But as soon as I walk through the door, I can smell it again. Frank's aftershave. The smell is pungent, overpowering the hallway, seeping up my nostrils and making me nauseous. I fall back against the wall, my breath catching. Benji dashes in and out of the house and darts around me, restless and agitated again. It's broad daylight and I'm afraid.

But then my fear morphs into fury. I think of poor Alyssa and Dylan and all the other souls in the world who have suffered because of Frank. I remember the life of oppression I lived at the hands of my cruel husband. And I remember what he made me become, how he took me apart piece by piece until I was broken. I push myself off the wall and stand square in the middle of the hallway, with my hands on my hips.

'You're pathetic!' I scream. 'You're a useless, pathetic man and that's why you're still here. Because no one else wants you, even when you're dead!'

A door slams hard, making me jump. My bravado evaporates and I call for Benji and dash out of the cottage again, locking the door behind me. Enough is enough. I can't take any more sleepless nights and looking over my shoulder in my own home. I can't cope with finding objects in the wrong place or smelling my dead husband.

I'm not going back to that house until Frank is gone. I'm going to find a way to get rid of him, once and for all. But until then, I need to stay somewhere else.

As I'm walking, I call Beth.

'I've had enough,' I tell her. 'Can we stay at your place until the psychic supper?'

'Yes,' she says, and I can hear relief in her voice. 'I think that's a good idea.'

'What is it, Beth?'

'I'm sorry, Maggie, but the cottage is giving me the heebie-jeebies. I thought I could handle it, but I'm exhausted. I've not been sleeping well.'

'You should have told me.'

'I know, but I didn't want to upset you any more than you already are.'

'Did something happen? Did you see a ghost?'

'No, it's not that.' Beth pauses. 'I can't explain it. It's like a strange energy. A *feeling*. And maybe I'm overreacting because I'm tired, but I'm scared for you, Maggie.'

Her words send a chill down my spine. 'What do you mean?'

'I just think you need to get out of there.'

My heart feels like it's going to stop. 'Do you think I'm in danger?'

Beth hesitates. 'I don't know. That's the problem. I just don't know.'

24

When I walk into the pub with Beth, it strikes me how much has changed in less than a year. I was so nervous when I went to the first psychic supper. I was afraid of being out of the house, at having to talk to other people, and my social anxiety was sky-high.

I'm nervous now, but for different reasons. Beth is by my side and Alyssa has messaged to wish us good luck, even though she thinks we're mad to be doing this. I've made some amazing friends, I have a job that I love and the most wonderful dog. I'm fit and healthy and I have a new-found confidence that I never could have imagined when I was with Frank. For a short while, I thought I'd found happiness with Gary too. But that hope was shattered, along with what was left of my sanity, and that's the reason why I'm here. I'm a desperate woman, willing to go to any lengths to get my life back. The thing is, I'm not sure what I'm more afraid of: Zara having a message for me or Zara not having a message for me.

Beth and I find a table in the unfamiliar pub and we sit down, smiling politely at the other guests. Beth launches into conversation with them but I'm too anxious to engage so I just give a glassy smile and hope they don't think I'm being rude. The food, when it arrives, tastes like cardboard in my mouth. Every minute feels like an hour. I just want to get this over and done with, for better or for worse. I spot Zara walking around, purposefully fading into the background. No one else has noticed her but I watch her every move and realise that she's reading the room. Then she turns to me and I hurriedly look away. I can still sense her gaze though, as I force myself to take another mouthful of food, and it makes me queasy.

I take it easy on the wine because I'm already wound up like a coil, but Beth keeps topping up my glass. I think she's nervous too but she's masking it by talking incessantly to the other guests. In contrast, I'm almost mute. I half listen to the conversations. One woman wants to connect with her sister. Another lost her mother. Everything feels too loud, as though someone has turned the volume up. I can hear every clatter of a fork, every hoot of laughter and it echoes around my head, making me want to shrink inside myself.

When Zara walks into the middle of the room I hold my breath. This is it, the moment I've been waiting for. The food I've forced myself to eat curdles in my stomach. The wine rises back up my throat, leaving an acrid taste in my mouth. I've put everything into this moment but I'm still not sure if it's going to solve my problems.

Zara begins with a similar spiel to the first time I saw her, telling people that she might not have messages for everyone and so on. But soon she's away, and she sidles up to another table and gives a message to a man from his wife. Next is a young woman who lost her father recently. She goes on and on, making people laugh and cry, but I can't enjoy it. My body is on high alert, energy surging through me every time she comes near our table and then fizzing out when she changes direction. I take a sip of wine and my hands are shaking. Beth seems to be getting more into it, but she keeps stealing glances at me to make sure I'm okay. I try to give her a reassuring smile but it comes out as a grimace and she places a hand reassuringly over mine.

'Relax,' she whispers. 'It's going to be okay.'

We're getting to the end of the session and Zara still hasn't come anywhere near our table. I'm beginning to lose hope and my disappointment is crushing. Why did I think that this evening was going to be the answer to all my prayers? I need to come up with another plan, and fast. Maybe I should talk to the vicar again, persuade him to help me.

But then Zara starts to walk towards us and I hold my breath. I feel everyone on our table tense in expectation. She stops when she reaches us and closes her eyes, breathing in and out deeply. Then she opens them again, but her expression is glassy and I can't tell who she's looking at, if anyone. All I can do is wait to see what happens next.

'Frank is here.'

My stomach drops and I remove my hand from under Beth's and cover my mouth. I can't believe this is real. It can't be a gimmick because Zara has mentioned my husband by name. Whatever is going on in this room, however she does it, any shred of doubt I had about Zara's capabilities vanish. She's reached my husband and that means that I finally have a chance to communicate with him. I'll tell him to go away and leave me alone, I don't care what anyone else thinks of me. I'll do whatever it takes to make Frank leave for good.

'He says he's sorry.'

I frown in confusion. This was not what I expected. Frank has never once apologised for anything. What exactly is he sorry for? Ruining my life or haunting me even after he died? Hope surges through me as I wonder if this is the turning point. The pivotal moment where Frank and I somehow manage to find some semblance of peace.

Zara is concentrating hard, frowning as she listens to whatever it is she is hearing, or channelling. The seconds pass and I think that I might pass out with fear and anticipation. Everyone else melts away, until it feels like Zara and I are the only two people in the room. And Frank of course, but I can't feel him and I can't smell him. It's nothing like it is at home, when he's all around me, all the time. It's different here.

'He loves you. More than he's ever loved anyone.'

Hope shatters into shards of glass. Whoever this person is that Zara claims to be talking to, it's not Frank. He would never say anything like that. I realise with a disappointment that feels like a punch in the gut that she's simply telling me what she thinks a widowed woman wants to hear. I already know she eavesdrops as people are having their dinner, so she has an idea of why we're all here before she starts. She must have overheard me mentioning his name when I half explained to my fellow guests why I had come along this evening.

I've been conned and I want to cry, right here in the middle of the pub. I've been such a fool to put so much expectation on this evening and the realisation is crushing. The people around me come back into focus, every sound acute again. I'm back in reality and I loathe it. Because I know now that I'm not going to walk away with any answers.

I'm so lost in my own misery that I almost miss what Zara says next.

'Going to France with you was the happiest time of his life.'

I have never been to France with Frank. I frown at Zara, deeply frustrated and ready to call her out for being a fraud, but she's not finished.

'He says it's time to move on. To forget about him and live your life. Keep going on your adventures and he'll always be with you in spirit.'

Adventures? What on earth is this woman going on about? I hardly look like the worldly, well-travelled type. I'm not like Beth. I shoot my friend an incredulous look, but she's smiling at me. She's happy for me, I realise. She thinks that this is the closure I need.

What the hell is going on? I try to think of explanations. Perhaps Zara has got it wrong and her message is for Beth, not me. But Beth's partner was called David. I picture the photograph she showed me on her phone. He looked nothing like Frank. The image dissolves again and is replaced by Frank. I don't know what to think, how to respond.

People are beginning to stare. Someone at our table is supposed to be reacting to Zara. Crying, or smiling, or thanking her. But no one is saying anything.

Beth finally breaks the silence. 'It's Maggie's husband,' she explains to the others. 'I think she's in shock.'

They all cluck sympathetically and Zara moves away. I don't call after her and ask her to deliver a message to Frank because I'm too dumbfounded.

A woman sitting opposite me, whose name I don't remember, leans forward. 'What a lovely message from your husband. I hope it gives you some peace.'

Peace? It's given me anything but peace. I can't get my head around what's just happened. I'm trying to work out if Zara has simply thrown some generic stuff out there to see what resonates. She mentioned France, but lots of British people go on holiday to France. It could have been a stab in the dark, which she was wrong about.

Beth loves France. Alyssa and Dylan went to France on their honeymoon. No. I shake my head vigorously. I'm overthinking this.

'Are you okay, Maggie?' Beth is looking at me with concern.

'I have to go,' I say, standing up and immediately feeling light-headed.

'Wait, I'll come with you.'

'No, you stay.'

'Maggie, wait!'

I glance at her. 'I want to be alone.'

It's the second time I've fled one of these psychic suppers. My head is swimming with confusion and unanswered questions, but the unsettled feeling is growing stronger, fuelled by the wine I've drunk too much of.

I rush back to Beth's flat, letting myself in with the spare key she gave me, and sit down on the sofa with my phone. Without really knowing what I'm doing I start googling car accidents involving loose horses and it doesn't take long to find an article on a local newspaper website. I skim the words, feeling guilty for thinking, even for a fleeting moment of madness, that the message might be for Beth from Frank. I'm such a fool.

I laugh as nervous energy spills out of me. I'm so paranoid. It's what Frank has done to me. I let someone claiming to be a psychic mess with my head and I won't do it again. My momentary relief quickly dissolves as I consider my options. The psychic supper has not solved my problems and I can't stay at Beth's much longer. The flat is too small and Benji and I are just getting in her way. I'll have to go back to the cottage, which is the last place I want to return to. And given Zara's disastrous performance this evening, I don't think asking her to come round and do an exorcism is going to help. Can I convince the vicar to try?

My head is spinning from the wine. I can't find a clear path through all this mess. I can't make it stop. I'm about to put my phone down when a photograph further down the news article I was reading catches my eye. It's of a family on holiday, a man and his partner, along with two smiling children. I read the caption, then reread it, and time stops, leaving me suspended in disbelief, flailing for a grip on reality.

The man in the photo is the motorist who died and I recognise it as the same photo as the one Beth showed me, although in hers the rest of the family have been cropped out. The woman is his partner and her name is Anna. She is quoted further down the article, paying tribute to her wonderful David and saying that the accident happened on his birthday. She had prepared a special meal, she says, and was waiting for him to come home when the police turned up on her doorstep.

My heart is pounding so loudly I can almost hear it, along with the cogs turning wildly in my mind. The poor man who died in that accident was not Beth's partner at all. This was not her tragic story to tell, it was someone else's and she's stolen it. Why would she do that? Why would she lie about something so horrific?

But I don't have time to even begin to figure it out because just then, I hear the front door open, followed by Benji barking. Moments later, Beth walks into the room.

25

I had long suspected that Frank had affairs. He worked away so much and I imagined he had a woman in every port. Sometimes I found lipstick on his shirt or the faint whiff of perfume on his jacket. I didn't hate those women, I pitied them for having to put up with the degradation that Frank had stopped inflicting on me because I was too disgusting. Occasionally I dreamed that he would leave me for one of them and I woke up with a brief surge of hope. Then, I felt guilty for wishing Frank on some other innocent soul.

It wasn't until we moved to Hertfordshire that I had solid proof of Frank's indiscretions. He left his laptop on when he went to the bathroom, and as I was walking past, I saw an email on his screen that he was writing. He had addressed it to *E* and as my eyes skimmed over the words, I could barely believe what I was reading. The email was so tender and affectionate. It was, to all intents and purposes, a love letter. It ended with a promise that he would see *E* next week and he was counting down the seconds.

I moved away quickly when I heard the toilet flush and by

the time Frank emerged, I was safely ensconced in the kitchen. But I couldn't stop thinking about that email, the words I'd read. I wasn't angry that Frank was having another affair. No, what distressed me was the way he wrote to this woman, as if she was the most important and special person in the world. I wondered who she was and why she deserved Frank's adoration when all I had experienced was contempt. I agonised over what was so wrong with me that Frank couldn't express any affection towards me when he could do it so freely towards another.

I thought about it all the time, until it became an obsession. I wanted to see more, to understand this unknown side to a man I'd been with for thirty years. But I never caught his laptop unlocked and unattended again. I tried to log on once, when Frank was out, but I couldn't guess his password and after several attempts, I eventually gave up.

I should have left him. But then I should have done that years ago. Fear of the repercussions held me back, as they had always done. Frank would hunt me down and destroy me, not because he loved me but because he would be humiliated, and that would make him very, very dangerous. Frank did not like to be made a fool of. And he didn't like a woman disobeying him. Or at least, he didn't like me disobeying him.

He was Jekyll and Hyde. Because out there, in the part of his world where I didn't exist, he was charm personified. A man who wrote tender letters to his latest amour, telling her she was beautiful and special. Who counted down the days until they could see each other again. And who was so manipulative that he probably made these women fall deeply in love with him, until they would do anything for him. Anything he wanted them to do.

And I wondered, time and time again, who E was.

* * *

Beth walks into the room and crouches down to greet Benji. I watch her every move, study her facial expressions. I'm looking for evidence that she's hiding something.

'Are you okay, Maggie?' she asks. 'I came home early as I was worried about you.'

'I'm fine,' I say, my eyes never leaving hers.

'Are you sure? You're still looking a little peaky. Shall I make us a cup of tea?'

Beth heads over to the kitchen before I can answer and fills up the kettle. I look around the flat and realise that there's not one photograph of Beth and David. There are some of her in destinations around the world, a few group photos with her friends, but that's it.

E. Elizabeth. *Beth*. The sudden and unexpected move to Hertfordshire that Frank never explained and I never truly understood. Did we relocate so that he could be closer to her? I want to ask her outright if she knew Frank but I'm afraid because if she did know him, if she's E, then she also knows that I'm his widow, yet she's still forged a friendship with me. In fact, she's gone out of her way to insert herself into my life. What does she want from me?

Beth brings me a cup of tea and sits down next to me. I instinctively move away and she looks at me in surprise.

'Maggie, what's going on? Talk to me.'

But I'm frozen, too afraid to verbalise what I'm thinking. What if Beth is dangerous? And part of me, the rational part, is still wondering if I've got this wrong again.

I'm going round in circles, but I keep coming back to the same thing. E. Zara's message from Frank which I know for certain wasn't for me. I doubted Zara at the time, but she was right about the back door key. Could that message really have been for Beth?

Sensing my unease, Benji comes and sits by my feet. Beth is still looking at me.

'You're upset about what Zara said,' she says solemnly.

I barely nod in response.

'Talk to me,' she repeats.

But I can't. All I can think is that I need find a way to get out of this flat without Beth realising that I'm on to her. I'm scared of Beth now that I'm seeing her with different eyes. She might not be the person I thought she was and if she's not my friend, then who is she?

I stand up abruptly. 'I'm going to go back to the cottage.'

Beth looks at me in surprise. 'Really? Are you sure?'

'Yes.'

I can barely meet her eye as I begin to pack my things.

'Shall I come with you?'

'No,' I say quickly. Too quickly. Beth's eyes narrow as she appraises me.

'What's going on, Maggie?'

'Nothing,' I say, this time more slowly. I'm buying time, thinking on my feet. 'I guess the message from Zara has reassured me that Frank's not out to get me. And I can't stay here forever, it's not fair on you. I think that the time has come for Benji and me to go home.'

Beth slowly puts her tea down on the table and for a second, I think she's going to try to stop me. Visions flash before my eyes of her locking me in the flat, imprisoning me inside like Frank used to do. But she simply nods.

'No problem. Call me if you need anything at all, okay?'

'Thank you.'

I start gathering my belongings, throwing them into my holdall, and then call for Benji.

'Thank you for having me,' I say as I dash for the door, praying that Beth hasn't locked it while I've been packing. But the door opens easily and Benji pushes past me to get outside.

'I'm sorry I can't give you a lift,' she calls after me. 'I've had too much to drink.'

'I've called a taxi.'

'I'll message you tomorrow.'

I close the door behind me and scurry down the steps to the ground floor, praying that the taxi is already there which, mercifully, it is. But the driver takes one look at Benji and shakes his head.

'No dogs,' he says.

I curse under my breath. In my haste to leave, I forgot to check whether pets were okay.

'Please,' I plead. 'He's very well behaved. He'll be no bother.'

'No dogs,' the man repeats before yanking down the handbrake and driving away.

Panic surges. I can almost feel Beth's gaze on me from the upstairs window. I don't want to go back up there again and I don't want to hang around on the street either. I start walking, with no idea which direction I'm going in. It's late and ominously dark. Then I think about the hotel where Gary and I stayed, and I can just about remember where it was. I head in that direction, hoping that it's still open and I'm overwhelmed with relief when I arrive and see the lights on. I step inside, bathing in the warmth of the cosy interior, and spot the landlady behind the bar. She smiles with recognition when she sees me.

'Hello again,' she calls.

'Hi.' I walk up to the bar. 'I'm so sorry to bother you. Do you know any dog-friendly taxi companies?'

She nods. 'I know the owner of the local firm, I'll call him now. Gary not with you?'

'No,' I say and suddenly I wish that he was. I wish it so much that it hurts. While the landlady calls the taxi firm, I reach for my phone and try to call Gary, but it goes straight to voicemail. He's probably asleep. I have no idea what time it is in Australia. I can't think of anything else but Beth. And Frank. And Beth and Frank. I want to be wrong.

The landlady hangs up and beams at me. 'A car will be here in ten minutes.'

'Thank you,' I say gratefully.

'Do you want a drink while you wait?'

I hesitate. I've had too much already but the idea of a calming tipple is tantalising. 'A bourbon with ice,' I say, before remembering that I've just asked for Frank's drink of choice. And then I have a thought. I pull out my phone and find a photo of Frank.

'Do you know this man?' I ask the landlady, holding my phone up.

She squints at it. 'Yes, I recognise him. He drinks in here sometimes. Not for a while now though.'

'On his own?'

'No, with a friend.'

I scroll through my photos until I find one of Beth. I took it when we were out walking and she's grinning at the camera, her windswept hair in her face. She looks beautiful.

'This friend?' I ask.

The landlady gives me a suspicious look. 'Why are you asking?'

'Please,' I beg.

She shakes her head. 'No, I don't know her.'

'But it was a woman he was with?'

'Yes.'

My face must crumple because the landlady looks concerned. 'Are you okay?'

'Yes,' I say, downing my drink and wincing as the bourbon burns my throat. Tears of relief prick at my eyes. I was wrong, Beth is not E after all. I'll call her tomorrow and apologise for being off with her. It occurs to me that she might have been having an affair, not with Frank but with David, the married man who died. If I'm right, maybe she'll tell me in her own time or maybe she won't. It's her secret to keep, I decide, and it's not my business to pry. I've got enough to worry about myself, without adding Beth's dramas to my list.

I hear a beep outside and I stand up, unsteady on my feet. 'Thank you.'

'You take care of yourself.' I feel the landlady's gaze on me as I make my way shakily outside to where the taxi is waiting. My vision is blurry as I climb in with Benji jumping up next to me. The driver tries to make conversation, but I don't engage and he eventually gives up. By the time we get back to the cottage, I feel like I might throw up. I pay the driver and step shakily out of the taxi, looking up at the house which is shrouded in darkness. I can't believe I've come back here. Perhaps I should have gone back to Beth's flat after confirming that she wasn't E. I could be snuggled up under a duvet on her sofa right now, sleeping off my drunken haze, with Benji lying on my legs.

I fumble for my keys and it takes a few attempts to get them in the lock. I'm never drinking bourbon again, it's tipped me over the edge. Although all the wine hasn't helped and nor has the stress of the evening.

The cottage is bitingly cold and I can see my breath in the air, but at least it's silent and still. No doors slamming or overpowering smell of aftershave. Benji dashes off to the kitchen in search of his food bowl and I head into the living room, turn on the light and walk to the fireplace to ignite the gas fire. And that's when I hear it. Footsteps on the stairs.

I freeze on the spot, paralysed by fear. My drunkenness evaporates as my mind and body stand to attention. I'm too scared to turn around as a floorboard creaks in the hallway, or as I hear the kitchen door close, followed by Benji's frantic barking.

A pungent smell of Frank fills the room, plunging me deeper into abject terror. By the time I hear the flick of the light switch, obliterating the comforting glow of the ceiling lamp, I've closed my eyes and started to pray. I've entertained other theories as to what was happening in this house. I've blamed Gary, Dylan, Alyssa, Beth. I've almost turned on each one of my friends, one by one. But I was right all along. It was always Frank.

He's finally come for me.

26

Another floorboard creaks close behind me. He is here, in this room. I don't know how, I can't begin to understand it, but I know that he is. I can feel him and it terrifies me beyond words. Beyond comprehension. Beth warned me that I might be in danger and her chilling words come back to me now. I should never have returned to this cottage.

I have no idea what he's going to do to me, how he will hurt me. He's a ghost, not a real person, and yet I can sense danger, and I know that it will end here, tonight. But I still don't open my eyes because I'm not ready to face it. I don't know how to defend myself against something inhuman and I've never been able to defend myself against Frank, even when he was alive. I can feel myself shrinking already, reverting back to the weak, feeble person I used to be. Ready to submit to whatever Frank wants. His control wraps itself around me like tentacles, squeezing me tight and leaving me breathless. Each second is excruciating, and I feel like I've been in this room for years and not minutes.

It is so quiet that I can hear him breathing. How is that even possible? He's dead. Surely he's dead? Is there any way he could be alive? I'm reliving the past, trying to think straight. I saw his body. Was I wrong? Have I been fooled in a way I don't understand?

I can't be wrong. And yet he feels so real. Why hasn't he come for me? Why is he just standing there, watching me? Why can't I move? Even in my panic I realise that this eternal torture can't go on. I need to open my eyes and confront the danger I'm in. I have to at least know what I'm dealing with. It takes every ounce of strength to force my eyes open. To lift my head up and look into the mirror so I can see what is standing right behind me.

I gasp. There's a figure only a few feet behind me. My heart hammers in my chest as I squint in the darkness and slowly the figure comes into focus. Cold, hard eyes bore into mine and I search them looking for answers to the unanswerable. Then I recoil with horror.

I'm staring directly at the person who has been tormenting me.

And it's not Frank.

My legs buckle as I finally understand what's been going on. It's not a ghost, it was never Frank, but they made me believe that it was. They wanted to scare me, to drive me to the edge of sanity and who knows what beyond that. But before I have time to ask why, something smashes into my head and I crumple to the floor.

* * *

I wake up with an excruciating headache. I'm disorientated and my mouth is dry. I can hear Benji barking and scratching at the kitchen door and my first thought is that I need to go to him. But when I try to move I can't. Then the memory of what happened comes flooding back to me, as powerful as a tsunami. I start struggling but something is restraining me. I look around frantically and discover that my hands are bound together behind me and my legs are tied tightly to the chair I've somehow ended up sitting on. The rope is digging into my flesh and every move I make to free myself causes pain to shoot through my wrists. I open my mouth and discover, with a surge of blessed relief, that at least it's not covered. I may not have my limbs, but I still have my voice and I get ready to scream louder than I've ever screamed before, hoping the neighbours will hear me.

'Make a noise and your dog will pay the price.'

She is standing in front of me, clutching an iron poker in her right hand. She looks like a completely different person without her easy-going smile. She looks menacing. Evil. I stare at this woman, who now feels like a stranger, and realise that she must have been waiting for me in the cottage when I got home. She's as ready as I am for this to end.

My mind is racing as I figure it out, the pieces finally coming together to form a coherent picture. Beth *is* E after all. She's the woman my husband was writing love letters too, the one he couldn't wait to see. Frank must have seduced her into falling in love with him, just as he did to me all those years ago. And when I met her, she was grieving someone after all, it just wasn't the person I thought it was. It was *my* husband. Is that why she inserted herself into my life? Was her plan all along to end up at this very moment?

But why tonight? Then it hits me. It was the psychic supper, Zara's message from Frank to Beth. Beth realised that I was on to her and decided to act. But what I don't know yet is why. What it is she thinks I've done to her to deserve this.

'Why are you doing this?' I ask her, my voice trembling.

'Because you need to suffer like I've suffered. You need to feel the pain I've felt.'

'How am I responsible for that?'

Beth's face contorts with fury. 'You took him from me.'

My head is still throbbing, but I try desperately to think through the pain. To figure out how Beth's mind is working so that I can attempt to reason with her. She's angry with me for reasons that I don't yet fully understand and I sense that my only hope is to keep her talking. Maybe I can convince her to let me go. She may not care about me, but I could persuade her that it's a better outcome for her if I leave here unharmed. Frank's already ruined enough lives without destroying Beth's too. Because if she goes ahead with what I fear she's planning, she'll end up in prison for a long time.

Or maybe she'll get away with it. The prospect horrifies me. And then another thought, even worse, creeps into my head. Maybe she doesn't even care. The woman standing in front of me seems beyond reason, devoid of rational thought. And that makes her lethal. But I have to at least try and so I consider how I can draw her into a conversation and maybe distract her. I think of possible ways to neutralise Beth by telling her what she needs to hear.

'How long were you having an affair with Frank?' I ask her.

'Four years. He loved me, you know. More than you.'

'I know he did.'

Her eyes narrow. She wasn't expecting that. 'He hated you.'

I nod. 'Yes.'

She looks confused. My response has momentarily disarmed her, taken some of the wind from her sails. But then her expression hardens again, like she's remembered why we're here. She points the poker at me accusingly.

'Why didn't you just let him go, Maggie?'

'I didn't stop him.'

Now she's incredulous, a gamut of emotions playing across her face. A face I've seen many times over the past few months but now feel like I no longer recognise.

'I know all about you,' she spits. 'Frank told me everything.'

I have no idea what Frank has told her, although I suspect it's lies. I now just have to work out how to convince Beth of that too. My life may depend on it. And I'm not prepared to die tonight because if I do, then Frank has won, again.

I take a deep breath. Try to block out the noise of Benji's distressed barking, the pain in my body and the deep-rooted terror in the pit of my stomach.

'What did Frank tell you about me?' I ask.

She looks at me like I'm something she stepped in, her beautiful face ugly with hate. 'You made his life a misery, always blaming and threatening him.'

I nearly laugh, despite the horrific situation I'm in. 'I never threatened Frank.'

'Come on,' she scoffs. 'You told him you'd kill yourself if he ever left you. What kind of person uses emotional blackmail to trap someone like that? The same sort of person who would make up lies about a good man who can no longer defend himself, I suppose.'

I look at Beth, wide-eyed and incredulous. 'That's not true.'

She ignores my denial. 'I told him it was all bluster and that he should leave you. But he said he was afraid you'd do something stupid. He felt sorry for you and now I've met you, I can see why. You're pitiful, Maggie. You're nothing.'

She sounds so much like Frank. But this time I refuse to accept the accusations levelled at me. I am not pitiful and I am not nothing. I am stronger than Beth will ever know. Because she doesn't really know me at all, she can't when our entire friendship has been a lie.

'It was you,' I say quietly.

'Excuse me?'

'You were the one who made me believe that Frank was haunting me.'

Beth laughs, throwing her head back so I can see her teeth. 'It was so easy. You're such a bag of nerves, aren't you, Maggie? So jumpy and paranoid. It didn't take much.'

'You never believed in ghosts.'

'Of course I didn't. For goodness' sake, who believes in ghosts?'

I think back through all the incidents, trying to work out how Beth was responsible. How she got access to my house so many months ago. 'How did you do it?'

'It wasn't *hard*, Maggie. Actually, it was the psychic who gave me the idea. When she mentioned the back door key and you got all freaked out, I realised that was my opportunity. So I got in one day when you'd gone to the shops and left a window open, and I stole the key and had a copy made. After that I had all-hours access to your home. I'm still not sure how Zara knew about the key. Maybe she really *is* psychic. It's quite creepy actually. But anyway, she did me a favour.'

I think about the day I found the back door key on the kitchen table and fretted about how it had moved from the drawer. It must have been Beth, replacing it after she'd had her copy cut. And then after that, she could let herself in and out whenever she pleased without me knowing. It was probably her behind the shed that day, when I saw something moving. But I got the locks changed, so how did she get in after that?

As if sensing my train of thought, Beth says, 'You momentarily scuppered my plans when you changed the locks. But it wasn't hard to get a new set cut. Your hapless beau, Gary, left them on the bar at the pub when he was having an afternoon drinking session. I had new copies made and the keys returned before he'd even realised they were gone.'

And when I had the locks changed a second time, I willingly gave Beth a spare set. I thought I could trust her. How wrong I was. But it doesn't explain why Benji has been getting so agitated. Benji knows Beth, he adores her. So if it was her in the house then why was he getting so riled?

Realisation dawns. 'You wore Frank's aftershave when you came, didn't you?'

'Yes. And his clothes. He had a whole wardrobe at mine, you know. It was like home to him. When he told you he was away on business, he was just a few miles away, in my bed.'

If her intention is to make me jealous, it hasn't worked. After years of being married to Frank, I no longer cared whose bed he was in as long as it wasn't mine.

'I wanted you to smell him,' Beth continues. 'To see him in the dark and think he was still here, haunting you. And it worked perfectly, because you were in a right state. You even started imagining he was in bed with you. Oh, how that made me laugh.'

'Did you tamper with the boiler to make it cold in the cottage?'

She smiles maliciously. 'Yes, that was me too.'

'And move things around?'

'Yes.'

'What about the smashed window?'

'I paid a kid to do it. Told him if anyone asked that the order came from Gary.'

Oh no. My heart shatters as I picture the look of hurt and confusion on Gary's face when I blamed him. I accused an innocent man of a crime he didn't commit and turned people against him. He fled to the other side of the world to get away from it all. And if I hadn't fallen out with Gary, he would still be here, with me. I might not even be in this god-awful situation. I have to tell him how sorry I am. I must get out of here so that I can make amends. I look at Beth and a trickle of anger absorbs some of my fear.

'You were controlling the TV weren't you? When it flickered on and off.'

'Yes, I was just outside with a universal remote. It was quite fun, actually.'

'Why did you put *Unfaithful* on?'

Beth shrugs. 'I just turned the TV on and that's what was playing. But actually it's quite fitting, isn't it, given the circumstances.'

It was a coincidence. Beth had no idea of the meaning of that film to me and yet I completely fell apart after that. I lost all rational thought and reason.

Beth looks at me condescendingly. 'I've been watching you for months. You're a sad old woman, Maggie. Everyone thinks it.'

Her words sting this time. They are the least of my worries, but my world is falling apart and it crushes me that the person I thought was a close friend thinks so little of me. She befriended me to get her payback, and it feeds on my insecurities. Was Alyssa pretending to like me too? And Gary? Was everyone laughing at me this whole time?

She's manipulating me and I'm playing right into her hand. She wants me to feel demeaned and isolated, just as Frank did. Maybe they were suited to each other after all. If only the damned man had left me for Beth, then none of this would have happened. I have no idea why he didn't, and I guess I'll never know now as the only person who can tell us is Frank. But I suspect that he wanted to have his cake and eat it. To have a placid wife at home who he could bully and torment, but to also have a bit on the side for him to treat like royalty.

Jekyll and Hyde again. That was my husband and I'm only now understanding the full extent of his deception. It makes me think of Gary. It doesn't matter how much Beth tries to persuade me otherwise, I know that Gary was not pretending to like me. His feelings were genuine, as were mine, and yet I drove him away. The one person I can trust is not here because my so-called friends convinced me he was guilty.

It all started at the psychic supper. If I hadn't gone, I would never have met any of them. And that makes me wonder how much of it was orchestrated.

'Did you know who I was when we first met?'

'Yes,' Beth admits. 'I'd been fascinated by you for ages but all I had was your name. I searched all over the internet for you when I was seeing Frank but I couldn't find a single social media profile or photo. You really are a loser recluse with no friends, aren't you?'

'So how did you find me?'

'After Frank died, I came to the village. He'd told me where he lived so I hung around, waiting for you. But you took your time didn't you, Maggie? You didn't leave the house for weeks. I was getting bored, to be honest with you, and I nearly gave up. Then one day there you were, putting your sunglasses on as though you didn't have a bloody care in the world.'

'You followed me?'

'Yes. And when I saw you take a photo of the psychic supper poster, I decided to buy myself a ticket just in case you turned up. When you did, I knew then that it was fate. That Frank had brought you to me. It was his final gift to me, his permission to exact my revenge.'

'Was Alyssa in on it too?'

Beth frowns. 'No, Alyssa doesn't know anything about it.'

'But you let Gary take the blame.'

She shrugs. 'I was raging when you and Gary shacked up. Seeing you looking like a lovesick teenager boiled my blood. You don't deserve to be happy, not after what you did to Frank. But actually it turned out to be quite handy. I was worried that the kid I'd paid to smash your window might blab, and having Gary to pin it on worked a charm.'

So, she's acting alone at least. Is there any way I can get a message to Alyssa? I have no idea where my phone is and I can't move my hands so there's no chance of calling her. I can't scream because I'm scared that Beth will follow through on her threat to hurt Benji. He's gone quiet now and I know with a brutal foreboding that no one is coming to help me. The long night stretches ahead and I don't even want to think about how it might end. But I can't give up, not while there's a tiny slither of hope. At least with a living person, I know what I'm dealing with. I'll take Beth over the ghost of Frank any day. I decide to stick to my plan to keep her talking for as long as possible. I need to make her understand that she's wrong about Frank and that he's the enemy, not me. I just hope I can convince her.

It may not work but I've got nothing to lose and everything to gain.

'Frank lied to you,' I tell her gently. 'He lied to you about everything.'

'You're the liar!' She rushes at me and screams so hard that her spit lands on my face. I wince as I see the poker come towards me and I close my eyes and wait for the impact. But it doesn't come and when I open them again, she's pacing around the room.

I change tactic, realising I made a mistake. 'I'm sorry,' I say. 'I know you loved Frank.'

I'm not even sure that she hears me. She seems far away, lost in her own thoughts. 'Thank God Frank had that vasectomy. You would have been a terrible mother.'

My first reaction is to scoff. Frank never had a vasectomy, so it just proves that Beth didn't really know him at all. But then another thought seeps in and it makes me feel sick.

'What did you say?' I ask, my voice quiet and cold.

This gets her attention again. She turns to me with a smirk. 'You didn't know, did you? Oh wow.'

'You're lying.'

'I'm the liar now, am I? Ha! First Frank and now me. You really are a piece of work, Maggie. Frank had a vasectomy years ago. He always knew he didn't want to have children, it was one of the many things we had in common. I remembering him telling me about it. He had to see a psychologist before they'd do it because he was so young. They tried to talk him out of it, if I recall. He was in his early twenties at the time.'

My hands are freezing cold, but my blood is boiling and my body is pulsating with rage. Instinct tells me that Beth is not making this up. She has no reason to and the details are too specific. All those years I tried to conceive, it was never going to happen for us and Frank knew it. He let me take the blame, used it as a tool to diminish me. He was even more vile than I thought possible. The image that I've held in my mind of Frank and I at the dinner table with our children shatters into a million pieces and I wish I could stab him through the heart with one of them. He stole my dream, my future. He took every single part of me.

I'm struggling to get it together. I need to stay alert because I'm in terrible danger, but I'm falling apart, destroyed by this revelation. Struggling to comprehend how someone, even a man as reprehensible as Frank, could be so deceptive. So cruel. I turn my head away from Beth so she can't see my tears and take a moment to recover. When I look back, she's watching me, her head cocked and her face full of mirth.

'Did I upset you, Maggie?'

I hate her too, in that moment. Almost as much as I hate Frank. I force myself to engage with her, to try to use this information to my advantage.

'I had no idea that Frank had a vasectomy. Which proves that he lied.'

'To you, yes. Probably because he knew you'd be a useless mother. He never lied to me. We had a very open and honest relationship.'

'He lied to you every single day, Beth.'

'No, he lied to *you*. Because he was scared to leave you. And it killed him.'

It's like she's hit me again. 'Excuse me?'

'You drove him to death. Why do you think he was stressed? Why was his blood pressure so high? Because you made his life a misery. He was trapped and he couldn't see a way out. He was exhausted from living two lives. I told him to leave you and I'd take good care of him. I begged him, but he said no. He was an honourable man, and he didn't want to abandon you. It literally killed him. *You* killed him.'

She starts crying, grief spilling out of her. I am struggling to believe she's this upset about Frank. He doesn't deserve her tears. I'm surprised he even managed to seduce someone so fit and healthy given how out of condition he was in his last few years of life. But then I remember the email I read on Frank's laptop. The tender way he wrote to Beth. He made her feel special, like she was the most important person in the world, and she fell for it. I can't blame her because I was intoxicated by

Frank when we first met. I would have done anything for him back then, no questions asked, and he was never as loving to me as he was to her. In fact, he treated me like dirt for our entire marriage. And lied about his vasectomy while I spent years dreaming of a family. And anger explodes inside me. My head is telling me that I need to pander to Beth so she doesn't lose her temper again, but my heart has gone head first down another path.

'Frank was a cruel, disgusting man,' I shout. 'He abused me for his own pleasure. He degraded me, insulted me, threatened me. He said he'd kill me if I ever left him.'

'That's not true!'

'Yes, it is. And I never tried to run because I was afraid. He isolated me from the world, so that I had no one to turn to and no self-esteem to believe I deserved better. For Christ's sake, he blamed me for not being able to have children when he knew all along that it was impossible. He was the worst kind of human being.'

Beth seethes. 'I knew Frank. I knew him better than you, and he'd never do anything like that. He was a good man, a kind man.'

'He deceived you!' My voice is rising further now but I can't pull myself back. 'Just like he deceived everyone else. Do you know that he conned Alyssa's husband into investing money and he lost it all? Who knows who else he's lied to?'

'Stop it!' Beth is furious but I've gone too far now, I'm beyond reason too.

'Do you really think you're the only person Frank had an affair with? Do you honestly believe you were the only woman? There were loads of women. Dozens.'

'Stop it!' she screams again, but I can't.

'He treated his other women like angels, while he treated his wife like dirt, but he was never going to leave me. That's the truth of it, no matter what he told you. I honestly wish that he had left, but he needed me. He needed to *own* me to feel powerful.'

'Shut up! Stop talking!'

'He used you, Beth, just like he used everyone he ever met. The only person Frank ever cared about was himself. The rest of us were just toys in his games.'

Beth is seething. 'How dare you say these awful things about the man I loved.'

'I can say whatever the hell I like, because I was his wife for thirty years. I knew Frank better than anyone. He was a monster. And I'm glad he's dead.'

Beth runs at me but this time I don't flinch. I don't beg. I'm not the person I used to be. I'm not the weak woman who capitulated to Frank and I won't capitulate to Beth either. There's nothing I can say that will change her mind because Frank brainwashed her and there's no way I can physically get myself out of this situation but, oddly, I'm not afraid any more. A thousand thoughts run through my head in those few seconds as she comes for me but one clear message fights over the noise and brings with it a sense of unexpected and innate calm. If this is how it ends for me then I will go down with my head held high.

I square my chin and stare directly into her eyes. I want her to see me while she does it. To realise she hasn't broken me. That she doesn't scare me.

I'm still looking at her when she hurls the poker into the side of my head.

27

I open my eyes and see Frank gazing at me. He's the Frank I first met. Young, handsome, sultry. For a moment my heart soars at the sight of him and I want to run to him and fall into his arms. I want to smell him, to kiss him, and to know that he is mine. *I love you, Frank.*

Then I remember. Moving to London, our marriage, what came after. The guilt of never living up to his expectations. The fear, the shame, the desperation. The lies.

Frank is dead, so if I can see him then I must be dead too. I look down at my hands and they are worn and wrinkled. I am me, now, but Frank is thirty years younger. And I'm confused and disorientated. When I look up again Frank is walking towards me but now I'm afraid of him. As he lifts his hand into the air, my fear accelerates. He is going to punish me. I open my mouth to call for help, but I can't. I try to lift my feet but they're cemented to the ground. He's getting closer. He's coming for me and I can't get away. I will be trapped with Frank for all of eternity.

Then I hear a voice in the distance calling my name and it takes me a few seconds to recognise it, as two worlds collide. It's Gary. Lovely, kind, self-deprecating Gary. I smile at the sound of his gruff tone. The voice is getting stronger and I want to go to it. I try to lift my feet again and this time it works, and I step backwards once, then twice. Frank's face contorts as he speeds up, reaching out an arm to stop me. He's so close that I think he's going to grab me. I step backwards again and then I fall. I'm plummeting downwards but I'm not afraid, I'm exhilarated. Because I understand in that moment that I have finally escaped.

Slowly I open my eyes and see Gary staring down at me. I try to smile but it's too much effort, so instead I focus on his face, studying his blue eyes, every wrinkle on his skin which has been tanned by the Australian sun. He's saying something but I can't work out what it is. It doesn't matter. All that matters is that he's here. He came. The room is flashing with blue lights and I can't remember why. Gary moves away and some other people fill the space. People in green jackets. Now they're talking to me too, but I don't know what they're saying. I'm cold. And so very tired. And when sleep pulls me down again, I don't resist.

When I wake up next, I'm disorientated. And I'm in agony. My head feels like it's about to explode. What's that noise? Wincing, I turn my head and see Gary, asleep in a chair. Where am I? Am I in a hospital? Why am I here? Did I have a heart attack? A stroke? Why isn't Gary in Australia? Did I miss my shift at the pub? Where is Benji?

Something pricks at the edges of my mind. A bad thing happened. What was it? Did I have a nightmare? Was it something to do with the cottage being haunted?

It comes to me then, slowly at first and then speeding up with intensity. The cottage isn't haunted, Beth just made me think it was. She tried to kill me. That's why my head hurts so much. Do I have brain damage, is that why I can't speak? As fear surges, my heart starts racing and somewhere an alarm goes off, and then people are running into the room and Gary's waking up and it's chaos. Someone puts a hand on my arm but I'm reliving what happened in the cottage and I'm frantic. I can't calm myself down. I feel something sharp in my arm and suddenly the world softens at the edges. I'm peaceful again, floating away into the sunset and it's heavenly. I'm on a boat, with Gary by my side, drifting towards a sandy beach with the sun beating down on us. And then I fall back into blissful oblivion.

A few hours later I wake again, and Gary is holding my hand.

'You're safe,' he says immediately.

I frown, confused, but this time it doesn't take me as long to remember.

'Beth,' I whisper.

'She's been arrested. You're safe.'

I try to sit up and feel a sharp stab of pain.

'My head...'

'You're okay. Your skull was fractured, but you'll be fine, Maggie.'

I wince and adjust my position so that I can see Gary better. 'Aren't you in Australia?'

'I flew back last night.'

I'm tired, so very tired, but I need to stay alert so that I can understand what happened. 'How did you find me?'

Gary looks like he's on the verge of tears. 'When the plane landed and I turned on my phone, I had a voicemail from Paula. She's the landlady of the hotel in Harpenden we stayed at. She said you'd been in that evening and seemed really distressed and out of sorts. She was worried about you, so I went straight from the airport to the cottage to check on you.'

He looks away as a single tear trickles down his cheek.

'Go on,' I croak.

'When I arrived, I heard screaming. I tried to open the door but you must have changed the locks again. Well, I panicked and smashed the door pane to get in.' Gary looks down at his hands and I see then that they are bandaged.

'I found Beth attacking you, Maggie. She was hitting you over the head.'

Hearing him say the words aloud makes it even more real. 'She was trying to kill me.'

'But why? I don't understand.'

It's an effort to talk but I summon up the strength to get the words out. 'She was in love with Frank. They'd been having an affair for years.'

Gary's eyes widen. 'Are you serious?'

'Yes. She convinced herself that I was the one who stopped them from being together. And then she blamed me for causing his death.'

Gary's face is pale. 'All the crazy stuff that happened in the cottage. Was it her?'

'Yes. She wanted me to think it was Frank. You saved me, Gary. I could have died.'

I'm crying now too and Gary wraps his arms around me and holds me gently.

'I'm so sorry,' I say to him, weeping onto his shoulder. 'I'm sorry I blamed you.'

'Shh, shh, it's okay,' he whispers into my ear. 'It's okay.'

'It's not okay, I'll make it up to you.'

'Maggie, you have nothing to make up for. I'm the one who's

sorry. I should never have gone to Australia and left you alone. I'll never forgive myself...'

There's a kerfuffle at the door and Alyssa appears, unkempt and frantic.

'Oh, Maggie,' she says, putting a hand to her mouth and I realise that I must look awful. Alyssa rushes towards me. 'I've just heard, and I came straight here.'

I don't have the strength to explain what happened again, so I look at Gary and he understands. He starts telling Alyssa and she stares at him in horror.

'How did we miss this?' she says. 'How did we get Beth so wrong?'

'We all did,' Gary says. 'None of us realised what was going on.'

I interject. 'The landlady of the pub in Harpenden told me Frank used to drink there. But when I showed her a photo of Beth, she didn't recognise her. So who was Frank with, if it wasn't Beth?'

'Could he have had another woman on the go too?' Alyssa asks.

I wouldn't put it past him. But would he really have the gall to meet another woman in the same town as his lover? Beth could have walked in at any moment.

'We'll find out,' Gary promises. 'I'll call Paula later and ask her.'

'And if there's anything I can do to help, let me know,' Alyssa adds. '*Anything.*'

I look between Alyssa and Gary, and even though I'm in a hospital bed with a head that feels like it's going to explode and limbs so tired I can barely move them, and although I nearly died last night, something resembling happiness settles over me.

Because Frank was wrong. I am not nothing and I am not alone. I am loved. And I deserve to be happy.

He did not win.

A slow smile settles on my face and Gary and Alyssa look at me, perturbed. I'm supposed to be horrifically traumatised and yet here I am, grinning like a Cheshire cat.

'She's on a lot of meds,' Gary explains to Alyssa.

He's right, I'm dosed up to the eyeballs. But that's not why I'm smiling.

* * *

The doctors insist that I stay in hospital for observation. Flowers and cards appear until there's no room left to put them. Gary barely leaves my side, although I make him go home and get some rest at night. Alyssa pops in and out and Mark, who is looking after Benji, comes to visit too. But as the meds wear off, reality kicks in and when all my guests have gone, I relive what happened to me over and over again. I'm too afraid to fall asleep because I don't know what I'll dream about. Who will come to me in my nightmares.

The police come to see me. They tell me that they found a bottle of sleeping pills in Beth's coat. They're working on a theory that she was going to force me to take them, so it looked like I'd killed myself. I consider this for hours. Everyone would think I was heartbroken over the death of my husband, followed by my failed relationship with Gary. The whole village knew I thought the cottage was haunted. Would it be a giant leap for me to want to end it? Possibly not. But Beth never got her chance because I wound her up so much, she lost control and attacked me. Oddly, provoking her might have saved me.

But I still have so many unanswered questions. Who was the

person that Frank used to drink with in Paula's pub? And how did Dylan meet Frank?

I get my answers over the next few days, thanks to Gary and Alyssa. Gary learns, through Paula, that Frank used to meet potential clients in her pub. The area is wealthy, a good place to strike up conversations with unwitting investors, particularly women. Gary's asked around and a few different pub landlords recognised Frank. It seems he worked the entire area, apart from the village pub, which he had clearly decided was too close to home.

Before we moved to Hertfordshire, Frank had done the same in London, and that's how he'd met Dylan. Dylan had recently become a dad for the second time and was proudly showing baby photos to his colleagues when Frank, sitting quietly at the bar, congratulated him and offered to buy him a drink. They got chatting and an increasingly drunk and emotional Dylan admitted that he'd grown up without a father and wanted to be the perfect dad himself. He confided that he dreamed of giving his children the best possible future and Frank said he knew how to make it happen. Told him stories of his own children's experience at one of the best schools in the country and made Dylan yearn to be able to give his kids the same opportunities.

Except there *were* no children, it was just another thread in Frank's web of deceit. Along with his stories about owning a huge country house. All lies. He had preyed on Dylan's vulnerability and used it to his advantage, just like he had probably seduced women and persuaded them to part with their money. Had that been his plan for Beth too or had it purely been about sexual attraction? I know it wasn't love, because Frank only loved himself.

There could be dozens of people out there who are angry with Frank or nursing a broken heart. Maybe there are more women like Beth who blame me for keeping Frank from them. Or maybe there are other women like me, who lived in fear of him. And yet he got away with it all, or at least he died before his past caught up with him. Like me, his victims remained silent.

The story has been picked up by the press. Gary had to fend off a reporter who was hovering in the hospital corridor. I am dreading seeing my name in the news, but I know that when the full story comes out, it will make the headlines because it's a scandalous story. I'll have to sit through a court case while distressing information about my marriage is divulged. I might have to give evidence too. My most fervent hope is that Beth pleads guilty and saves me the trauma of a trial. But something tells me that she'll want her voice to be heard.

I have highs and lows. There are moments when I feel so surrounded by people who care about me that I know I can tackle whatever comes next. Then there are other times when I'm gripped by anxiety about the future. Even though I know that the cottage isn't haunted, I don't want to live there any more, not after what happened. And although I understand now that Beth was behind it all, I still can't stop thinking about the two psychic suppers we went to. Both times, Zara claimed to be communicating with Frank and I can't disprove it. That's the one thing I can't pin on Beth and I'm wondering if Zara really is psychic.

And that means Frank might not have gone away.

It's Gary who comes up with the suggestion. His son has offered to buy his house from him. He and Sophie are happy and settled there and so they've agreed to a private sale to save costs. Gary's selling it to him for less than it's worth, but it means that his son's family will have a home to call their own and he'll have some money in his pocket.

'What if you sell the cottage too? Then together, we'll have enough money to move away,' he says.

'Where will we go?'

'Anywhere you want.'

The village is the only place that has ever felt like home to me. And if we left, I'd be letting down Alyssa, when I promised to look after her children. I'd have to quit my job at the pub and I'd be taking Gary away from the place he's lived in for most of his life.

But it's tempting, so very tempting. To walk away from all of this and start afresh. Perhaps we could even move to Australia, somewhere so far away that I know Frank will never be able to reach me. Maybe I'm crazy to be considering moving away with a man I've only known for a few months, but life is short. I've lost too much of it already, being married to Frank. I want to take the risk with Gary, because I know that he's nothing like my husband was. He's kind, honest and caring, and he saved my life.

My mind is made up when I'm finally discharged from hospital and Gary drives us back to the cottage. I stand on the garden path, looking up at the house.

'I can't go back in there,' I tell him.

He nods, as though he was expecting it. 'We'll go back to mine. They can put up with us for a few weeks until we've made a plan.'

Sophie is much warmer when we move back into Gary's place. She even makes an effort with Gary. Perhaps it's because she's realised that she was wrong about him, or maybe it's simply that she knows it's not a permanent arrangement and the house will soon be hers. But she doesn't make us feel unwelcome and for that I'm grateful. The baby, Emilia, is a doll and although Sophie is still overprotective of her, I get a few cuddles, breathing in her gorgeous baby smell and watching her giggle and gurgle. It still reminds me of the life I never had but I'm too old now to contemplate that path and I've made peace with it. And I feel safe in the house, and when I'm wrapped up in Gary's arms at night. He's there when I need him, but he also respects my need for a bit of space. Some time on my own to process what happened. He doesn't overcrowd me and for that I'm grateful.

I put the cottage on the market, and Gary and I discuss our next steps. It turns out that moving to Australia is not an option as neither of us qualify for a visa and anyway, I'm not sure I want to put Benji through the stress of the relocation. We consider the south coast and talk about living by the sea. One weekend we drive down to Devon to scout out potential locations. The future sparkles with possibilities but I can't stop thinking about letting down Mark and Alyssa and the wrench I would feel at leaving the village. And I think constantly about Beth too. About Frank and this whole devastating mess.

I understand then that I don't need a ghost in my house to feel haunted.

I tell Gary that I need more time to decide what to do and he agrees. So the days turn into weeks and we're still holed up at Gary's place, getting in the way and testing Sophie's patience. I know it can't go on forever, but I'm waiting for something.

At first, I think I've worked out what it is when Beth pleads guilty to attempted murder and is remanded in custody to be sentenced at Crown Court. I am so happy that we've avoided a trial and I assume that I will finally move on for good. But instead, I lie awake at night, imagining her in a prison cell, her future snatched from her. And I can't hate her for what she did to me. My anger is aimed directly at Frank because he ruined her life too. I want to release all this negative emotion and finally be free, but something is still holding me back.

One afternoon, when I'm not working, I go for a walk and find myself standing outside the church, staring up at the building which has stood for hundreds of years. Which has seen people come and go, has witnessed their tears and guilt and confessions. I take a deep breath and go inside, walking up the aisle and sitting on a pew halfway down.

I don't know how long I'm there for but after a while, the vicar sits down next to me.

'Hello, Maggie, how are you feeling?' he asks.

I hesitate, before answering honestly. 'Lost,' I say.

He nods. 'That's understandable. You've been through a lot.'

'I don't know how to get past this.'

'You must be patient, Maggie. Give yourself time to heal, physically and emotionally. And remember, it's our challenges that make us stronger. They make us who we are.'

'I can't forgive,' I tell him, knowing that makes me extremely unchristian.

He probably thinks I'm talking about Beth when he answers. 'You are angry and you have every right to be. But the anger will fade in time and you *will* find peace again.'

'When I came to you months ago and told you I thought Frank was haunting me, you said I should look to the living. I've thought about it many times. Did you know?'

The vicar is silent for a moment. 'I was talking about you, Maggie. I could tell you were troubled by something. I believed that was the source of what was happening.'

'So you really think that Frank is gone?'

'Yes, he is at peace now.'

I don't particularly want him to be at peace, but I do want him to be gone.

'So why do I feel like it's not over yet?'

'Because you haven't let him go.'

I stare at the vicar, aghast. 'I want him gone more than anything.'

He nods. 'Then let him go, Maggie.'

'And how exactly do I do that?'

'By forgiving yourself.'

'For what?'

He smiles and takes my hand. 'For whatever it is you blame yourself for.'

28

It was the email that did it. Not the years of control and coercive behaviour. The cruelty and the imprisonment. No, it was one simple email that had tipped me over the edge.

When I read Frank's love letter to E, I didn't care that he was having another affair. But what I did care about was the realisation that he could be so loving towards a woman, because it proved that he was capable of kindness. He could be a good man, a caring person – or at least he could pretend to be – and yet he had made a deliberate and conscious decision not to be like that with me. He had chosen to hurt me, to diminish me. He had violated my adoration of him and squeezed the life out of me for his own sick pleasure.

My fury built inside me like a dormant volcano coming back to life. I simmered over the life I could have lived, the life that Frank took from me. I began to look at him with contempt and hatred, scarcely able to breathe the same air as this vile man. And yet I still feared leaving him. I had no money, no job, no confidence, no friends. And I was convinced that anywhere I went, he would find me. I even considered a women's refuge, but

I knew he'd track me down eventually. I could tell the police what he had done to me, but I suspected that Frank would charm his way out of it. He'd make up lies about me, he'd unravel my allegations piece by piece, and then he'd punish me for it afterwards. I knew how many domestic abuse allegations went unprosecuted. And I knew what often happened to the women who made them. I could not be a victim any longer.

I would never be safe while Frank was still alive. I would never be free. And suddenly I realised how much I needed to be. I had to salvage what was left of my life before it was too late. Frank had taken too much of me already and my need to protect the tiny portion that was left became an addiction. The only way to make sure that Frank never hurt me again was to kill him. And somehow get away with it. I lay awake at night considering my options. I talked myself out of it and then back in to it again. I planned. I plotted.

And then I decided.

It was an incredible risk. It wasn't even prison I feared, because I'd be safe there, where Frank couldn't get to me. It was the fear that I'd fail and he'd find out what I tried to do. And the repercussions of that were unthinkable. But I was prepared to take the gamble because for the first time in a very long time, I had a purpose again.

I had read a news article online a few months previously about a woman who poisoned her husband's food with eye drops. Just a small amount, over time. She hadn't gotten away with it but then her husband didn't have a history of heart problems or a doctor telling him he was a dead man walking if he didn't take medication and change his lifestyle. Frank was on the edge anyway, so he only needed a gentle nudge to push him over. And it was so easy, to walk into the chemist and buy the small bottle for only a few pounds.

The Widow's Husband

The first time I contaminated his food, my trembling hand hovered over his microwave chicken curry. Was I really going to do this? Was I going to poison my husband? And then I remembered the email and I squeezed the bottle, watching the clear drops fall into the food. I sat opposite him at the kitchen table as he took the meal without thanks and shovelled forkfuls of it into his mouth, and I felt afraid and exhilarated. And for the first time in over thirty years, I felt something else too. Control.

It became easier after that, almost second nature. And as Frank's health ailed, his GP simply repeated his advice to take statins. I sat next to him in the surgery, nodding my agreement at the doctor and feeling elation when my stupid husband still refused to accept the prescription for no other reason but ignorance and arrogance.

In the days before Frank died, he deteriorated. He was nauseous, disorientated and he took to our bed. He didn't even have the energy to be cruel to me. In fact, he seemed almost grateful that I was there, looking after him. He knew he was vulnerable and he probably hated it but he needed me more than I needed him. I brought him poisoned food and watched him with almost clinical fascination. I slept beside him every night, listening to his grunts and moans. I think I had detached myself from the situation by that point because it was the only way I could cope with it. With what I was doing. In my head, I was playing a character in a television show and I half convinced myself that none of it was real.

Except that it was real because one day I woke up and Frank was dead. And it hit me like a ton of bricks. I had killed my husband. I stared at his lifeless body with horror, relief and abject terror. It took me a good hour to gather my senses and call for an ambulance. And then I watched as they confirmed his death and carried his body away. I forced myself to act like a widow should, contacting friends and family, organising the funeral. I waited for the repercussions, a post-mortem to be ordered, the police to turn up at my doorstep.

But there was never any suspicion, only sympathy. The GP confirmed Frank's heart condition and his refusal to take medication. The death was considered natural and no post-mortem was requested. Frank was buried and everyone moved on. Everyone but me.

For a couple of months, I remained imprisoned in my home, not because of Frank but because I was too afraid to step foot outside. Part of it was the legacy of my marriage but another part was my fear that people would see straight through me. That they would somehow know what I had done. And with so much time to think, I wondered if I deserved to be happy. I had killed another human being, I was the worst of the worst. I had nightmares about it, visions of Frank coming for me, telling me he knew what I'd done. And every time I woke up screaming, vowing to hand myself in the very next morning.

But I never did. And, as the days, and then the weeks, went by, I began to remember why I had done it. What I had risked to finally be free of the monster who had terrorised me. And it would all be for nothing if I continued to live like a victim.

So I took my first tentative steps out into the world. And no one saw through me, no one suspected me. Slowly I realised that I really had been given a second chance and I had to embrace it. It became easier with each day that passed and perhaps I would have moved on quicker if it hadn't been for Beth, making me think that Frank was haunting me. But the truth is that I made it easy for her because I was haunted anyway, by what I had done.

When Beth attacked me, I wondered if my day of reckoning had finally come. If this was my punishment for killing Frank. For a brief moment I thought she'd worked out what I'd done. And when I survived, it made me question things all over again. Did I deserve to be alive? Would I ever truly be free with the guilt hanging over me constantly? When the vicar said I needed to forgive myself to let Frank go, I finally understood what I needed to do. I had to make my confession, not to him, but to the person I cared about the most.

And so as Gary and I walk along the footpath that cuts through the farmland, taking the same path Beth and I had taken on our first walk together, I tell him everything. I know that I could lose him, and my freedom, but it isn't fair to lie to him any more. If we are going to build a future together, he has to know who I really am. And if he can't move past it, or if he calls the police and tells them, then I will accept my fate.

He listens without once interrupting me. And when I'm done, his silence continues. We walk and walk and I wait for his response. I brace myself for his disgust, his outrage and his declaration that I deserve to be in prison.

And then he finally speaks.

'If I'd had the opportunity to meet the bastard, I'd have killed him myself.'

'Don't say that, Gary.'

'I'm serious. Frank Rossi was an absolute weasel who destroyed the life of every single person he met. Look at the damage he left in his wake. He turned you into a broken wreck. He swindled Dylan. He made Beth so crazy that she tried to kill you. And that's just in one tiny village. Who else is out there that he hurt and manipulated?'

'But I'm a murderer.'

'No.' Gary shakes his head. 'It was self-defence.'

'You know it wasn't.'

'Yes, it was. It was the only way you could be free of him.'

I consider this. 'But I'm not free of him, am I? Everything that has happened since has been because of Frank.'

'But it's over now. Beth's in prison, the cottage is on the market. Frank's gone and you're still here. So make the most of it, Maggie. And don't, for one second more, feel guilty about what you did.'

I close my eyes, taking in Gary's words. 'Can you still be with me, though, Gary, knowing what I've done?'

He takes my hand and squeezes it. 'I love you.'

'That's not an answer.'

'Well then, here's your answer. If you'd done nothing, if you'd stayed with Frank for the rest of your life, refusing to stand up to him, giving up and giving in, then that would have been harder for me to understand.'

'I'm a killer,' I remind him.

He shakes his head. 'No. You're a survivor.'

I pause and listen to the sound of birds calling to each other above us. To the distant hum of a tractor. It calms me. It's done now and I can't go back and change it, but I can move forward. I can find a way to live with what I did to my husband. Because it wasn't the cottage that needed an exorcism, it was me. It's been me all along.

'I don't want to leave the village,' I tell Gary, and I swear I see relief on his face.

'Are you sure? A change of scene might help you move past all this.'

'I'm done hiding. This is where our life is. Alyssa and the boys, my job. Your son and granddaughter. This is where we belong.'

'I've already agreed to sell the house to my son, though.'

'That's okay, we can find somewhere else together. Somewhere new for both of us so it's still a fresh start. We don't need a lot of space.'

'And you're absolutely certain?'

There are so many things in life that I'm uncertain about, but this is not one of them. I reach up and kiss him gently on the lips. 'Home is where the heart is, and mine is here.'

He puts his arms around me. 'And mine is with you. Always.'

Then we walk back to the village centre together, hand in hand, instinctively heading in the direction of the pub. And with each step we take, my feet – and my heart – feel lighter.

It's taken me half a century, but I've finally found myself. I know who I am now. I'm a survivor. A woman who has learned to stand up for herself, to fight back. I am strong and capable. I deserve to be loved. And I will never, ever, let anyone control me again.

We reach the pub and Gary turns to me with a cheeky glint in his eye. 'May I treat my beautiful lady to a glass of wine?'

I smile. 'Go on then. But I'm having a beer. And I'm buying.'

* * *

MORE FROM NATASHA BOYDELL

Another book from Natasha Boydell, *The Doll's House*, is available to order now here:

https://mybook.to/DollsHouseBackAd

ACKNOWLEDGEMENTS

Thank you to everyone who helped this book to become a reality – the first round's on me! From my friends and family to the incredible team at Boldwood Books, I appreciate your support every time I disappear head first down the rabbit hole of writing a novel and emerge, months later, exhilarated, dazed, confused and in need of some editing.

Special thanks as always to my editor, Isobel Akenhead, for working with me to make *The Widow's Husband* the book that it is. And to everyone at Boldwood for your expertise, enthusiasm and dedication. I am so thrilled to have signed another publishing deal with you and I can't wait to release more books with you over the coming years.

To my fabulous author friends, Keri Beevis and Nikki Allen, who are always a joy to chat to and keep me sane and motivated. You are my companions on the rollercoaster journey of being an author and I'm so glad I get to share the highs and lows with you.

To my old friends, new friends, mum friends – special mention to Emma and James Newall, Jenny and Mark Hawthorne, Sarah Mountford, Amy Smart, Louise Garrahan, Louise Newsome, Laura Walmsley, Joana Oliveira – thank you all for your unwavering support and your enthusiasm even after all this time (and many, many books!).

To my family, Jon, Alice and Rose. Thank you for everything.

And finally, to you, my reader for coming on this journey with me.

ABOUT THE AUTHOR

Natasha Boydell is an internationally bestselling author of psychological fiction. She trained and worked as a journalist for many years, and decided to pursue her lifelong dream of writing a novel in 2019, when she was approaching her 40th birthday and realised it was time to stop procrastinating! Natasha lives in North London with her husband, two daughters and two rescue cats.

Sign up to Natasha Boydell's mailing list for news, competitions and updates on future books.

Follow Natasha on social media:

- facebook.com/NatashaBoydellAuthor
- x.com/tashboydell
- bookbub.com/authors/natasha-boydell
- instagram.com/tashy_boydell
- tiktok.com/@natasha_boydell

ALSO BY NATASHA BOYDELL

The Fortune Teller

The Perfect Home

The Doll's House

The Widow's Husband

THE *Murder* LIST

THE MURDER LIST IS A NEWSLETTER DEDICATED TO SPINE-CHILLING FICTION AND GRIPPING PAGE-TURNERS!

SIGN UP TO MAKE SURE YOU'RE ON OUR HIT LIST FOR EXCLUSIVE DEALS, AUTHOR CONTENT, AND COMPETITIONS.

SIGN UP TO OUR NEWSLETTER

BIT.LY/THEMURDERLISTNEWS

Boldwood

Boldwood Books is an award-winning fiction publishing company seeking out the best stories from around the world.

Find out more at www.boldwoodbooks.com

Join our reader community for brilliant books, competitions and offers!

Follow us

@BoldwoodBooks

@TheBoldBookClub

Sign up to our weekly deals newsletter

https://bit.ly/BoldwoodBNewsletter

Printed in Dunstable, United Kingdom